THE SUBSTITUTE WIFE

Brides Of Little Creede Book 1

CICI CORDELIA

SOUL MATE PUBLISHING

New York

THE SUBSTITUTE WIFE

Copyright©2018

CICI CORDELIA

Cover Design by Syneca Featherstone

Published in the United States of America by

Soul Mate Publishing

P.O. Box 24

Macedon, New York, 14502

ISBN: 978-1-68291-632-2

ebook ISBN: 978-1-68291-609-4

www.SoulMatePublishing.com

To Harrison and Retta Osborn,

the inspiration for The Substitute Wife

A true-life love story from the Old West

In memory of Carol Anderson

My Mom and biggest fan

You will forever be missed

-Cheryl

Acknowledgments

A huge thanks to Crystal Lovejoy and Carol Anderson (sisters) for the family history lesson that sparked the idea for our story. (Cheryl Yeko & Char Chaffin, aka: CiCi Cordelia)

Introduction

In the later 1800s, the silver mining craze easily caught up to the level of frenzy gold fever had already created, and men flocked to the Colorado Territory to try their luck at staking a mine and making a fortune. Colorado reached statehood in the summer of 1876, when silver fever was high. These newbie miners brought their sweethearts, their wives, and their families, enduring untold hardships in their bid for instant wealth. Some established themselves first, then sent for those sweethearts and family members to join them.

Their stories were amazing, thrilling, dangerous—and endlessly inspiring.

Chapter 1

Chicago, Illinois
March 1878

The earsplitting whistle made Retta Pierce choke up as she hugged her sister goodbye on the train platform. Jenny's slight frame trembled in her grip, and Retta fought back her worry.

Too thin. Too frail. Shoulders drooping, as though too heavy to hold up.

"There must be a better way, Jenny," Retta murmured, stricken. "It's just not right—"

Her sister's features took on that stubborn look Retta knew so well, indicating there'd be no changing her mind. "And what would be right, Retta? For Papa to really hurt you the next time he feels the urge to beat the devil from your soul? For him to finally slip and hit Addie?" Tipping up Retta's chin with two shaking fingers, she smiled gently. "That darling girl is the best thing that ever happened to this family, no matter how her skunk of a father ran off and left you."

Jenny glanced over to where their Aunt Millie stood under the metal portico, holding two-year-old Adeline in her arms. The desolate flapping of a loosened, rusty panel, noisily vibrating in the chilly breeze, only added to the solemnness of the day. Moisture gave a sad sheen to her aunt's eyes as she cuddled the toddler closer.

Retta's sigh was as broken as her heart. "No, of course

not. But to leave you when you need me the most . . . Please, Jenny. Don't ask."

The dark circles around Jenny's blue eyes gave her complexion a grayish cast. She shouldn't be standing out in the wind like this, as sick as she was. She could barely stay upright. But Retta knew all too well her sister's inner core of strength, because Jenny was cut from the same cloth as their beloved mother, gone three years now. "Mama wouldn't want me to desert you," Retta began, only to be silenced by her sister's dismissive wave of one skeletal hand.

"Mama would do exactly what I'm doing." She shoved a wrinkled pouch into Retta's shabby reticule, ignoring her protests. "Take it. You think I would leave Mama's rubies to rot in Papa's strongbox?" She snorted weakly, but her disdain was evident. "It's your future, darling." Her voice dropped to a wisp. "It's my legacy to you."

Fighting back tears, Retta held on to her sister's fingers when she would have pulled away. "You can't go back. Papa will know you took Mama's necklace, and will beat you for it." She gripped her bag between whitened knuckles, then gasped at the clinking sound coming from within. "Are those coins? Jenny, where did you get them?"

Jenny drew herself up, straightening her shoulders, and for a shining moment Retta saw her sister as she'd been, before consumption ravaged her body. "My dowry. Yours, now." She patted the reticule in Retta's fist. "There's a letter folded inside with the coins. You take that letter to Harrison. It explains everything. Tell him I wish for him a happy life. Tell him I'm sorry."

She dashed wispy locks of dull-brown hair off her perspiring forehead. "I'm going to stay with Aunty until, well, until . . ." Her chin firmed. "I will be safe and well-cared for. By the time Papa sobers up enough to realize we both left him, it'll be too late to do anything about it."

A rambunctious boy bumped them as he sprinted across the wooden platform to keep up with his family. "Oh, Jenny," Retta murmured sadly, steadying her sister when she nearly lost her footing.

Retta blinked away fresh tears as Jenny gave her hand a final squeeze, before she eased away.

Aunt Millie transferred Retta's sleepy daughter into her arms then whispered in her ear, "I know, child. She wouldn't admit anything but I know how sick our Jenny is. I'm taking her back to Dewfield with me. I promise you I will never say a thing to your father, and I'll care for her faithfully."

"You'll keep in touch? You'll write?" Retta clung to her aunt's vow, even as everything inside her demanded she remain to care for Jenny herself.

"Yes, indeed. Have no worries." Millie curled a supporting arm around Jenny's thin shoulders. "I'd best be getting you back to the house, darling girl. A nice cup of cocoa and a nap will do you wonders. Just you wait and see."

An errant tear tracked down Jenny's pale cheek that she quickly batted away before offering an encouraging smile. "Harrison is a good man, Retta. Be happy. All I want for you and Addie is to have a good life. Promise me you'll give him a chance."

Retta's stomach clenched with fear and uncertainty, even as she hesitantly agreed. For the love of her sister, she'd acquiesce to her final wish. Though it'd been four years since Jenny had last seen her fiancé. Who knew what kind of man he was now?

Jenny traced a slender finger down Retta's cheek. "I love you, little sister."

Blinking through a flood of tears that fell silently against the top of her sleeping daughter's head, Retta whispered, "I love you, Jenny. I'll hold you in my heart forever."

There were no final goodbyes, just an assortment of

promises and encouraging murmurs, before Aunt Millie guided Jenny from the platform, toward a waiting hackney.

Struggling for composure, Retta held Addie close. As the March wind whipped around her ears, she watched them go until their figures merged into a single, blurred image, and the train whistle blew its final, 'All Aboard' warning. Only then did she allow the conductor to help her with her baggage.

Harrison had reserved a sleeper for Jenny, an extravagance to be sure, but safer for a woman traveling alone. *What will he do when I arrive instead?*

Blinking furiously, Retta guided Addie through the doorway. Inside the cramped compartment, she laid the sleepy child on the narrow bed and covered her with the only blanket she could find. Addie cuddled into a ball, snoring lightly. Retta brushed the tangled golden curls from her fair brow, trying to envision what sort of future awaited them out West.

Love for her child stiffened her spine. Her baby—her world.

I'll make a better life for you, I promise.

Even if she had to travel halfway across the country and marry a stranger to do it.

~ ~ ~

Outside Little Creede, Colorado
April 1878

"Well, Copper," Harrison Carter said soothingly, stepping onto the wagon plank and settling himself on the wide wooden seat, "time to pick up our girl."

One of the first things he'd done when coming out West was to capture and tame his wild mustang. But even after years of building trust with his old friend, the burnished stallion still had a bit of a rebellious streak. Tossing his silken mane with an indignant whinny, Copper turned his head and gave Harrison an annoyed stare, while adjusting to the pull of the wagon straps. The horse was more than capable of handling the heftier burden, though Harrison knew Copper hated it. Three other horses—two mares and another stallion—were stabled at the ranch, but Copper remained Harrison's favorite.

With a cluck of his tongue, he gently steered the horse and wagon toward town.

Jenny was due in before dusk, and Harrison would be there, waiting. It was the least he could do after the brave girl traveled all this way to marry him.

She's not a girl any longer.

No, Jenny would be all grown up. But he'd bet she was still that sweet, innocent young lady he'd met at Missy Brower's wedding in Bolster. Harrison had known right off she was the one for him. After a short courtship, he'd proposed, and she'd shyly accepted, allowing him to steal a kiss from rosy lips he swore he could still taste.

A scant few months of betrothal adjustment had gone by too fast, before he and his brother Frank left Illinois. For a chance at a better life, they'd set off for Colorado Territory to make their fortune in silver, from the mines their uncle left them in his will.

Faithfully, Jenny had waited for him. Very soon, she'd be in his arms.

As the wind died down and the air stilled, Harrison whipped off his Stetson and blotted the sweat from his brow with his forearm. Damn, he hadn't expected it to take so long to get the silver mines up and running. Talking Frank into joining him had been tricky enough, without years of struggles and hardship adding to the mix. At times, they'd come close to chucking it all and returning to Bolster with their tails between their legs. Only the dread of having to listen to a multitude of 'I told you so' from family and friends, kept them out West.

Harrison studied the barbwire enclosing the south border of his land and caught the last glint of the low-hanging, late-afternoon sun. The fencing, brand-new, surrounded most of the three hundred acres Uncle Norton had left him. With the mines producing strongly, Frank's house almost finished, and Harrison's lacking only a few pieces of furniture, the Carter Brothers' future shone brightly. A plan to buy up more of the surrounding land was in the works as well.

And not a moment too soon, for a man needs room to grow a family. Harrison broke out in a wide grin as he raised his eyes to Cascade Mountain and its lower summit that served as a backdrop to their ranchland. Judging by the sun's angle against the closest ridge, he should reach Little Creede in plenty of time to meet the stagecoach . . . and finally put his arms around Jenny.

Closer to town, the rough-scrabbled trail smoothed out and widened. Low brush and dried-out clumps of prairie grass gave way to greener patches speckled with late-spring wildflowers. Bonney Creek bubbled noisily, its runoff from the higher range dumping the last of the melted snow from the previous winter into its generous rock bed. Once he and Frank secured those extra acres, North Bonney would cross neatly over their extended property line. Someday his and Jenny's children would play in that creek.

Maybe even Frank's children too, if the cranky bugger ever cheered up enough to attract a woman who'd be willing to marry him. Harrison chuckled at the thought, and Copper snorted loudly as if in response.

Higher grasses opened to a trail fork leading to several other smaller silver mines located in the hills. Carter Brothers Mining sat higher than most, where the ore formed deeper but proved more plentiful. Yes, their workers had to toil a bit harder, but the rewards had been great. Satisfaction settled in Harrison's gut like smooth whiskey as he urged Copper into an easy canter, the wagon rolling along on well-oiled axles.

Up ahead, Little Creede's assortment of outbuildings and newer structures came into view. The town was growing a mite too speedily in his opinion. Harrison guided Copper along the rutted street, nodding to several miners he recognized as they ambled the wooden sidewalks. A pair of older women paused in front of Loman's Mercantile and tittered behind work-roughened hands as he tipped his hat to them. He tried not to frown at the sight of their worn, faded day-dresses and shawls. No doubt these were miners' wives, come to town for supplies.

The life of a miner wasn't easy. He knew that firsthand. But his Jenny wouldn't suffer callused fingers and mud-stained half-boots. He'd make sure of it.

Harrison's mood lightened as the carriage station came into view. Excitement grew in his chest and he urged Copper at a faster clip down Main Street, noting the dust churning in the distance. The stagecoach, six horses pulling its load of travelers and baggage, would arrive very soon. The north end of Cascade Station came into view and he couldn't wait a second more. He eased Copper into the wagon lot, barely pausing for a complete stop before he jumped down and flung the straps around the nearest post.

"Ho, Carter, you collectin' that lil' gal of yours?" Moe Parker called to Harrison as he strode toward the station.

Harrison didn't even slow down, passing the grizzled miner who owned one of the larger spreads between Little Creede and Silver Cache. "That I am, Parker." Harrison managed a perfunctory nod as his legs ate up the distance and the dirt path gave way to wooden planks, ignoring Moe's raspy cackle behind him. He probably looked like an overeager young fool, but damn it all, it'd been nearly four years, and he could almost taste his Jenny's welcoming kisses . . .

The coach doors flew open and a few men jumped out, striding off toward the Lucky Lady Saloon down the street. Anxious for his first glimpse of Jenny, Harrison watched as two more travelers disembarked. The stage held roughly six to eight people and so few women traveled West by themselves. Surely Jenny would be easy to spot, with her silky brown curls and those huge blue eyes—

He hurried along the platform, squinting, worry forming along with the anticipation of seeing her again. What if something happened along the way? Ten days on a train was difficult enough, but over two weeks stuck on three different stages held its own kind of danger. Anything could have gone wrong.

A slight young woman with a crown of golden hair stepped from the coach. Something about her rang a distant bell in his memory. She held out her arms, a soft smile forming on her face. Harrison found his lips curving at the sight of a little girl with thick, bouncy curls as bright as the sun. The child jumped into her arms with a squeal of laughter and she swung the tot around amongst happy screeches.

Then she turned toward Harrison and her bright blue eyes locked onto him. Her smile faded as she perched the tiny lass on her hip and slowly walked toward him.

Glancing over her head at the gaping door of the stage, Harrison frowned when no one else stepped out and the drivers began unloading baggage from the roof of the coach.

What the hell—?

He started for the nearest driver, when a gloved hand touched his arm.

"Are you Harrison Carter?"

The slender, golden-haired woman had stopped before him. Looking down, Harrison stared into eyes the exact same color and shape as Jenny's. But there the similarity ended. This woman was very young, barely big enough to carry the little girl who gazed at him with deep-brown eyes, her thumb in her mouth.

"Is your name Harrison?" the lady repeated, drawing his attention back to her delicately lovely face.

Harrison nodded briefly. "It is."

She expelled a breath and fished in her bag with her free hand, drawing out a slip of badly-wrinkled paper. "This is—I mean, I'm—" She stuttered to a stop, held out the paper with fingers that visibly trembled, and whispered, "I'm Retta. You might not remember—well, I'm Jenny's sister." She waved the note.

With a sudden sense of foreboding, Harrison took it from her.

Slowly he opened it, while she fidgeted beside him and the toddler she carried yawned and snuggled against her shoulder. Harrison started reading:

Dearest Harrison, please forgive me—

His head came up as a horrible, breaking sensation tore through his chest. He didn't want to read any further.

He had to.

Meeting the eyes of Jenny's sister—who would have been just a tad short of sixteen, last time he saw her— Harrison spotted the glitter of tears on her cheeks before he managed to return his attention to the letter.

A few minutes later, he crumpled the note in one shaking fist. Unable to spare another glance toward the bearer of the most agonizing news he had ever received, Harrison strode toward a trio of shabby bags piled on the platform, hefting two of them under one arm and grasping the third in his free hand. "These all you've got?" he ground out.

"I don't think I should—"

"*Are these all you've got?*" He tried and failed to keep the fury from his voice.

"Y-Yes," she stammered, as the child in her arms whimpered.

Above the roaring in his ears he managed a rasping, "Fine. Follow me." He stomped off toward his wagon.

After several moments, he heard the hesitant click of her boots on the wooden platform behind him, the sound of the child's soft whimpers echoing in the gentle, early evening breeze.

Chapter 2

Dying. Grief held him in an iron grip, and Harrison's heart ached at the thought of the beautiful girl he'd fallen in love with, wasting away over fifteen hundred miles from here. This was not how he'd envisioned the day ending. He flicked the reins to encourage Copper to get moving. Clamping his jaw, Harrison ground his back teeth together, struggling to keep from snarling at the girl, his supposed 'substitute wife,' sitting meekly on his right.

The sound of her timid voice reached his ears, along with the jingling of coins. "Jenny sent along her dowry." There was a short pause, before she hesitantly continued. "She wanted you to have it, Harrison."

He didn't dare look at her. Not yet. If he did, he might lash out in anger, and she was already frightened enough. She'd put as much distance between them as the wagon's bench seat allowed, holding her child protectively in her arms. Sucking a thumb, the little girl clutched the front of her mother's dress. Her big eyes filled with wariness as she stared at Harrison, before she finally gave in to sleep.

"Keep it," he gritted out, snapping the reins to get Copper moving faster.

Goddammit, he'd never harmed a woman or child in his entire life, and he wasn't about to start now. But how in the hell was he supposed to take this stranger as his wife, when his heart belonged to Jenny?

Jenny. Images of her lovely face flashed before his eyes, and he inhaled deeply, trying to control his pain and anger at the loss of his dream. Jenny had spoken fondly of her sister in their letters, and he knew all about the drifter who'd passed through their little hometown, seducing Retta and leaving her with child, before riding off again. Considered a soiled dove, she'd become a disgrace in Bolster.

Now she was his burden. What was Jenny thinking?

Am I really going to marry her?

Did he even have a choice? In her letter, Jenny had pleaded with him to wed Retta. She'd called him a good man. An honorable man. A man she could trust to provide for her sister and niece so she could die peacefully, knowing they'd be well cared for. What kind of a man would he be if he threw them onto the streets?

A real bastard, that's what. Rounding the bend, Reverend Matias's church came into view, ending Harrison's internal conversation. "Let's just get it done," he muttered under his breath, tugging on Copper's reins.

Hopping to the ground, he finally met Retta's blue-eyed gaze, reminding him so much of Jenny's. Which angered him all over again, and for a moment he couldn't speak as he fought to reel his temper back in. But he was angry with everyone right now.

Jenny.

This girl and her child.

God.

Even the damned Reverend for what he was about to do, tying him to a woman not of his choosing.

Squaring his shoulders, Harrison walked to her side of the wagon and lifted his arms. "Give me the girl." The words came out gruffer than he'd intended.

Retta lifted her chin in a defiant manner. Her clear blue eyes clouded with suspicion. "Why?"

He blinked. Her sharp response wasn't what he'd expected. Retta's timidity so far hadn't been very inspiring, but now it was as if he saw her for the first time. The woman staring down at him appeared ready to do battle. Pink stained her pretty cheeks and her lush full lips pursed in annoyance. Long, pale curls escaped from her bonnet, framing a very appealing, sweet face.

His blood heated.

And that, too, angered him.

"We're getting married." Harrison didn't even try to hide his annoyance when he spoke to her. "Now, give me the girl."

For a moment, he thought she might refuse, and almost hoped she would, even if that meant letting Jenny down. But then Retta's shoulders drooped, transforming her into the meek woman he'd met at the coach station. She nodded and handed down her daughter.

A sliver of guilt tamped his anger to a slow boil as he took the sleeping child and tucked her in the crook of one arm, holding his free hand up to help Retta from the wagon.

Twenty minutes later, he exited the church a married man. The Reverend hadn't blinked an eye when Harrison showed up with a stranger to marry, though he must have wondered. But he didn't so much as ask whose child Harrison held throughout the ceremony, while a tearful bride spoke her vows.

~ ~ ~

What have I done? Retta couldn't quite believe she'd wed the grim man at her side. He'd barely spoken a word to her since she'd arrived on the stagecoach. And when he did, he seemed furious. During the short ceremony, hard steel threaded his vows. It'd taken every ounce of strength in her not to snatch Adeline from his arms and run out of the church.

"Mama," Addie said sleepily, snuggling into her arms, "thiwsty."

Retta pressed a kiss to her little girl's forehead, then gathered much-needed courage, addressing the man she'd married only minutes earlier. "May I have some water?"

Her breath froze in her lungs when she met his icy gray eyes. A scowl darkened his face. "There's a canteen tucked under your seat," he growled.

"Thank you," she whispered, hating the insipid sound of her own voice. She'd spent years being ridiculed by the 'good' townsfolk of Bolster. Abused by her father, too. Yet she'd managed to hang on to her pride, keeping her head high and her eyes level with every scornful stare she'd met.

What was it about *this* man that intimidated her so?

Breaking contact with his piercing stare, she placed Addie onto the wide spot between them, then reached under the wooden bench to locate the canteen. After quenching her thirst, her daughter snuggled back down in her arms and fell asleep.

Retta tenderly brushed the curls from Addie's face. *Poor darling.* She hadn't yet napped this afternoon. Overwhelmed with love for her babe, she pressed a kiss to her chubby little cheek.

When Harrison spoke again, the deep resonance of his voice sent a tiny shiver through her. Wondering what her wedding night would bring, her thoughts flashed back to her experience with Addie's father, Cal. Unpleasant memories, not something she was eager to repeat.

Will I have a choice?

"Retta, are you listening?" Harrison's exasperated tone snapped her mind from thoughts of the past.

She met his eyes over the top of her daughter's sleeping head, hugging her tighter as though that'd save her from her husband's temper. It hadn't worked against Papa and she doubted it'd work against this man either, who appeared upset with her. The question was, how bad would it be?

As long as he doesn't touch my baby, I can survive anything.

He scraped back thick, brown hair with a broad, long-fingered hand and demanded, "Tell me about Jenny."

Retta found it impossible to look away from his commanding stare. She wet her dry lips before saying, "Everything should have been in the letter."

Harrison's eyes lowered to her mouth. His jaw flexed before he slapped the reins to get the horse moving faster. "Humor me."

With a deep breath to settle her nerves, Retta spent the next hour, the length of time it took to reach his ranch, to talk about her sister. The happiness they'd shared growing up, the sorrow of their mother's death, and their father's downward spiral into a bottle. Jenny's sickness that'd come upon her so viciously. Everything, all the way up to Retta's departure at the train station. The only thing she didn't discuss was her father's escalating need to 'beat the sin' out of her, and her disastrous liaison with Cal.

Retta's voice cut off when she caught sight of Harrison's home, tucked at the foothills of a low mountain range. A medium-sized ranch nestled in a cluster of trees, with a wide, shaded porch facing the magnificent view. Jenny had said Harrison was successful in the silver mines, but this was more than she'd envisioned.

The buckboard rolled to a stop before a long iron gate, and without saying a word, Harrison hopped down to open it, then pulled the wagon through, closing the gate behind them. It was getting late and the setting sun graced the area in soft shadows of reds and golds, giving the home a calming, picturesque quality. In contrast, a cloud of tension hung in the air, growing thicker and darker with each passing minute.

Retta nervously licked her lips again, uneasiness churning harder in her stomach. Shivers snaked up her spine.

What would this man expect of her tonight? Their wedding night. *You can do this, Retta,* she assured herself, *just close your eyes and think of something else.*

Harrison took Addie from her before helping her down. The jostling movement woke her daughter, and a few drowsy moments passed before she realized she wasn't being held by her mama any longer. With a wail, her lower lip trembling, she held out her hands as fat tears fell from her big brown eyes, so identical to Cal's.

Frowning fiercely, Harrison eased Addie back into Retta's arms. Collecting her bags from the bed of the wagon, he strode up the steps and deposited them on the wide-planked porch before unlatching the sturdy split-door and flinging both open.

Rooted to the spot, Retta told her feet to get moving, but they weren't listening. As hard as she tried, she couldn't force herself to enter his home, and into a life she didn't choose. A life with this implacable stranger. All the things Jenny told her about him had been wrong. He was neither kind nor gentle. Whoever he'd been years ago, he wasn't that same man today.

Too late. There'd be no going back for her now. That'd ended when she'd allowed Cal to doggedly coax her into submission under the stars on a hot summer night.

Harrison pinned her with stony eyes, brows drawn down. "Coming?"

Retta gulped, but slowly stepped onto the porch like a prisoner on her way to the gallows, which was exactly how she felt. By the time she approached the threshold of the narrow but functional foyer, anger seemed to ooze from him.

Silently he scooped up her bags. "This way."

Trying to ignore her rising anxiety as he led her into the house, Retta took in the spacious parlor. Harrison lit one of the wall lamps, filling the dim interior with the faint smell of kerosene and a soft golden glow. Although lacking any sort of feminine touches, the room appeared comfortable. A stone fireplace covered part of one wall. A tufted sofa and matching chair took up space across from a lovely formal dining set, framed by a huge picture window, perfectly smooth without a single ripple. She couldn't conceive the cost of glass for such a window. Many of the fancier houses in Bolster couldn't boast an extravagance like this.

Harrison strode from the room and she followed, more intimidated than ever. He brought her to a long, wide kitchen, taking a moment to light another sconce. Floor-to-ceiling shelves on one side of the sink area held an assortment of pottery and dishes. A simple block table and four chairs filled the middle of the room. On the other side, a thick wooden slab with a satiny finish provided a functional place to knead bread. Shiny copper pots and pans hung from a rack near the cast-iron cooking stove, which looked new and unused.

Her gaze lingered on its fancy scrollwork. Cooking on such a luxury would be a true joy, and for the first time since she'd boarded the train in Chicago, Retta felt a rush of anticipation. She loved to bake.

One corner held wooden barrels, and a narrow door against the far wall had been left ajar, cracked open a good six inches. She stared curiously, and ventured, "Root cellar?"

"Yes. Could be bigger, deeper. More shelves, too. But it's enough for now." He eyed Addie, snoring softly on her shoulder. "I suppose the girl still nurses?"

Retta felt her cheeks heat at the very private question. "N-No, Adeline can drink milk from a cup."

Her new husband grunted. "Might consider an ice box, then. I'll order one from Silver Cache."

"Where would you get ice?"

"Got access to plenty of ice up there." Harrison jerked his chin toward the window and the mountain range beyond.

Along the higher elevation, she spotted snow. Mesmerized by the sight, she perused the craggy dips and soaring summits.

Then she started when Harrison advanced toward her, his eyes on Addie.

Retta stiffened. As exhausted as she was, if he tried to harm her girl in any way, she'd fight him.

A gruff chuckle near her ear indicated he'd reached her. "Relax, Retta. I don't bite."

He smelled of leather and dark spice. Such a combination under different circumstances would have appealed to her. Right now, she just wanted it, *and him*, to go away.

His broad chest brushed her shoulder when he continued past her, carrying her bags down a short hallway and disappearing through a door. Her heart raced as apprehension filled her, wondering if the room was for her and Adeline, or her and Harrison.

Of course it's for me to share with Harrison. I'm his wife now.

A heartbeat later, he returned, a determined expression on his face. Stopping in front of her, far too close, he peered down at her with unreadable eyes. "It's getting late. Put the child down for the night. Use the room across from ours, on the left. Then go to bed, you've had a long trip."

Across from ours . . .

That answered her question about the sleeping arrangements. She ran her tongue across her teeth, searching for some moisture so she could speak. "Maybe I should stay with Adeline tonight. She might wake up frightened, being in a strange place."

Harrison's face hardened. "No. You're my wife, your place is with me." He indicated a back door at the end of the hallway. "I'm going to tend to my horse. When I return, I'll expect to find you in my bed."

With that, he strode away without a backward glance and slammed out the door.

Retta sucked in a deep breath, her legs shaking beneath her as the finality of her situation crashed down on her.

Oh, Lord. What have I gotten myself into?

~ ~ ~

Pausing outside the back porch, Harrison stomped the excess dirt from his boots. He'd remained in the barn far longer than intended, brushing Copper until he gleamed, then lingering while the feisty mustang chomped oats and hay. Scraping out hard-packed muck from Copper's hooves, digging stones from the wagon wheels . . . it all took time.

Stop stalling. He had a wife waiting for him inside. Not the one he'd expected, but she was his nevertheless. He had to deal with her sooner or later. *Later, preferably.*

With a self-deprecating snort, he entered the hallway leading to the kitchen. Prying off his boots, he dropped them next to the stove; first one, then the other, each dull *thud* on the floor echoing his bleak mood.

What now? The woman was afraid of him, not that he blamed her. He hadn't exactly been welcoming toward her or the girl.

The girl. The child had a name. *Adeline.*

He scrubbed a hand through his hair and blew out an impatient breath.

Not only was he wed to a woman he didn't love, he was an instant father. To a dainty little female, no less. Hell, if he were a bettin' man, the money would have been on his brother ending up in a shotgun marriage. Frank was as wild as Harrison was steady.

And there'd be no living with the ornery cuss when he found out.

Enough moonlight filtered through the window that Harrison didn't bother with a lamp as he headed for the sink. A few hard jerks on the pump filled the tin washbowl halfway to the rim, enough to scrub his hands and soak his head.

Straightening, he tossed back his damp strands, sending drops flying. Harrison sluiced the excess off the back of his neck, the cool water soothing some of his tension.

The lone wall sconce in the parlor still glowed, and he strode over to lower the wick until it blinked out. Women didn't much like the smell of smoldering kerosene, so he flipped the snuffer in place to keep the smoke from stinking up the air, then headed down the back hallway toward his room.

Our room.

Harrison found himself dragging his heels as he thought of the woman who waited for him in the big feather bed he'd ordered from Silver Cache a few months ago. When he'd built the frame and set the bed-slats, he'd anticipated the happy reaction of his bride-to-be. Maneuvering the thick mattress in place and smoothing on the soft linens he'd dried in the sun, he'd pictured the delight on her beautiful face. A handmade quilt he'd also found, bright with embroidered flowers and tiny birds, completed the marriage bed he'd share with—

Not Jenny, goddammit. Pausing at the half-open door, Harrison inhaled deeply. Squeezing his eyes shut, he pinched the bridge of his nose between his finger and thumb. His bride's pale, frightened face etched onto the backs of his lids. *I can't do this.*

Turning, he trudged back to the kitchen and the bottle of Old James he kept under the sink. Pulling a tumbler from the side cabinet, he splashed in two fingers of bourbon and downed it in a single gulp. Harrison eyed the remaining fifth, which looked to be a goodly amount. He had bought the bottle right before Christmas, and he'd never been much of a drinker.

That might just be changing tonight.

Wiping his damp mouth on the back of his sleeve, Harrison poured another.

Chapter 3

Retta came awake abruptly, jerking upright in the bed. She must have dozed off despite the attack of nerves that had kept her hunched in the pillows, clutching the bedsheets until her knuckles throbbed. Exhaustion had gotten the better of her.

Shoving tangled hair out of her eyes, she peered across the room toward the door she'd propped open so she could hear Addie if she awoke anytime throughout the night. Earlier, half-spooked, she'd set a lamp burning on the low dresser against the opposite wall before climbing into bed.

She strained to hear any noise, any tiny sound of distress. When Addie's sweet little snores reached her ears, a sign she slept deeply, a hiss of relief escaped Retta's lips.

The darling hadn't raised a bit of fuss when Retta had laid her down, asleep almost before she could fasten a fresh diaper and pull a nightgown over her girl's curly little head. She'd trimmed the wick in the wall sconce until it burned low, then tucked Addie in securely.

Fully awake now, Retta did her best to relax into the pillows. A futile attempt. She wouldn't easily fall asleep again. A faint clinking in the kitchen told her Harrison had finally finished his nighttime chores. She couldn't imagine what he might be doing. She only knew he'd soon enter the bedroom. Once here, would he shed his clothes and pounce on her?

Fresh panic had her breaking out in icy chills. *Maybe if I pretend to be asleep, he'll leave me be.*

His image flashed in her mind. The man was so big and brawny. Much larger than she remembered from the one time she'd caught a glimpse of him back in Bolster when he'd shown up to collect Jenny for a barn dance. Hard-muscled from laboring in his mines, no doubt. His wide hands, long-fingered and work-hardened . . . how would they feel against her tender skin? Would he be gentle or cruel? What if those hands slapped and his fingers pinched and probed, instead of caressed?

Like Cal.

God, stop thinking about it. She was his wife now, legal and binding. Her husband could do as he liked and nobody would stop him. Marriage gave him power over her.

Nausea gripped Retta's stomach, pushing bile up into her throat. It was all so unfair. First Cal. Then her sweet sister falling ill. Now this. Trapped forever in a loveless marriage to a hard man.

Her eyes burned with unshed tears as she tortured herself with a litany of the ways Harrison Carter could cause her pain, and it didn't matter what Jenny had said about his warm, caring nature. Nor did it matter how gently he'd held her little girl while they'd stood before the preacher and repeated vows neither one of them might ever be able to keep.

Scuttling across the bed, her cotton nightgown snagging around her knees, Retta's singular thought was to scoop up her child, the only bright spot in her otherwise drab life, and escape out the door. To run as fast and as far as her legs could take them.

She managed to untangle herself from the voluminous material and gain her feet, only to shrink back in apprehension when the hallway floorboards creaked, closer and closer.

Then, a heavy exhale right outside the slightly ajar door. *Harrison.*

Teeth chattering, Retta dove for the bed and burrowed under the covers. Eyes squeezed closed, the phrase *pretend you're asleep, pretend you're asleep, pretend you're asleep* became a mantra in her mind.

The sound of the door clicking shut sent her into fresh panic. A few seconds later, the mattress dipped on the far side of the bed. In the anxiety-laden quiet, she heard the rustling of clothes, the chink of a belt buckle, the whisper of a shirt. She breathed in and out as quietly as possible. Biting her bottom lip to stop it from trembling, Retta curled into the tiniest ball of shivering flesh possible, trying to will herself into unconsciousness.

Sudden heat engulfed her shoulders, her spine, the backs of her legs, as she felt him nestle close. One large, muscled arm curved around her waist and tugged her against his *completely* naked body.

She swallowed a whimper, her limbs locked so tightly she ached. He adjusted slightly, as if searching for the most comfortable dip in the feathers, his wriggling movements fusing him against her quaking frame.

Please—

"I know you're awake, Retta." His deep rasp vibrated in her ear.

Startled, she jerked, which brought her even closer to his hot, firm flesh. Refusing to contemplate the meaning of that heavy firmness, now pressing into the small of her back, Retta froze. Still, a tiny sob burst from her throat.

He stroked her arm with fingers every bit as rough-hewn as she'd imagined. "Shh. You don't know me." His mouth stirred the hair at her nape. "I don't know you." He brought her around to face him, and the shock of this new position made her gasp and slam her eyes shut.

Sighing, he cupped the side of her head with one wide palm and pushed her cheek into his shoulder, his thumb rubbing along her jaw. His other hand slipped over her nightgown and rested lightly on her hip.

The heat of his fingers burned through the thin cotton material. His nakedness, pressed against her, was terrifying, yet at the same time the gentle way he held her was a comfort.

"Look at me." The command in his tone left her no choice but to obey.

With a nervous gulp, she opened her eyes and met his level gaze. In the dimness from the lamplight, his eyes glittered, their expression shrouded. The smoky hint of bourbon washed over her face.

Her heart sank. He'd been in the kitchen, drinking. Heaven only knew how much. Liquor and lust made for a very bad combination. She'd learned that the hard way.

"I'm not the kind of man to demand or force. Nothing's gonna happen tonight."

She blinked. Could she believe him?

His hands were careful with her, easy. Non-threatening. "I can't—" He broke off and ground his teeth so hard she heard them gnash. Finally, he muttered, "I know you had a rough time of it. I saw Jenny's note. You're not ready. Neither am I."

Her cheeks heated from such unfamiliar and intimate contact as they lay facing each other. The man was a contradiction she couldn't figure out. One moment a growling bear, the next a gentle giant. In a situation like this, what kind of man would put off taking advantage of a woman whose body he had every right to use?

"As my wife," he continued, in the same easy tone, "you'll eventually have to get used to my touch."

Retta's tense muscles slowly loosened. She wouldn't be able to deny her new husband forever. But at least for now, she was safe. Inhaling, she detected a trace of lye soap and the natural musk of a man who worked hard. The mixture of scents further soothed her.

Hesitantly, she let her fingers unclench, though they remained pressed against his chest. The skin covering all those muscles felt smooth, with a hint of silky hair.

He was so warm that Retta relaxed.

"That's better." He stroked her hair, brushing at her curls. "I'm sorry we got off to a rough start. I won't lie to you, this is hard for me. I . . . care for your sister." He exhaled roughly. "I don't much remember you, but if this is Jenny's final wish then we must abide by it."

He tipped up her chin with two fingers. "You agree with that?"

Retta searched his intense gaze for any sign of treachery, and found none. Slowly, she nodded. "I— Yes, Harrison."

"All right, then." He brought her cheek back to his shoulder, and she felt a yawn shudder through him. "Tomorrow we'll sit down and talk. Figure out what we need to do to make this work." His arms kept her pinned to his side.

Too weary to worry about their intimate position, she mumbled, "Goodnight, Harrison."

"Goodnight, Retta," came his soft reply.

~ ~ ~

The faint sound of snoring awoke him, right before he became aware of the warm woman next to him, her silken arm draped across his bare stomach, her cheek resting close to his heart. But what surprised Harrison the most was to find himself holding her.

He lay perfectly still, not wanting to disturb the moment, enjoying the feel of Retta pressed against him. One of her long, slender legs, free from the constraints of the cotton gown she wore, hitched across his thigh. A smile curved his lips. The cumbersome material, meant to cover her from neck to toes, had failed in its attempt to keep him disinterested.

Inhaling her clean, fresh scent, Harrison entwined one of her golden curls around his finger. It felt damned nice having a woman in his bed. Unbidden, his shaft hardened. He could no more stop his body's reaction to her, than stop breathing.

Always mindful of his innocent bride-to-be back home waiting for him, he hadn't lain with anyone, though he'd used his hand when desperate urges overtook him. As often as the girls at the saloon tried to entice him, Harrison had resisted, much to his brother's amusement. Frank wasn't under the same constraint and he partook liberally of their charms.

Tucking the pale tendril behind his wife's ear, Harrison let his thumb linger against the base of her throat, all too aware she wasn't the one he loved, but his body didn't understand the difference. It'd be too easy to tug her beneath him and enjoy his new bride. She was no virgin, and he doubted she'd deny him.

Disgusted with his train of thought, as well as his desire for her, he lifted Retta's arm off his stomach and placed it by her side, then slid from the bed, careful not to wake her.

Though she was now his wife, he knew she wasn't ready for his touch. Jenny hadn't actually spelled it out in her letters, but he'd been able to read between the lines. Retta hadn't exactly been a willing partner when her daughter was conceived.

Scowling, he raked his fingers through his hair, studying the delicate beauty asleep in his bed, determined to ignore the way his cock bobbed with eagerness. Overcome with the sudden urge to track this Cal bastard down and put a bullet between his eyes, Harrison figured if he ever saw the man, he might do just that.

Spinning away from temptation, Harrison quickly dressed, shoving his swollen appendage into his trousers and carefully buttoning up. He'd promised Retta patience, and he was a man of his word. Heading into the kitchen, he set kindling and wood in the stove to start heating the griddles. Three eggs, nestled in their basket and collected from yesterday, weren't enough for all of them, so he'd check his laying hens before he began anything else. Whatever he ended up collecting could be cooked up alongside slabs of the pork shoulder from Sunday dinner.

Frank planned on stopping by today to meet Jenny. *Well, this oughta be fun.* Self-restraint wasn't his brother's best quality, and who knew how he'd react to finding Retta instead? Harrison didn't want her upset. Even though she wasn't the woman he'd expected, she was now his responsibility, as well as the child. Harrison took his duties seriously, and would do right by both.

Grief tightened his chest as he recalled fond memories of Jenny and their far too brief time together. It was hard to believe that only yesterday, he had awoken filled with happiness and hope for the future.

A sigh shook his chest. *Yesterday seems so far away.*

Now, his future was uncertain, wed to a stranger. Though his heart would always belong to Jenny, the only way forward was to gain his new bride's trust.

Harrison trudged outside to the chicken coop with a spare basket to scrounge for more eggs.

A few minutes after he returned to the kitchen, he heard the girl stirring. Certain Retta was still sleeping, no doubt worn out from her long journey, Harrison set the half-full basket down on the floor and headed into the spare bedroom. The tot had crawled from the bed and now stood in the middle of the room, one fist clutching the edge of a blanket. The rest of it dragged behind her tiny frame.

When her sleepy gaze landed on Harrison, it held no fear this time.

Harrison vowed to keep it that way. If he was going to persuade his new bride to stay with him and make this marriage work, the first step would be winning over her daughter. *Careful, all good intentions pave the road to perdition.*

Plastering on a fake smile, not ready to admit he knew nothing of how to handle a child, he said brightly, "Are you hungry, little lass?"

Addie nodded. Thrusting her thumb into her mouth, she tugged the end of the blanket to her face and mumbled, "Potty."

Harrison sniffed. From the smell of it, a diaper change was already in order. His day was just getting better and better. For one desperate moment, he considered waking up Retta, then remembered the dark circles under her pretty blue eyes and the weariness in her voice.

He rolled his shoulders back. *I run a profitable silver mine. I can handle one small child.*

The closer he got to Addie, the less certain he was of that. The babe smelled worse than a dead carcass that'd baked in the sun a good long while. Glancing around for a clean diaper, he spotted one of the newfangled things lying on the dresser, along with a change of clothes Retta must have laid out.

"Potty," the girl whined again.

"Yeah, I'm working on it. Hold your hosses." Harrison scooped up the items off the dresser, turning back to Addie. The stench of that soiled diaper grew stronger as he approached. He wrinkled his nose. "What *did* your mother feed you yesterday?"

It couldn't have been anything good.

At the sharpness of his tone, the girl's lower lip trembled as her eyes welled up.

Forcing another smile to his lips, Harrison squatted down in front of Addie. "Hey, sweetheart, you ready for some grub?"

The child blinked, two tears tracking down her cheeks. Then with a sniffle, she nodded. Tossing the diaper and clothing across his shoulder, Harrison tried to tug the blanket from her pudgy hands, but Addie wouldn't let go, instead looking perilously close to crying again.

"All right, you can keep it." Wrapping the blanket loosely around her, Harrison scooped Addie up and strode briskly down the hall, over to the fireplace. Laying the child on the woven rug in front of it, he noted sourly how the diaper had leaked onto the blanket. "Let me get some water to clean you up with." He pointed a finger and ordered, "You stay here."

Harrison hurried to the foyer and lifted the pitcher of water he usually kept on the spare washstand, pouring some into a bowl. When he turned around, he nearly stumbled over Addie, who was now standing right behind him, still hanging on to the end of the dirty, smelly blanket. He frowned, not used to being disobeyed.

The toddler plucked her thumb from her mouth and burbled, "Hungwy."

Harrison eyed the trail of pee Addie had left in her wake, the hem of her little nightgown damp. The overstuffed diaper had fallen off about halfway across the parlor and now lay in a stinking mess on his oak planked floor.

"Holy. Hell." Again, he thought about waking Retta, then dismissed the idea. "I can handle this."

"Hungwy," Addie repeated with a pout.

"Yeah, I heard you the first time," he muttered to himself, feeling a bit panicked. Reentering the parlor, Harrison plopped the bowl of water onto the table and collected babe and blanket, placing both on the polished surface. "Let's get you cleaned up." He refused to think about what now smeared across his former fine piece of dining furniture.

"Mama," the child wailed, twisting around and trying to crawl off the table. Her poop-covered bottom stuck out from beneath the filthy gown.

Grabbing the girl by the leg as gently as possible, Harrison slipped his hand between her birdlike shoulder blades and eased her over onto part of the blanket. "Adeline, lay still," he said sternly, hoping his usage of her full name would compel her to obey.

Addie stared accusingly, her lower lip trembling worse than a drunk gunslinger's shootin' arm.

Tension gripped him. If things had played out the way they were supposed to, he'd still be in bed, holding his exhausted and well-loved wife in his arms. How in blazes had his life come to this?

Jenny's lovely image flashed in his mind, and his heart constricted.

Because Jenny asked me to, that's how.

Addie sniffled again, but finally did as commanded, giving Harrison a chance to dampen a cloth and clean her up, before tossing the soiled rag and her gown onto the floor. Then he cursed under his breath, recalling what both contained. A puddle of pee had settled into the wood from where the child dribbled across the room. Well, he'd have to deal with it later.

Somehow, he managed to hold down the squirming Addie long enough to get the diaper on and tied in front, willing it to stay put. Her pinafore buttoned down the front and this he managed to wrestle on despite her wriggles.

He hefted the child to return her to the rug so he could clean up the mess littering his table and floor. As he swung her into his arms, Addie patted his cheeks with both hands and smiled at him sweetly. In that moment, she looked so much like her mother that Harrison found himself smiling back.

Right about then, his annoying brother charged through the door separating foyer and parlor, coming to a screeching halt within smelling distance of the soiled diaper. His rounded eyes took in everything, brows arched quizzically.

As usual, Frank resembled a wild man, his full beard unkempt and his long dark hair in knots. God only knew what he'd been doing that had torn out both knees of his pants. His shirt was equally ragged, the wool stained and badly wrinkled. He stank of cheap perfume and blood.

Something involving women, whiskey, and no doubt brawling. Then again, today *was* hog-butcherin' day. Might explain the blood stink.

Addie blinked at Harrison, then at Frank. Her tiny mouth opened and she let loose with a screeching, "Mama."

~ ~ ~

From a deep sleep, Retta shot up at the sound of her daughter's cry. "Oh my God." She unwound herself from the heavy quilt and made it to the spare bedroom before her mind had fully cleared from sleep. Her heart sank at the sight of an empty bed. Images of Harrison hitting her baby made her stomach wrench, and she doubled over for the briefest second to catch her breath before charging out of the room and running down the hallway.

Reaching the parlor, she took in the morning sun pouring in from the largest window. Her father would have beat her for sleeping so late. Then she spotted Harrison, holding her wriggling daughter, who waved her arms around like a dervish, shrieking at the top of her lungs.

By the time Retta's fuddled mind registered the intimidating man in the doorway, she was about ready to faint. With his mane of hair and full beard, the behemoth resembled a black bear she'd once seen in a painting hanging on the wall of Bolster's First Bank and Trust.

Retta quickly closed the distance between her and her child, facing a scowling Harrison.

She held out her arms, locking her shaking knees to keep upright. "P-Please give her to me." Despite her enforced bravado, there was no stopping her instinctive flinch when he made a move toward her. Eyes pinched shut, the sound of her panicked breathing roared in her ears before she managed to wrestle her emotions under control.

Opening her eyes, Retta took in Harrison's glowering expression. His flexing jaw made him appear to be chewing on a particularly tough piece of meat. Without a word, he dumped Addie into her arms. Immediately quieting, her daughter clung to Retta's neck, shuddering and damp from sobbing.

Retta glanced toward the bearded man and found a matching scowl on his face. Edging back, she reached behind her with her free arm and gripped the corner of an occasional table. What would these men do to her and Adeline? Making amends to Harrison had to be her first priority. Her husband could do whatever he wanted with her.

She licked her lips. Unable to meet Harrison's penetrating stare, she focused instead on his chest. If it was just her, she'd hold her ground, but she had her little girl to think about. "I'm sorry I overslept." She swallowed hard. "It won't happen again."

The silence in the room grew thick with tension, and Retta braced herself, shielding her daughter against the blow she feared was coming.

The deep voice of the man across the room growled out, "What the hell, Harrison?"

Retta instinctively met his stare. But instead of ire, his frown held confusion. Her gaze lowered to the floor, holding her baby closer. Everything had happened so fast she'd been running on instinct, but now her mind scrambled for a way out of this mess. What could she say to appease these two men so they didn't hurt her and Addie?

"Not now, Frank." Harrison's voice sounded weary, but it didn't hold the anger she'd expected. "Retta, look at me," he said softly.

Addie had grown calm, her thumb in her mouth, her other hand playing with Retta's hair. But though her worry had receded some, Retta couldn't bring herself to look at him.

"Retta," Harrison repeated, placing a finger under her chin and forcing her head up. The gray eyes that met hers were gentle. "I would never hurt you or Adeline. You don't have to fear me. Ever."

Could she trust his words? After every brutal beating from her drunken papa, he'd promise the same thing. But that never stopped it from happening again.

Still resting his fingers under her chin, his eyes searched her face. "Would you like to meet my brother?" Before she could utter a word, Harrison nodded toward the bearded mountain man. "Frank, I'd like to present my wife, Retta Pierce Carter. And this little cutie is her daughter, Adeline. My daughter now."

The way he claimed her and Addie, the sudden, possessive gleam in his eyes, caused her emotions to churn.

Footsteps drew near them. Retta found herself meeting another set of familiar gray eyes.

When Harrison's touch fell away, she felt a moment of regret, then resolutely faced his brother.

Chapter 4

All their lives, Harrison had dealt with Frank's surly nature. And though only a year older, Frank tended to think of himself as some kind of second father to Harrison and their baby sister, Vivian. It would no doubt get worse next year when Vivian and their widowed mother finally joined them in Little Creede.

Overbearing and often downright sarcastic, Frank at least treated women with respect. Harrison preferred not to think about the way his brother acted around the bar maids he dallied with. Wasn't any of his business.

Frank crossed muscled arms over a massive chest and studied Retta. Harrison waited to see what would happen next. Frank's thick brows formed a straight line over his eyes. Since his brother would be an integral part of her life here in Little Creede, she'd have to learn to get along with the curmudgeon. But given Frank's usual orneriness, Harrison remained ready to jump to her aid.

The bright morning sun backlit Retta's frilly cotton nightgown, revealing a suggestion of gentle curves and soft shadows. Harrison flexed his jaw, fighting against a growing awareness of his bride. To his credit, Frank's regard of Retta never wavered below eye-level. Good thing, or Harrison would have been obliged to punch him out purely on principle.

He was impressed at the way Retta held her ground, given her fear only moments earlier. She took in her new brother-by-marriage from the top of his unkempt hair to the tips of his mud-coated boots. Though her eyes widened a bit at the hog's blood slashed across Frank's work shirt.

Finally, she parted her lips and murmured, "Mister Carter. I'm pleased to make your acquaintance." The words were uttered softly, politely.

"Missus Carter." Frank offered a quick head-nod, before regarding Harrison. He tugged on his beard. "Wanna tell me what happened to Jenny?"

A choked cry sounded from Retta. Addie, who had been curled contentedly against her mother, started whining.

"E-Excuse me, please." Without another word, Retta hurried down the hall with Addie, carrying her toward the spare bedroom. The door slammed shut, but not before they both heard the sound of her crying.

Harrison scrubbed rough palms against his eyes and muttered, "Well, shit."

Frank grabbed his arm and dragged him toward the front door. "All right, little brother. Outside, now. And start talkin.' I want to know what the hell is goin' on."

~ ~ ~

Slumped on the edge of the bed, Retta cradled her daughter, stroking her damp, tumbled curls. Adeline was such a happy, bouncy child, despite two years of exposure to a grandfather who disliked her very existence. Shy at times, yes. But usually not overly-clingy. Retta hated that circumstances had put her in a position to cause her darling any kind of anxiety.

Addie cuddled closer, gripping the high-necked collar of Retta's nightgown. "Mama." Her breath stuttered out in a sigh.

Retta pressed a tender kiss to her forehead, nuzzling the satiny skin. Her arms tightened as she rocked her little girl, until Addie's eyelids drooped. Glancing toward the door, Retta struggled with her own emotions.

Hearing her sister's name on a stranger's lips had hurt her heart. Of course, Harrison's brother would know of his betrothal and the imminent arrival of Jenny. Seeing another woman—in a nightgown, no less—holding a child, had to have shocked him. Frank Carter appeared to be a gruff sort of fellow. She supposed several years of hard mining would do that to anyone, even to the genteel dandies she'd seen now and then in the parlors of Bolster. How could it not?

And yet, Harrison seemed different. Perhaps because he'd had Jenny waiting for him, someone's love to anticipate and build upon. *And instead, he got me.*

What would the townsfolk think? Would she once again become the subject of ridicule?

Overwhelmed with a sense of loneliness, and missing her sister, Retta blinked away tears. Feeling sorry for herself wouldn't help. Neither would suffocating grief. Jenny was in good, safe hands. Aunt Millie would take such excellent care of her. God willing, Jenny would thrive far past the shortened life other consumption sufferers must have dealt with.

I have to hold on to that hope.

Easing Addie into a more comfortable position against her shoulder, Retta wiped at the damp trails on her cheeks and took in a deep, cleansing breath. Her duty now was to her child. Her husband. And her new life here in Little Creede.

A soft knock on the door broke into her musings. She swallowed against an aching throat and managed a calm, "Yes, come in."

Harrison's wide shoulders filled up the open doorway. He studied her and Addie for a long moment as her heart raced. Parting his lips to speak, he paused, then nodded toward her little girl, a question in his gaze.

Retta offered a faint smile. "It's all right. You won't wake her." She gestured toward the edge of the mattress with her chin.

Harrison crossed the room, seating himself gingerly, and resting his elbows on his thighs. "I'm sorry—"

"Listen, I—"

Retta's breath caught, as a sliver of fear curled in her belly for interrupting him. Papa would have backhanded her for such impertinence.

When Harrison lifted a large hand to gesture for her to continue, Retta flinched. Everything she had thought to say clogged up in her lungs, along with her breath.

For a brief instant, anger flared across his face, before his expression smoothed, revealing none of his thoughts.

He spoke, his tone soothing. "Retta, you have nothing to fear from me or Frank. My brother may seem a bit rough, but he's a good man. And I would never harm you or your daughter."

She shifted nervously. Was he telling her the truth? As Addie wriggled slightly, yawning, Retta repositioned her against one shoulder and rubbed her back gently. "Does Frank like children?"

"Steamed, with potatoes and extra gravy, I suspect." At her shocked gasp, Harrison grinned. "Sorry," he said, though he didn't sound sorry at all, "just teasin'."

The ball of tension inside her began to loosen as she dared to believe Jenny's vow that Harrison was a decent man. Her stiff shoulders relaxed.

He studied her with a thoughtful expression. "He deals with children well enough." Reaching out carefully, Harrison stroked Addie's curls with a gentle palm. "She's a sweet child. I bet she'll wrap her Uncle Frank right around her little finger."

He rose, extending his hand. "Want to find out? Will you let me introduce you properly to my brother? I talked to him. Explained a few things."

Retta fingered the silk ribbon at the high neck of her nightgown. Heat rose to her cheeks. "I would like that, as soon as I, um, make myself decent." She stood, cradling her daughter. "Five minutes?"

"Take your time." Harrison ambled toward the half-open door. "And, Retta? I think you're charmingly decent, as is." He firmly shut the door behind him, leaving her gaping and hot with a flush she swore now covered her from head to bare toes.

~ ~ ~

Frank lounged against the window, staring out, as Harrison checked on the coffee pot. He worked silently, using a bit of pork fat to grease the skillet he'd set on the griddle, then cracking eggs into a shallow bowl. "Want them scrambled?"

Frank turned from the window and fixed him with a frown. "Why isn't your wife cooking breakfast?"

"Because she's exhausted, you jackass. With what happened yesterday— Look, I'm not going to explain it all again." Harrison grabbed a fork and started whipping the eggs into a foamy mess. "Just be nice. Can you do that?"

Frank glowered, his bushy brows forming a straight line over his eyes, and dropped into the nearest chair. "I'm always nice to women." He crossed his arms over his chest.

"Sure you are," Harrison said sarcastically. He dumped the eggs into the hot skillet and stirred them. "Make yourself useful and pour the coffee."

As Frank expelled a loud, put-upon sigh and lumbered from his chair, there was a movement in the kitchen archway. Retta appeared, wearing a brown gathered skirt and a white ruffled blouse, her hair tied back with a scrap of lace. Addie rested in her mother's arm, her thumb firmly plugged in her rosebud mouth, drowsily content.

Retta ventured forward then halted, glancing from Frank, to Harrison. She looked utterly lovely, standing there in her sensible clothes, their plainness somehow framing her stunning features, making them stand out in the sunny room.

Under his steady perusal, a lovely blush stained her cheeks. Then Frank cleared his throat, and the moment was lost.

Pulling the skillet off the griddle, Harrison wiped his suddenly damp hands on the seat of his trousers and moved toward his wife. He gently caught her elbow and guided her forward, until she stood between him and Frank. "Can we try this again?" At her brief nod, Harrison gave her arm a squeeze. "Retta, may I present my brother, Frank."

A dimple appeared at the corner of her mouth when she sketched a quick, graceful curtsey.

"Mister Carter, I apologize for my earlier outburst of emotion. I am surely glad to meet you," Retta murmured. Shifting Addie to free up a hand, she held it out to Frank.

With a sober expression, he took her fingers in his big paw, and brought them to his mouth. Retta's eyes widened as he pressed a brief kiss across her knuckles and rasped, "I sure didn't mean to make you cry, ma'am."

He might have said more, but just then Addie's thumb popped out of her rosy little mouth and she giggled, staring straight at her new uncle. Before Harrison could react, she lifted her tousled head from Retta's shoulder and stretched the wet digit toward Frank in a kind of babyish salute. Her lips parted in a smile that revealed pearly teeth.

Letting go of Retta's hand, he gaped, first at the young girl, then her mother who looked just as surprised. It was the first time Harrison had ever seen him at a complete loss. "Uh," Frank began.

"Hi," Addie's childish peep broke in. She wriggled, reaching out to Frank and bouncing in Retta's arms.

"I think she wants a hug," Harrison managed somberly.

Taking a hasty step back, Frank's dark eyebrows crawled up in horror. "I'm all dirty."

Retta spoke up. "I don't think she'll mind." She loosened her grip on Addie.

His new daughter latched on to Frank's shirt lapels. He grabbed her around the waist, then stood frozen as the tiny girl faced him squarely and rubbed her pudgy fingers over his eyelashes, sighing in delight.

"She likes the feel of eyelashes," Retta offered helpfully. Her gaze met Harrison's, bright humor washing away the last of the worry he'd spotted in her eyes earlier.

Nodding, he cleared his throat. "Yep, Uncle Frank does have some uncommonly pretty lashes."

"You—" Frank began then clamped his jaw shut and managed a tight-lipped smile aimed at his brand-new niece who had jabbed her wet thumb in one of his ears.

Retta clapped a hand over her mouth to stifle a laugh that held an edge of obvious relief.

"You can hold her," she managed. "She likes to be hugged."

Gingerly, as if he held live gunpowder, Frank brought Addie to his chest, then gaped again when she laid her head trustingly against his shoulder and puffed out a tiny sigh. Her thickly lashed eyes fluttered, then closed. She popped her thumb back into her mouth.

"Um, maybe I should sit down. I don't want to drop her." Hastily, Frank scuttled to his vacated chair and sank onto its hard surface, Addie molded to his chest like a little barnacle. With a hint of panic in his voice, he asked, "Is she hungry? She can, um, have some of my eggs."

A wide grin covering his face, Harrison moved to the stove and grabbed the skillet's handle. "Coming right up." He paused, then added with a grin, "Uncle Frank."

Chapter 5

Pulling in on the reins in front of the mercantile, Harrison clucked his tongue softly, the brief command enough to bring the enormous bronze-colored horse to a stop. Retta tightened her grip on Addie as a precaution, but the sturdy buckboard wagon only shuddered a bit. As the horse—Copper, she recalled—tossed his head and snorted, she ran a quick hand over her bonnet to assure it hadn't blown sideways on the trip into town.

Harrison jumped down and moved to her side. "I'll take Adeline."

For a frozen moment, Retta's hold tensed, then Addie squirmed on her lap, both arms reaching out toward her new papa.

"You, my girl," Retta chided gently, "are a flirt."

Over the past week, her daughter had grown fond of the handsome man who smiled at her as if she were the most important two-year-old in the world.

Concern for Addie's wellbeing aside, Retta knew she had to find a way to stop borrowing trouble. Here they were, in much better circumstances, her precious baby happy and content.

Find your trust, Retta. Especially after all Addie had been through in her short life. With a self-chastising sigh, Retta loosened her hold and allowed her daughter to clamber off her lap and into Harrison's embrace.

Swinging Addie to his hip, he secured her in place with one brawny arm and held out his other hand for Retta. Careful to hold down her skirt, she climbed from the wagon and gasped when he unexpectedly curled his free arm around her waist and swung her to the ground next to him. "Oh, my."

His breath warm against her forehead, he murmured, "That first step is a doozy. I wouldn't want you to end up in the dirt with your pretty clothes all mussed up."

Studying the apparel she'd donned earlier that morning, she chewed her bottom lip. "I'm not dressed properly for a town visit." Her serviceable blue twill skirt would look out of place anywhere but in the kitchen of her new home. She brushed at a streak of dust. "I should have worn a dress, and—"

"Retta." Harrison eased away and stared down at her, his thick brows drawn together. For a moment he looked so fierce, she trembled at incurring his anger. Her fear must have shown on her face, because his expression immediately softened.

Jiggling Addie on his hip, he laid a hand on Retta's shoulder and coaxed her toward him. "Look over there, in the doorway of the mercantile. See that lady?"

Retta swallowed her anxiety and obediently glanced to the side. A woman stood on the wooden slat boardwalk, a squawking hen under one arm and a rough-woven basket hooked over the other. She wore a man's duster, the heavy, oiled cloth crusted with dirt. On her gray-frizzed head sat a ragged porkpie hat, and the frayed legs of what appeared to be dungarees peeked out from the hem of the duster.

She caught Retta's stare and tossed a wink and a raspy, "How-do?" her way, before striding toward a line of horses tethered to a rail. The only thing remotely feminine about the woman's apparel was the buttoned and laced-up pair of boots on her surprisingly narrow feet.

"Now," Harrison said near Retta's temple, "that's Hattie Frick, one of the Jinks' Mining women. Her husband has a claim there and she comes to town twice a month for supplies and such. If she can walk through Little Creede wearing men's britches, and nobody blinks an eye, then I think folks around here will say you sure look mighty pretty today."

The possessiveness in his tone made Retta's heart race, her stomach twirling pleasantly at the caress of his hand on her shoulder. When he dipped his head toward her, for one breathless moment she thought for sure he'd kiss her.

But he only studied her closely, then adjusted one of her bonnet ribbons, before offering his unencumbered arm. "Let's see what we can find at the mercantile. Fabric, I'd wager. And those sewing gewgaws you ladies always seem to need."

"You mean, buttons and thread?" she asked, fluttering her lashes at him, even as her cheeks heated at her own daring. How would he react to her teasing?

Judging by the wide grin on his face as he steered her toward the open shop door, Harrison didn't mind a bit.

Inside, Retta found herself amazed at the well-stocked shelves, not at all what she'd envisioned a mercantile in this wild country to contain. Barrels of pickles, potatoes, and apples rimmed the walls. Tall, wide jars of eggs in brine and pig knuckles in vinegar took up space on wooden tables along with jams and preserved meats. Overhead, slabs of dried venison and backfat hung from the ceiling. Other tables held everything from calico and linen, to ladies' slippers and bonnets nestled next to cowboy hats, boots, and kerchiefs. She spotted a bolt of dark-red brocade, propped against the end of the table.

She turned in a circle, trying to close her astonished mouth. Harrison crossed to her, still carrying Addie. Retta blinked up at him, dazzled by the sunlight that filtered in from the shop window, sparkling brightly over everything. "I don't know where to begin," she confessed, as Addie wriggled to be let down. "No, darling, settle yourself," she admonished the restless child.

"Mama, down," Addie begged, squirming harder.

"I can keep her with me," Harrison offered. "Got to collect an order I placed for steamed wood. For the wagon wheel," he explained, when she shot him a puzzled look. "It'll only take a few minutes, and Missus Loman—she runs the mercantile—has a hound that just birthed a passel of puppies. They'd probably lick Addie into a stupor." He grinned when Addie let out a squeal.

"Oh, that would be wonderful. You don't mind?" Retta asked, dubiously.

"Don't mind a bit." He bounced Addie a few times. "What do you say, Addie girl? You want to see some puppies?"

"Puppies," Addie screeched, attracting the attention of a few store patrons who looked their way and smiled indulgently.

"Guess that settles things," he decided.

"You aren't actually going to get a you-know-what. Are you?" she asked anxiously.

"Nah, I wouldn't do that to you. Not while you're still getting used to everything around here." He offered a wink. "Buy what you need, all right? I have an account." With that, Harrison carried the giggling Addie out. The door closed behind them.

After introducing herself to Silas Loman, the proprietor, Retta selected a rather battered straw basket with a crooked handle and slipped it over her arm. It would hold the buttons and thread Harrison had teased her about, as well as the sack of meal and jar of honeycomb he mentioned wanting. Her first priority—bunting for a blanket and some calico for dresses—sent her in the direction of that table of fabric delights she had spotted when she first ventured in.

While sifting through a bowl of whalebone buttons, she found a length of pale-blue sprigged muslin that would make a sweet little pinafore for Addie, and if she had any left over, she could fashion a few pairs of bloomers to match. Eagerly she added it to her growing pile of selections. A folded square of yellow seersucker caught her eye, and she shook it out over the surface, delighted to see several wide yards. With summer coming, both she and Addie would benefit from lightweight nightgowns made from the soft material.

As Retta reached for a gray-stripe bolt, envisioning a new shirt for Harrison, her gaze fell on the dark-red brocade again, the rich fabric just begging to be made into a fancy gown. *What an unexpected find.* She stroked the beautiful material, smooth and cool beneath her palm, and visualized the style of gown this lovely bolt might create. Something with an off the shoulder drape, caught up in sweet little dropped cap sleeves with perhaps a matching spencer, the softly ruched train trimmed in black bugle beading to play up the fabric's red sheen—

"You should buy it. I do believe it would look lovely against your hair." The deep voice held roguish familiarity as well as charm.

Retta dropped the brocade and spun, coming face-to-face with a complete stranger. Handsome, well-dressed, wearing a diamond-tipped stickpin through the high starched collar of his pristine white shirtwaist. His charcoal wool morning coat, exquisitely tailored, fit his trim frame perfectly, and his pinstriped trousers boasted a precise crease. She'd never seen a man so nattily-dressed, including patrons at an opera she'd once attended with Aunt Millie in Chicago.

The man appeared to be in his late thirties. With gray wings of hair at his temples, offsetting his dense black, pomaded locks and the mutton-chop sideburns on either side of his lean cheeks, he cut a dashing figure. Yet the pierce of his gaze, eyes so dark they appeared as black as his hair, unsettled her. Retta hastily retreated, then froze as he advanced.

"I apologize for my forward behavior, miss. I am afraid too many days living in the uncouth wilderness of Little

Creede has stunted my manners." He swept into a graceful bow. "Slim Morgan, at your service. I own an entertainment establishment here in town." He straightened, offering a smile. "I shall feel quite desolate until I know your name, young lady."

"I'm Retta Carter. And I really should finish my chores, Mister Morgan." She clutched her basket to her chest and strove to remember her manners, flustered at the attention she was receiving from this charming man. "Perhaps we'll meet again sometime—"

"I am counting on it, Miss Carter." He tilted his head, looking faintly puzzled as he stroked a finger over his waxed mustache. "I know a Carter. Two of them, in fact." Leaning closer, he murmured, "Dare I presume you to be their sister?"

The man looked so charmingly hopeful, Retta couldn't help but unbend a bit. "No, sir. Not their sister. In fact, I'm—"

"Mama," the high, childish voice of her daughter broke in, just as Harrison strode up with a thunderous expression on his face. Curled on his shoulder, Addie held out her arms.

Retta smiled, scooping the child out of her husband's grasp. Though happy and relieved to see him, the look on his face gave her pause.

Nervousness fluttered through her belly. Even though he'd assured her he'd never raise a hand against her or Addie, she still had her doubts.

"Harrison, have you met Mister—" she began hesitantly.

"I know who he is." He sent the man a scowl.

Slim Morgan didn't utter a word, but his lips twitched, as if he found the entire situation amusing.

"We need to go, Retta." Harrison bit out each word, setting his hand on her shoulder. "The wagon's ready."

"But—"

"*Now*, Retta." Sparing only a scant amount of time to gather up the fabric she had chosen, Harrison urged her toward the front.

Whatever bond she'd felt earlier had shattered. Disappointment raced through her. She had a lifetime ahead of her with this man, and by God she wouldn't be treated this way. Reaching deep inside, she finally found the courage she'd been missing since stepping off that coach in Little Creede.

Out of earshot from the fabric table, she dug in her heels. "Harrison, please. I must pick up a few more items." Unmoving, she faced her husband and stiffened her spine. "Whatever is wrong?"

"I don't want you talking to that son of—that man," he muttered. "What did he want? Did he touch you?" His hands fisted at his sides.

"What? No, of course not." She broke off when he caught hold of her arm, his eyes narrowing as his gaze bore into her. "Do let me collect my things." She eased away slowly, then tugged a bit until he finally released her, looking none too happy about it.

Several young miners chose that exact moment to burst into the store, crowding the doorway, stomping clumps of dried mud from their boots.

Harrison released a growling breath, plucking her daughter from her arms. "Fine. We'll wait outside with the wagon." Addie rested her chin on his shoulder with a yawn, and his face softened, glancing down at her. With a brief nod to an older woman standing near the front of the store, he exited the building.

The woman held out her hand for Retta's basket. "I'm Betsey Loman. I'll take that, my dear. Such pretty ribbon." She smiled gently as she lifted out the spools of ribbon Retta had chosen for trim. "I have a bag for the buttons. Ah, there it is." She dug out a drawstring pouch made of burlap. "You know, I fancied that yellow seersucker myself." She nodded toward the fabric, folded neatly atop the other three Retta had chosen. "Cut off a good four yards of it to make a dressing gown." She gestured toward her ample bosom. "Though I might have been better off with five."

"Yes, ma'am."

"Oh now, you just call me Betsey. Everyone does." She carefully counted out and set aside the needles Retta selected. "And you're Retta. Married our Harrison, did you?" When Retta blinked in surprise, Betsey flapped a hand. "There's very few secrets in a place like Little Creede, dear. Not to mention my store. Besides, I heard Harrison talking to you." She bundled ribbon spools and needles together and used a corner of the seersucker to wrap the items. "And that little darlin' of yours? Cute as can be."

"Thank you, Betsey," Retta began, then jumped as Slim Morgan sidled up behind her. She thought the man had already left the mercantile. Shifting uncomfortably, she swore she could feel his hot breath on the back of her neck. Which would mean he stood entirely too close to her for propriety.

Retta edged forward until the counter dug into her middle. It didn't much help, for she heard the click of his boots as he moved with her, step for step.

If Harrison looked through the window and saw the man standing nearly on top of her, what would he think? Would he blame her?

Lord, what should I do?

Thankfully, Betsey came to her rescue. "Mister Morgan, your wagon is stocked and ready." The shop-owner's tone held a not-so-polite frost. "I think you might want to get along on your way, now." She crossed to the door and swung it open, then waited there, her hands folded at her waist.

Hastily, Retta put needed distance between her and Slim Morgan. Offering a brief nod, she tucked her hands in her pockets. She didn't want the man touching her.

As if he'd guessed her thoughts, his lips thinned ominously, before he tipped the brim of his stylish black wool Slouch toward her, and strode out.

Wondering if she'd ever understand the vagaries of men, Retta retied her bonnet and held out her hand to Betsey. "Thank you for making me feel so welcome. I'd consider it an honor if you would stop by the ranch for tea. And with Addie's sweet tooth, I always have cakes or biscuits on hand."

Betsey clasped Retta's fingers, giving them a squeeze. "The pleasure's all mine." She hesitated, as if pondering her next words, then blurted out, "I feel obliged to offer some caution, dear. You might want to avoid Slim Morgan. He is no gentleman. And his behavior toward women is . . . unsavory, at best." She peered anxiously at Retta. "Do you understand what I am trying to say? You're a married woman, and in most of society that status alone carries protection and respect. But a man like Morgan doesn't care about such things."

Retta nodded. Oh, she'd had firsthand experience on the unsavory aspect of men who believed women were nothing more than a plaything for their lusts, uncaring of their feelings. All her instincts confirmed Slim Morgan was one of those men.

"I'll be giving the man a wide berth, Betsey. Never doubt it."

~ ~ ~

Beyond the corner of the mercantile, Slim Morgan leaned against the rough wood siding, cursing under his breath as the fine wool of his coat snagged on a splinter. Nobody in this pissant town cared about the niceties, such as sanding down the damned split logs before they built anything. Cheap was the name of the game.

Not me. After getting a taste of the better things in life thanks to a stint on *The Mississippi Empress* and its floating riverfront gambling hall, Slim had no intention of going back. Certainly not to the one-room, tin-roof hovel he'd escaped years ago, when he killed his father and raided the meager nest egg the miserable geezer had hidden in his ratty old mattress.

The coins weren't much but they'd bought him a spot on the Empress as an apprentice to Fast-Johnnie Dawson, an aging gambler with the slickest dealing style Slim had ever seen. He'd kept his nose clean and his ears open, learning all he could, before smothering Fast-Johnnie in his sleep one night.

Escaping over the side of the slow-moving riverboat with his earnings—and Johnnie's bulging coin purse—Slim had moved north for a spell, then west, where he'd won the only saloon in Little Creede, The Lucky Lady, in a card game. Sure, he'd cheated, but that was only a concern if you got caught.

He had a knack for making investments that paid off. Too bad his gambling habit ate up his savings as fast as he could earn it. At least as owner of The Lucky Lady he had easy access to all the women he could want. And he wanted Carter's new wife.

What a mighty fine woman. She'd look damn good in his bed.

All that silky yellow hair and those eyes, so wide and bluer than the sky. Her slender frame under her plain skirt and blouse made his cock leap when he'd stood close to her inside the mercantile.

Retreating further into the shadows, Slim focused on the pretty turn of Retta Carter's ankle as she climbed into the wagon and then held out her arms for the snotty-nosed rug rat who crawled into her lap. The girl's sticky hands clutched her mother at breast-level, and Slim broke out in a sweat as he imagined putting his hands in the exact same place. Stroking those full globes . . . maybe pinching the nipples hidden beneath lace and linen . . .

The sight of Harrison Carter, swinging up into the seat next to Retta, splintered Slim's fevered daydream. Clucking at the horse—a big, strong Mustang Slim coveted for his own—Carter drove the wagon down the dusty, rutted street.

"Goddamn," Slim muttered, adjusting himself in his pants. First, he'd find a willing whore at The Lucky Lady to take care of his immediate problems. After all, as owner of the damned place they were as much his property as the whiskey he stocked.

Then, he'd figure out a way to force the Carters to sell him at least one of their mines.

A grin spread across his face as he watched their wagon fade into the dust trail.

Maybe I'll see about taking Harrison's woman, too.

Chapter 6

Glancing outside as the sun slowly sank against a sky of brilliant orange and gold, Harrison took in a deep breath, expelling it slowly in an attempt to shake off his irritation at finding Retta talking to that skunk, Slim Morgan.

The man was a menace, a dirty, low-down scoundrel who would hang his own mother if there was a dollar in it for him. And his reputation with women was just as unseemly. Rumor was, he'd bedded a saloon girl south of Silver Cache, his treatment of her so rough she'd nearly died from her injuries. Because of his money and stature as a businessman, the poor girl had been too frightened to have him arrested, and fled East as soon as she'd healed enough to travel.

When he'd walked into the mercantile to find Retta chatting with the bastard, jealousy hit Harrison like a sharp punch to the gut. They didn't know each other well enough for love, but she belonged to him now. It was up to him to protect her.

If I find Morgan near my wife again, I'll put a bullet through his brain.

Harrison rubbed the back of his neck. It'd been a long, silent ride to the ranch, because he'd still been bristling over the incident. What had started out as a nice family outing turned quickly to shit, his bad temper threatening what headway he'd made with his new bride. It wasn't her fault the no-account bastard approached her.

I need to fix this, and fast.

Striding into the kitchen, he retrieved the bottle of whiskey and tossed back a shot, slamming the glass on the table, the burn in his gullet helping to clear his mind. The possessiveness he felt toward Retta unnerved him.

A piece of his heart already accepted her as his, though the rest still mourned for Jenny. Harrison glanced toward the hallway she'd bolted down earlier, carrying Addie to tuck into bed. That'd been some time ago.

Avoiding me, no doubt.

His jaw ticked. If they were going to make this marriage work, he couldn't let her put distance between them. Retta had to accept him as her husband. Not fear him.

She'd been hurt in the past, and he'd vowed to be careful of her feelings, to take things slowly. But it was time for his wife to trust him.

Tonight, she'd learn to accept his touch.

~ ~ ~

Retta smoothed silky curls off Addie's cheek. Her sweet angel had given up the fight twenty minutes earlier, and now slept soundly, but Retta couldn't find the courage to face her husband yet. A shudder quivered through her. She didn't think Harrison would actually beat her, but she didn't know him all that well. He'd been visibly upset the entire ride back to the ranch, and she wasn't sure what was in store for her once she left this room.

She stiffened at the sound of his heavy tread down the hall, scrambled to her feet, and moved away from Addie's bed. She didn't want her daughter awakened by his bad temper.

Retta watched with trepidation as the door slowly opened.

Harrison stepped inside, his gaze flickering over Addie, before focusing on her. The smile he offered held no traces of anger. She blinked, feeling off balance. A long moment passed as they stared at each other.

Finally, Harrison held out his hand to her. "Come on, Retta, it's late. Time for bed."

She ventured forward slowly. Deep down she knew he wouldn't hurt her, but that didn't stop her belly from flipping or her heart from pounding. The uncertainty of the marriage bed kept her on edge.

Maybe the best thing is to just get it over with. Her breathing became difficult as panic surged through her. Still, she let him take her hand, her fingers engulfed by his warm palm as he led her out of Addie's room, and into theirs. He guided her right to the edge of the bed before he loosened his grip.

The look Harrison turned on her was startling in its intensity. She stumbled a bit, bringing her palm to her throat in a nervous gesture Jenny had always teased her about.

His tense muscles visibly eased. "I'm sorry I lost my temper this afternoon. But Slim Morgan is not a good man, and I don't want you talking to him. Ever."

She nodded, still not trusting herself to speak for lack of breath.

Harrison lifted his hand and she couldn't contain a flinch. His mouth firmed as he tucked a curl behind her ear. "I want you to always remember you don't have anything to fear from me."

"A-All right." Was there more he wanted to say? She waited, but he didn't speak. Instead he began to unbutton his shirt.

"What are you doing?" she asked, swallowing in a panic.

"Getting ready for bed. I suggest you do the same."

She'd felt his hardness against her each night. Usually in bed first, she'd avert her eyes while he undressed. Now she couldn't take her eyes off him as he dropped his shirt to the floor, baring a broad chest, a dusting of dark hair leading down to the top of his trousers, which he was in the act of unbuttoning. *Oh, my.*

The expression on his handsome face reminded her of a predator studying its next meal. "Stop," she said breathlessly, bringing up her hand, palm out.

He paused, ready to pop open the second button to his trousers. He quirked a brow. "What?"

Scrambling for time, Retta tugged on her braid as her mind raced furiously. "Can you wait while I, while I—" Good Lord, she couldn't even form a coherent thought.

"You're my wife, Retta. I'm not going anywhere." He slipped the last few buttons free of their moorings, and all she could do was stand frozen while he removed his clothes.

Although she'd lain with Cal, Retta hadn't seen him completely naked that awful night. The brief glimpse she'd had of his manhood paled in comparison to what pointed in her direction right now.

Her knees wobbled as unease filled her.

"Retta." At Harrison's commanding tone, her gaze snapped back to his. Heat crawled up her neck, spreading across her face at being caught staring. "Come to bed."

He walked to the edge of the mattress, his backside just as impressive as his front. Hard muscles rippled with every step he took. Lifting the covers, he slid in. Relaxing against the wide headboard, he entwined his fingers behind his head to watch her.

Devilment sparkled in his eyes as his mouth curved into a teasing smile.

Retta licked her lips. She'd never seen such a magnificent sight, even if it did set her heart to pounding madly. As her husband, he had every right to the marital bed. She'd accepted that when she boarded the train in Chicago and traveled West.

Life holds few guarantees for a woman. Time to deal with the cards she'd been dealt.

Squaring her shoulders, Retta walked over to the dresser and retrieved her nightgown. Though unable to face him, she retained a bit of bravado as she disrobed completely, then dropped the gown over her head before turning around.

The passion she read on his face stole her breath, and she was unable to tear her eyes away.

Crooking two fingers, he beckoned her forward. "Come here, Retta."

The deep rumbling of his voice did funny things to her insides. Confused, she laced the nightgown up to her throat, so that not an inch of her skin was showing, before sliding tentatively into the bed next to him.

"Closer," he coaxed.

Daring a quick peek, Retta found him watching her with amusement, but she could also see desire in his eyes. That same desire had been on Cal's face right before he'd hurt her. She sucked in a panicked breath.

Harrison's brows drew down. "Retta, what did I say earlier?"

"That you wouldn't hurt me."

"And I'm a man of my word." He slid an arm beneath her, rolling her toward him. In a panic, she flattened her hands against his chest to keep him at bay. Her palms burned under his heat.

"I'm only going to touch you, Retta. Nothing more." He snuggled her easily, her body held tight against his hard, masculine frame. "You can touch me if you like, but that'll be up to you." His lips brushed against the curl of her ear. "We'll start getting to know each other."

"Just touching?"

Easing back to stare down at her, Harrison nodded solemnly, running his hand up and down her back. "Just touching."

The fear she'd been experiencing lessened, though tension still assailed her. Yet as his hand continued to make light passes over her skin, an unfamiliar tightening in her body overwhelmed her.

Her heart sped up, beating hard enough to rattle her ribs.

Harrison pressed a moist kiss to her temple. "You're a beautiful woman, Retta."

Warmth swirled in her belly at his compliment. No man had ever told her she was beautiful. "I am?"

"Yes. Very."

She inhaled sharply as his hand slid lower and cradled her bottom. When he gently squeezed, her next breath burst on a moan. Her body thrummed with an urgent need she didn't understand.

His lips nuzzled her ear as he eased her onto her back. Propped on one arm, his gaze moved over her. "You all right?"

"I don't know. I think I might have a fever."

His smile broadened. "May I kiss you, Retta?"

She licked her lips, suddenly wanting that kiss. His heated gaze fell to her mouth as she managed, "Yes, Harrison. You may kiss—"

That was as far as she got before his mouth, warm and demanding, covered hers. His tongue parted her lips and probed deep, exploringly. Caught by surprise, Retta gripped his shoulders and hung on, bombarded by new feelings and emotions she didn't know how to absorb.

When his tongue curled around hers she moaned into his mouth and tentatively kissed him back, hoping she was doing it right. Cal hadn't kissed her. Not once. Slamming the door shut on that memory, she instead lost herself in Harrison's heady kiss.

Suddenly, he broke away, lifting his head to stare down at her as if he wanted to devour her, his breathing as labored as her own. Those rigid muscles she'd been gripping now bunched under her touch.

Never breaking eye contact with her, Harrison tugged at the lace tie of her nightgown with fingers that held a tremor.

Her chest heaving, she couldn't look away from him. The feeling of something throbbing through her skin wouldn't go away.

The next thing she knew, cool air hit her breasts as her nightgown gapped. Careful fingers smoothed the fine linen from her shoulders, baring her fully to his marauding touch. Her nipples peaked and she shifted restlessly. God, what was he doing to her?

Harrison cupped her breast, rubbing his palm over her sensitized nipple, then pinched it. This time she cried aloud as a spear of pleasure tore through her.

"I'm going to kiss you here, Retta," he rasped, stroking his palm between her breasts until he held her steady, as if she might run from him.

Retta couldn't speak. Her body thrummed in the most pleasurable way, and curiosity held her captive as she breathlessly waited to see what Harrison would do next.

He lowered his mouth to her breast, nipping at the taut peak, soothing it with his tongue, repeating the action on her other side. Back and forth. Left, then right, until she lost track of how long he played with her this way. Her entire being came alive in a way she could never have imagined.

"Harrison, please."

"Shh," he soothed, gently kissing her nipples, flicking them with his tongue.

His hand slid down her leg, then slipped under the gown that had ridden to her knees. She tensed. Would he now slam into her the same way Cal had?

As though reading her mind, he whispered, "Trust me," and took her mouth again in a slow, dreamy kiss, his hand edging toward the juncture of her thighs. She instinctively squeezed her legs together, stopping him right before he could touch the part of her pulsing with an acute fierceness.

"Trust, Retta," he murmured against her lips.

He made no attempt to force her, but continued to kiss her with tender passion. As if with a will of their own, her legs fell open to allow him access.

"That's my brave girl." He cupped her intimately, his touch sending a riot of feelings through her. Retta arched into his hand, her breath coming in little pants. She bit her lip to hold back another cry.

But when Harrison slid a finger inside her, pumping, once, twice, three times, she could no longer hold back the high-pitched mewl that tore from her throat.

Growling, his fingers thrust deeper into her. "So damned beautiful. I need just a little taste to hold me over."

Retta barely heard him, lost in a cloud of passion. His fingers traced down her thigh, wringing a sob of protest from her lips.

A few seconds later, she froze when she felt him press a kiss between her legs.

Scandalized, she urged desperately, "Harrison—"

Before she could beg him to stop, he grasped her hips and lifted her, sucking her tender flesh into his mouth.

Fire exploded behind her eyelids, and she erupted with a pleasure so strong her ensuing shriek bounced off the walls. Groaning harshly against her quivering thighs, Harrison used his fingers to somehow prolong the acute sensation, rubbing and probing her slick entrance.

She convulsed as wave upon wave of bliss overwhelmed her. Never had she imagined a feeling like this, nor believed such heights of ecstasy existed. Not after what her first and only experience with a man had put her through.

Finally able to gulp air back into her starving lungs, she sank back against the pillows, boneless as one of Addie's rag dolls.

Harrison trailed moist lips over her heated skin until he reached her neck. Nuzzling her there, trailing along her jaw to the corner of her mouth, he kissed her so tenderly, it brought tears to her eyes. She tasted a strange musk on his lips and realized it had come from her. It should have shocked her. Repulsed her.

Instead, she collapsed in his arms, gripping his shoulders hard enough to make her fingers tingle with the same ache that lingered between her legs.

She felt him against her hip, huge and hot, a silk-covered shaft he could have already shoved inside her if that had been his intent. Without kisses, or gentle touches, or any sort of passionate overture at all. But he'd brought her to such unfamiliar, maddening, delicious heights . . . asking nothing in return.

Tentatively, Retta relaxed her hands. Slid them down his chest, enjoying the hair-roughened skin against her palms. While he traced his tongue in a lazy pattern under her chin, she trailed one hand lower, her curiosity a live thing.

She had never touched Cal.

She wanted to touch Harrison. *My husband.*

His swiftly-indrawn breath let her know he realized what her hand sought, and he pressed his forehead to hers, the skin along his brow damp with sweat. "Retta, you don't have to."

"I know." Two words, uttered almost soundlessly, but he must have heard them because he shuddered in reaction. "Can you—would you—" She paused, her cheeks flaming hot, then gulped and eased back.

He tipped her chin up, his gray eyes gone almost black. "What do you want?"

"Can you please keep kissing me? And sh-show me. What you want. What to do."

His sudden smile dazzled her as he bent to her mouth and his palm gently guided her lower, and then lower still. Until she fisted him, her fingers unable to meet around his girth. His lips took hers fiercely, yet his hand cupped hers carefully as she clutched his flesh and moaned on his tongue.

So hard, like satin-coated iron. So hot, with a heavy pulse that matched the thudding of her heart.

"Stroke it, root to tip," he rasped against her mouth. "Your hand feels so good."

"Like this?" She let her palm slide over him, fascinated with the way skin, so flexible and velvety, could cover something so steely. Her thumb brushed the very tip and the slippery wetness she found there was unexpected and thrilling. When she pulled gently, he groaned into their kiss and stole her breath as he pressed her hand down firmly on his heated flesh.

He broke off and rasped, "Harder, Retta."

Blindly, Retta obeyed, tightening her grip, stroking faster, then harder, worried she could be hurting him but unable to stop or let go, that wild heat building again, pounding in time with the thrust of his hips against her palm—

And when he threw back his head and shouted aloud, his shaft pumping thick and hot over her fingers . . . Retta buried her face against his shoulder and trembled, finding no shame in what she had done.

Only womanly pride.

Chapter 7

An odd pressure against Harrison's chest woke him slowly from a dream in which he held his warm and sated wife. His lips curved as he stroked a hand down soft, tangled hair, all too willing to slip back into slumber with her curled over him like a heated blanket . . .

A wet, heated blanket.

What the hell—?

Tiny, probing digits slid over his closed lids, along his lashes as he struggled to rouse himself. Prying open one blurry eye, he found Addie's gleeful face an inch from his, her hair a mop of ringlets around her cheeks and one pudgy finger extended toward him, no doubt reaching for his eyelashes. Resigned, Harrison held still and allowed the prodding intrusion. Those little fingers tickled, damn it.

"Hi," she crooned, flashing her pearly baby teeth, before yawning and tucking her head on his shoulder. Harrison rubbed her back and then grimaced as his hand encountered her damp diaper. Though Addie did well during the day, using the privy like a big girl, it would take a while yet for her to hold it in all night long. He decided he didn't really mind the sogginess or the smell, and let her slumber on his chest as he turned to the pillow next to him, expecting to see his sleep-tousled bride.

She wasn't there.

At first he worried he might have scared her off with his demands, though he knew she'd loved what he'd done to her last night, the way he'd touched her, tasted her. Then he cupped a hand over his new daughter's silky curls. Of course she'd never leave Addie behind.

Hearing muffled banging noises in the kitchen, he relaxed against the mattress. His wife was cooking him breakfast. Harrison drew the blanket up, cuddling Addie close as she snored softly into his neck. He'd remain here a bit longer and let his little girl sleep while he waited for Retta to come back to bed. Finding his own eyes growing heavy, he thought he might just doze a bit as well.

Sometime later, he woke to Retta lifting Addie off his chest. He blinked up at her and she blushed, but her eyes held a softness as she whispered, "Sorry, I didn't know she was this wet. Let me change her and I'll finish making breakfast." Carrying Addie over her shoulder, she exited the room silently.

Harrison rose up on an elbow and listened to the sounds of mother and child, soft chatter and tender admonishment. Addie might want to play, while Retta would try to pin her down, clean her up, and get her dressed. Clearly Retta was losing the battle, because he caught a glimpse of a bare little backside as Addie ran past the open bedroom door, giggling happily at being unclothed, while Retta chased after her.

"Adeline Marie, you get back here."

"Hoecake!" The one-word shriek echoed in the kitchen.

Harrison sniffed the air. Yep, smelled like hoecakes to him. Also smelled like she'd used the bacon fat he'd rendered last week. "Nothing better than bacon-fried hoecakes," he mumbled through a yawn.

Dragging his bones out of bed, Harrison yanked on his drawers and stumbled down the hall to the back door, intent on taking care of some pressing business.

By the time he fumbled into his trousers and made it to the kitchen to wash up, Retta had set a mound of golden cakes on the table, and Addie bounced on a chair, eyeing the stack with avarice. Harrison dug in a cupboard for the honeycomb

Retta had purchased last week at the mercantile. "I'd double that batch if I were you," he commented, bringing the honey and some plates to the table. "Frank can sniff out hoecakes a mile down the road."

"Is that where he lives?"

Harrison nodded. "His land butts up to ours. His ranch isn't as finished, though."

She flashed him a quick smile. "Making extra is easy enough to do."

Building on the progress they'd made, he crossed to the stove and brought her close enough for him to snag her around the waist and nuzzle a kiss to the back of her neck. Under his lips she tensed, then went limp. After making sure Addie wasn't watching, Harrison snaked a hand up her ribs to palm a breast.

She wasn't wearing a corset today and her soft flesh, covered by a few layers of linen and cotton, felt so good against his palm. "Mmm," he rasped against her ear. "Good morning, wife." He stroked her nipple and stifled a groan when it budded under the pad of his thumb.

"Harrison . . ." Her breath hitched but her head rested on his shoulder, neck arched as if begging for his mouth.

He angled her chin with a finger and caught her bottom lip in a nibbling kiss. Without giving her a chance to retreat, he spun her around and took her mouth in a hungry kiss. She'd been so receptive under his touch, and he wanted it again.

"Hoecake." Addie's demanding voice piped up behind them like a dash of icy water. Harrison broke off the kiss with a muttered curse that held no heat.

A fine tremor moved over Retta's delicate frame. "It'll only get worse if I don't feed her and then take her for a walk."

"Feeding and walking? Is she a child or a puppy?"

"Puppy," Addie hollered, jumping up and down on her chair.

"Adeline, sit." Retta glanced at Harrison with a sigh of exasperation. "Now you've done it. Gotten her all riled up." She dumped a thick hoecake on Addie's plate and drizzled honey over it, then grabbed a fork and cut the cake into bite-sized pieces. "She'll screech about wanting a you-know-what for days, mark my words." She handed the plate and a spoon to their daughter.

"Well, I've been thinking about getting a you-know-what for a while now," he mused, taking a seat next to Addie and tousling her curls. She looked up from her plate and beamed at him, all tiny white teeth and half-chewed breakfast.

"Oh? And since when have you been thinking about getting a puppy—oh, damn," Retta moaned, as Addie slammed down her spoon and bounced at hearing that word again.

"Since right about now." Harrison scooped up the dainty girl and rubbed beard stubble in her neck, loving her screams of laughter as his whiskers tickled her. "What d'ya say, sweetpea? You wanna go to town with me and Uncle Frank, and pick out a puppy?"

"Yes!" Addie wrapped her arms around his neck and peppered his face with sticky kisses.

Fifteen minutes later, with Copper hooked up to the buckboard and ready to go, Addie snuggled up next to her Uncle Frank and tugged at his beard. "Puppy, puppy," she chanted.

His normally ornery brother smiled down at the child with real affection in his eyes, then patted her on the head. "Hold on to your hosses, shortcake. You'll have your puppy soon enough."

~ ~ ~

The afternoon sun beat down as they left the mercantile, Addie clutching a squirming beagle puppy in her arms, the runt of the litter. Two mournful eyes stared out like a bandit from circles of varying shades of brown, split with a splash of white running over its snout and onto the top of its head. The pup's one outstanding feature was a perfect circle of gold fur, the size of a large thumbprint, nestled in the middle of its white forehead.

As the pup continued to give her face a soaking with its sloppy tongue, Addie's sweet giggle sang in the air. Each step she took, the pup slipped down her body, since the little tyke didn't have enough strength to hang onto the squirming animal.

To keep the puppy from dragging on the ground, every so often Frank patiently heaved the pup back up into her arms. It was a side of him Harrison had never seen before, and it filled him with a great deal of amusement.

When he opened his mouth to give his brother a hard time, Frank narrowed his eyes. "Don't even . . ."

Harrison grinned. "I didn't say anything."

After giving the puppy's bottom another shove, Frank straightened. Although he didn't smile, Harrison could easily read the laughter in his eyes as he thoughtfully tugged at his beard. "Quite a family you've got yourself, little brother. A bit more than you'd bargained for."

"That it is," Harrison admitted. "But I'm determined to make it work."

"Your bride seems as skittish as a newborn colt."

Recalling the hard way he'd greeted her at the train station sent a burst of guilt through Harrison. He hadn't handled the situation as well as he could have. "We had a rough start, but I'm working on it."

Frank leaned down to readjust the dog again. Addie peered up at him with a broad smile on her adorable face. "Tank you, Unca Fank."

Frank ruffled the top of her head. "Welcome, shortcake."

They continued down the dusty street, heading toward the wagon at a slow pace. Once she'd gotten her hands on the pup, Addie refused to relinquish him for either of them to carry.

"So," Frank began, "I heard Slim Morgan accosted your missus in the mercantile the other day. What're you gonna do about him? The man's a bad egg."

Harrison tensed as anger curled in his gut. "He gets anywhere near my wife again, and he'll be a dead bad egg."

Frank opened his mouth to respond, but was interrupted by Addie's wail. "Puppy!"

The dog darted past them, scrambling down the boardwalk, only to be blocked by Cat Purdue, a barmaid from the Lucky Lady saloon. With a husky chuckle, she scooped up the yipping beagle.

Harrison eyed the young woman warily as she scratched the puppy behind one floppy ear. She wasn't much older than Retta, maybe a year or two. Although Cat was strikingly beautiful, unlike his sweet bride, the shine of innocence had long worn off this one.

She wore a gown that fit snugly against a waist made wasp-thin by a fancy bodice that laced up the front. The low neckline bared creamy white shoulders and full breasts, set off by some kind of red material, covered in black netting. One side of the skirt had been knotted high, held in place with bright red ribbons, showcasing a shapely thigh peeking through black net stockings. Harrison recognized the costume of an entertainer. Not surprising, since Cat Purdue also sang at the Lucky Lady.

Tall and slender, Cat's dancing shoes brought her almost eye level to them. To Harrison's amusement, Frank hadn't taken *his* eyes off the lovely songbird, even as he frowned fiercely all the while.

Tumbled waves the color of deepest honey framed the face of an angel. Though this woman was anything but angelic. Harrison knew a little about her past, and the girl had been dealt a bad hand, for sure. It was hard living a virtuous life when your own father lost you in a game of cards—along with The Lucky Lady Saloon—to Slim Morgan.

Harrison took Addie's hand before she could run down the street after her dog. The way Frank tensed when Cat headed toward them, puppy in her arms, didn't go unnoticed. The woman's gaze locked on his brother. And she didn't look happy to see him.

Interesting. Although Cat regularly performed at the Lucky Lady Saloon, Harrison didn't think she worked as one of the whores, too. Though he couldn't know for certain, since he seldom entered the establishment. Frank normally kept his dalliances with women who offered no entanglements, and this woman had entanglement written all over her.

With the squirming puppy in her arms, she strolled up to them, hips gently swaying. The closer she came, the tighter Frank's muscles got as his jaw clenched. Even Addie seemed to know something didn't seem right, and waited silently at his side.

Reaching them, she murmured, "Hello, Frank." Her voice, soft and melodic, made her an invaluable source of income for the saloon. Men came from miles around just to listen to her sing. The fact she was stunningly lovely helped too.

Frank gave a curt nod. "Cat."

When it became obvious that his brother wasn't going to offer anything else, she sighed, then glanced down at Addie. "Did you lose something, pretty one?" She knelt and placed the ecstatic puppy into her arms, gently patting her cheek. "Be sure to hang on tight to the things you love, baby."

Without another word, she breezed past them and kept walking toward the saloon, head held high.

Chapter 8

Retta scraped the remnants of breakfast from the plates and stacked them in the metal dishpan. Water heated on the stove, ready for washing off all the stickiness only hoecakes and honey could manufacture. She hummed as she worked, fragments of a tune she and Jenny used to sing together when they cleaned up after a meal. She could almost hear their awkward harmony, almost smell the sweet lilac water Jenny loved to dash behind her ears—

If she's still alive. It'd been two months since she'd said goodbye to her sister at the train station.

A single, sharp pain pierced her, and Retta clutched a damp hand to her heart to ease it away. A sob caught in her throat, before she determinedly set aside the grief threatening to overtake her. Here, in this sunny kitchen with the fragrance of breakfast lingering on the air and a pan full of dishes, grief would have to wait. Jenny was safe back in Dewfield with Aunt Millie, well-cared for. Everything that could be done to make her comfortable and content, Aunty would surely do.

Now that Retta was settling in, she'd pen a letter to her sister, letting her know she'd arrived safely and that she and Addie were happy.

Someday soon, perhaps remembering their childhood together would bring fond smiles instead of tears and feelings of guilty abandonment. Retta could only hope.

"Enough of that," she admonished herself, as she attacked the dishes anew. With Harrison gone into town with Addie and Frank, she had plenty of time to set the ranch house aright. Maybe even change some things around more to her liking, and look through her patterns for the clothes she wanted to make for Addie. Busy work, indeed, and exactly what she needed right now.

Except as she rinsed and stacked dishes, she found her mind wandering far from Dewfield and centering on other things.

Such as the way Harrison touched her each night, in their bed . . .

"Oh, God." The oath shuddered from her mouth and pinged around the quiet kitchen like a stone skipping over water. The mere recollection of his mouth, his hands on her skin, made her woman's core clutch and moisten. How could something so immense exist inside her, yet not rip her apart as it built and then burst?

Retta dropped the plate she'd been scrubbing and sagged weakly against the waist-high slab of wood that served as a counter. Vaguely she registered the sound of the sturdy pottery shattering in the metal dishpan. "I'll clean it up later," she whispered, unable to concentrate on anything except her husband. How he touched her, kissed her. The words he'd groan as she clasped his length in her hand . . .

Her own heart pounding furiously, Retta abandoned all pretense of housework and sank into the nearest chair.

The way he'd hold her, his warm palm against her cheek as he pressed her close to his heart. His unlimited patience, never pushing her for more than she was willing to give. That, most of all.

Barely a month as Retta Carter, and her world had upended in the most amazing way. What could have begun as a travesty of a marriage had become a wide-open opportunity for affection and acceptance. For her. For Addie.

A firm knock on the front door had her jumping to her feet, whipping off her stained apron. She wasn't expecting anyone, but perhaps the mercantile lady—Betsey, if she recalled—had decided to pay her a visit. Retta hurried to the foyer, wishing she had anything besides cold hoecakes and leftover coffee to offer a visitor. Well, it wasn't as if she'd had much time to bake up a storm. Surely the woman would understand.

Smoothing the loose bun at her nape and weaving wayward strands back from her face with one hand, Retta rounded the corner to the narrow foyer . . . and stared dumbfounded through the split porch door at the sight of Slim Morgan, dandy-dressed and dapper as he stood with his hat in his hands and a wide smile on his mustachioed face.

His dark eyes moved over her in a way that shot unease right through her. Retta inched backward, wishing she had thought to close and latch both halves of the door. She couldn't imagine any harm befalling her in broad daylight, yet she wasn't naïve enough to think a man such as Morgan might not try something untoward.

"Mister Morgan, what are you doing here?" Her voice held calm reason when she felt none at all.

"Ah, Missus Carter. Lovely to see you again." Morgan stroked the brim of his hat with one long-fingered hand, a silver ring sparkling on his pinky. "I wondered if I might speak to your husband. I've some business to discuss with him." He edged toward the threshold.

Retta swallowed a relieved sigh to see the bottom panel firmly latched. The situation reminded her of a tonic salesman who'd once tried to gain entrance to the front parlor of her childhood home in Bolster by sticking his foot in the door. Her father had tossed him out on his ear.

A split-door open at the top—at the moment—wasn't much of a barrier, but it was better than nothing.

She folded her hands at her waist and strove to appear collected. "Might I ask what this pertains to, Mister Morgan? I was under the impression you and my husband are not very well acquainted." Not exactly true, but it served little purpose to repeat Harrison's thinly-veiled loathing of the man when she had no idea what might have caused it in the first place.

Morgan's gaze slid over her a final time. Inexperienced with men in general, still Retta recognized the look in those nearly-black eyes, and it made her skin crawl. He placed both palms on the half-door, effectively blocking any attempt to slam and latch the upper section. With one casual move, he'd lessened her ability to defend her home.

She hated it, but remaining civil and polite was her only recourse. With a fortifying breath, Retta held firm. "Mister Morgan—"

"Call me Slim. I would so enjoy watching those lovely lips of yours forming my first name." His smile broadened, revealing white, straight teeth. Neither the smile nor the teeth instilled any reassurance as he continued, "I must say, Retta, your presence in our little boomtown is a spot of fresh beauty." Lifting one hand from the edge of the door, he stretched it toward her face as if to cup her cheek.

Retta jerked back. "Sir, you had best state your business." She fought to keep from trembling and locked her knees. If she showed a speck of uncertainty or weakness, Morgan would take advantage, she was certain.

"Why, I would be most happy to, my dear. If you would please tell your, er, husband I have come to call." Morgan gestured with his hat toward the wagon barn. "I wonder, is he even at home? I took the liberty of peeking here and there as I rode up, and didn't see him. Or his buckboard." His smarmy smile sharpened. "Dare I hope you and I might be all alone in this idyllic setting, under the warm sun and the soft spring breeze?"

Tossing his hat aside, Morgan slapped his hands on the half-door again. Retta watched in horrified fascination as his fingers felt along the lock rail, this time finding the latch on the inside. *Her* side. He played with the barrel bolt, and her eyes widened as she realized he could easily slide the catch. Leap over the open jamb.

Or simply kick it in.

"So, pretty Retta," he purred, "Will you invite me in? Or shall I just . . . help myself?"

~ ~ ~

"Almost home, Addie." Frank ruffled the tiny girl's curly locks. She sat on his lap, clutching her pup to her thin chest.

The little beagle dozed for most of the trip back, and Addie's eyes drooped as well. Frank had ended up holding them both and hadn't complained once.

Harrison flicked the brim of his brother's Stetson. "You going to tell me what that little scene was all about with Cat Purdue?"

"Nothing to say, really. Things just didn't work out."

"Did you want them to work out?" He'd never known his brother to get attached to a woman, not even a speck.

"Doesn't matter now."

Ready to pursue the line of questioning further, Harrison guided Copper to the entry gate, then frowned to see it ajar. "I know we latched it." He brought the wagon to a stop. "Whoa, boy," he admonished the horse, then set the brake and jumped down. He'd taken two steps before he spotted the prints in the dirt. Four horseshoes, no wagon trail behind. "Damn, somebody else rode through. Single horse." He climbed back into the wagon and grabbed the reins. "Hold tight." He snapped the reins hard and urged Copper into a fast canter, the wagon rumbling and jerking as the wheels hit clumps of hardpacked dirt and rocks.

Frank braced himself on the seat and cradled Addie and the pup as they thundered over the trail toward the ranch. He squinted into the dusty air. "Son of a bitch, I know that goddamn horse."

As they got closer, Harrison growled, "*Morgan.*" He plied the reins, and Copper shot forward. As the ranch house loomed, he shouted, "Take it over, straight to the barn."

Slowing Copper barely enough for safety, Harrison jumped, landing in a tumbling roll to protect his head and eyes from the rough ground-scrub. He gained his feet and pulled his pistol as he ran toward the side yard, banking on taking Morgan by surprise before he could get to his horse, tied to the hitching post near the house.

Harrison sidled to the front of the wraparound porch, spotting Morgan's fancy boots with their brass-tipped spurs. A woman's low murmur confirmed his worst fear: Retta, facing the bastard down, possibly already in his filthy clutches. Snarling low in his throat, Harrison leapt over the side railing, pistol cocked—

Only to come to an abrupt stop and stare, gape-mouthed, at the sight of his dainty wife calmly pointing the cocked barrel of his Winchester repeater dead center on Slim Morgan's pale, high forehead. Harrison gave her a fast, encompassing glance to assure she was unharmed, before bringing his Colt level to Morgan's chest. A grim smile etched his mouth at the sweat rolling down the worthless cur's face.

Other than loose, silky tendrils escaping from her upswept hair and a smear of honey on her chin, Retta seemed remarkably composed.

"Retta," Harrison began, "you can put the rifle aside now."

"I'm all right, Harrison." She blew a tangled curl out of her eyes. "Mister Morgan would like to talk to you. He also tried to enter the house without my permission." Lowering the rifle, she un-cocked the barrel and set it aside. "I was very glad to see such a fine weapon hanging by the door." Her fingers shook when she smoothed them over her hair and inhaled deeply.

Brave girl. Smart, too, because only a stupid person didn't recognize danger when it stared them down.

"Go to the barn, Retta." Harrison never took his eyes off Morgan, his hand steady on the trigger. "Now."

"Where's Addie?"

"In the barn with Frank, waiting for you." Remembering how his wife's hand had trembled, he took a threatening stride forward. "Move away from the door, Morgan, and let the lady pass."

Morgan held his hands up in a surrender gesture, but the sneer on his face indicated otherwise, as he edged back.

Closing in, Harrison kept his gun pointed at the man, forcing him off the porch, then held his free hand out for his bride. "I'll be along soon. But first, Morgan and I have a few things to discuss."

Eyes as wide as a startled doe, she placed her hand trustingly in his. Harrison took a moment to enjoy the feel of her skin against his, before guiding her through the archway. "Stay inside until I come for you."

She nodded, ignoring Morgan completely, and with a dignified swish of her skirts she walked briskly toward the barn.

~ ~ ~

Harrison waited until Retta was safely ensconced in the barn, before gritting out between clenched teeth, "Tell me why I shouldn't fill you full of lead." He wanted to take the shot, but he wasn't a murderer.

Hands still held high, Morgan grinned, looking every bit a dandy in his expensive three-piece suit and high-dollar boots. But Harrison knew better. The man was as dangerous as a rattler. "Now, Carter," he said mockingly, "there's no need for that. I'm here on business, nothing more. I'm sorry if your wife got the wrong impression."

"Is that so?" Harrison wasn't buying it. He'd seen the lust in the man's eyes at the mercantile when Morgan looked at Retta.

"I'd like to make an offer on one of your mines. A very generous offer."

"The mines aren't for sale." Harrison lowered the weapon slightly, aiming at the man's privates, and cocked the trigger. "Stay away from what's mine."

Morgan's smile turned mean. "My men know I'm here, and if anything happens to me they'll avenge my death. It'd be a shame if something happened to that lovely wife of yours or her daughter."

Fury pounded through Harrison. This bastard just threatened his family. His finger twitched on the trigger, as he contemplated ending it right here. The only thing that stopped him was the sound of his brother's voice.

"Harrison," Frank said calmly, coming up to stand next to him, a rifle cradled casually in one arm. But Harrison wasn't fooled for an instant. Frank's posture indicated he was ready to take Morgan on if necessary. "Why don't you two put down the weapons and work it out?"

Hell, yes. He might not be able to shoot Morgan in cold blood, but that didn't mean he couldn't mess the dandy up a bit. A grin spread across Harrison's face as he slowly lowered his gun, handing it off to Frank. Morgan lifted a highly-polished Smith & Wesson from its holster and placed it on the square table positioned against the outside wall.

"I'd sure like you to reconsider," Morgan said. "At least listen to my offer."

Harrison met the man's calculating stare. "Not interested."

With a smirk, Morgan casually stepped off the front porch and closed the short distance between them. Balling his hands into fists, he lifted them up in a fighter's stance.

"I'll try not to damage you too much, since you have a new woman to satisfy."

The slur cranked up his anger, but Harrison maintained his control. Morgan was baiting him so he could get the upper hand. *Not goddamned likely.* With a flick of two fingers, he beckoned at the bastard. "Make it good, Morgan, because one punch is all you're gonna get."

"Cocky son of a bitch," Morgan ground out, before he swung in a wide arc and connected with Harrison's lower jaw, knocking him back. When Harrison only shook his head, pinning Morgan with a threatening stare and a grim smile, the idiot's bravado deserted him damned fast.

Morgan took another swing, but Harrison blocked it. Five seconds later, with a shot to the gut, and two quick punches to the face, Morgan lay flat on his back in the dirt, semi-conscious.

"Well, that was too easy." Frank sighed. "I was hoping for more entertainment. Want me to dump a bucket of water on him so we can try again?" His brother's tone held a hopeful note.

Harrison snorted, leaning down to toss Morgan's sorry ass over his shoulder. "That won't be necessary." He carried the skunk to his horse and threw him roughly across the saddle as Morgan began to rouse.

Frank walked up next to him with Morgan's gun, emptying the bullets onto the ground, before shoving it in the saddlebag.

"I find you at my ranch again, Morgan, I won't go so easy on you." Harrison slapped the appaloosa on the rump and sent him charging along the gate trail.

Cursing loudly, Morgan clung to the saddle. "This won't be the end of it, Carter," he hollered.

"I know." He strode into the barn where Retta and Addie were kneeling on the dirt floor, playing with the puppy.

Retta lifted a worried gaze to him. "Harrison," she breathed, relief flooding her voice. She stood and crossed to him, curling her arms around his waist and laying her head on his chest.

He skimmed a hand along her back. "Everything's fine." Glancing over the top of her head at his daughter, he asked, "Do we have a name for your puppy yet, Addie girl?"

Addie smiled, nodding vigorously. "Noodle."

Behind him, Frank laughed. Harrison grinned. "Noodle, huh? That's a . . . different kind of name. Why don't we introduce him to his new home?"

Addie scooped up her dog and ran outside, followed closely by Frank. With one arm securely around Retta's slim waist, Harrison led her toward the open barn doors.

She lifted her sweet face up to him as they strolled toward the ranch. "What happened to Morgan? What did he really want?"

"It's all taken care of. Don't worry, he won't be bothering you again."

Her fingers slid along his jaw, where he'd been hit. "You fought him?"

"It was nothing." Harrison glanced in the direction where Morgan had ridden off. They hadn't seen the last of the man.

Chapter 9

Harrison tossed the reins aside and jumped from the wagon seat, holding up his arms for Retta. "You sure you want to go in?" he asked—for at least the tenth time—as he swung her to the ground, supporting her elbow until her feet were steady.

"I'm already here. Sure, I want to go in."

On the other side of the wagon, Nell Washburn waited for Addie. Married to one of Harrison's apprentices, Nell had volunteered to keep an eye on Addie while Harrison showed Retta the mine operation.

Pushing her bright-red hair from her eyes, Nell brought Addie around to the back of the wagon. "See, all safe and sound, Mister Carter. Me an' the boys will take good care of her for you." She gave the excited Addie a wink. "And we got kittens—"

"*Kittens*," Addie shouted, jumping up and down, her curls bouncing madly.

With a groan, Retta protested, "Not a kitten. Oh, Lord. She loves them even more than p-u-p-p-i-e-s," she spelled in a low hiss.

"Er, sorry." Nell clapped a hand over her mouth. "Guess I should keep me lips buttoned." She herded Addie toward the narrow path leading to the miners' cabins, her guidance gentle but firm. "Cookies first, all right, young Miss Adeline?"

As Addie nodded eagerly and scampered along beside Nell, Retta tamped down her worry. Miners' wives and children were everywhere, all friendly and good-natured. Addie would be perfectly safe for a few hours.

She sucked in a deep breath, the air tinged with the raw ore the miners were carting out, and nodded to Harrison. "I'm ready."

Harrison eyed her up and down. Today she wore a black split skirt and a dainty yellow blouse with a pin-tucked bodice. "Did you bring an apron? Or a duster? You're going to get dirty in there."

"Um—"

"Never mind. Here, put this on." He whipped off his duster and draped it around her shoulders. "It'll keep you cozy if we descend."

Retta clutched the garment close. It smelled of musk and warm man, a delicious combination. "What about you? Won't you get cold?" He had rolled up the sleeves of his faded chambray work shirt.

"Not likely." He caught her hand. "Ready to see the mine?"

"Oh, yes."

"All right, then, but you have to be cautious as you proceed. Don't want you touching anything that might scrape up your pretty hands." He brought her fingers to his lips. The kiss he pressed on each set her heart pounding as emotion melted her from the inside.

Some of what she felt must have shown on her face, because his eyes went dark. "Careful," Harrison admonished against her fingers, "or I might shock half my crew by kissing you right here." He stroked his tongue over the delicate skin between her thumb and index finger.

A tiny moan escaped her lips at the exquisite caress.

Behind her, a masculine snort brought her to awareness. Retta tugged her hand from her husband's too-tempting mouth, and pivoted around. Heat bloomed in her cheeks at the sight of Frank leaning against the front wagon wheel, arms crossed over his chest.

"How-do, Missus Carter." He tipped his well-worn Stetson. "Can't find anyone more respectable to escort you around?" Mischief danced in his dark eyes as he nodded toward Harrison, then dropped his voice to a low drawl. "I've got it on good authority he lets puppies lick his teeth."

"Bad timing, fool," Harrison muttered softly.

Gathering her composure, Retta smiled, brushing a stray wisp of hair out of her eye. Harrison's brother could be so surly one minute, and ridiculous the next. "Are you going in with us?"

Frank straightened and swept off his hat, knocking it against his leg to shake off the dust, before he dropped it back on his head and adjusted the rim. "No, ma'am. Stayin' out here where it's breezy." He winked. "Maybe I'll head on over to the Washburn place and grab me a kitty." He grinned at Retta's squeak of alarm. "You know, to keep that ferocious dog of yours in line."

"Oh, Frank, that's not a good idea." Visions of dogs giving chase to spitting cats swirled in her brain. She thought of the mess they'd create inside her tidy ranch house, pictured claws shredding the furniture, and shuddered.

"Stop teasing her." Harrison settled one brawny arm around her shoulders. "How's about instead you hunt up Ben and Dub. Maybe take a walk around."

"Sure thing, old son." Frank shot off a cocky salute. "Careful, y'hear? That south shaft needs reinforcement." With a nod toward Retta, he strode off.

Retta tugged against Harrison's encompassing arm. "Is it really safe down there?"

"I wouldn't let you anywhere near the inside if it weren't." He guided her toward the entrance, handing her a bandana from his back pocket. "Tie this over your nose and mouth." Waiting until she obeyed, Harrison eased through the reinforced bracket, wide enough for two men. "Watch your step." He held his hand out to help her inside. "This is the main floor. North shaft goes down four levels. Might have to eventually go deeper."

Though she wanted to look ahead, down the long, dimly-lit shaft opening, Retta kept her eyes on her boots, feeling the suction of mud-coated boards and ground cover. Even this close to the entrance, the air already stifled her breaths. She couldn't imagine working any deeper and having to inhale the dust and specks of ore, the way these poor men had to endure. Harrison guided her further into the mine.

Along one rough-hewn wall, a sconce had been hung on a jutting rock. Harrison paused to light the thick candle, replacing the soot-streaked glass. He pointed to a piece of paper nailed to a makeshift frame. "Frank drew this up last year, when we completed the third level. Good enough to see what's below where we're standing."

Retta traced her finger over the box-like shapes. "Men stand in these?"

"Yep. Two men to a timber-set. One digs and the other collects the ore. When they have enough to fill a pallet, they bring it out." He indicated a pulley system constructed of ropes and wheels. "Most of our men can block out substantial chunks at once. Cart tracks only descend two levels from the surface, where the shaft is wide enough to handle a mule. Stack the pallet, pull it up, fill the cart, and the mule brings it out. Takes two men guiding the cart and the mule to make it out safely." The smile he gave her shone in the dimly lit shaft.

Suppressing a shiver, Retta tried to imagine what a fourteen-hour day must be like, and what kind of toll it had to take on a miner's body. These men worked from sunup to sundown and sometimes beyond, that much she already knew just by the little Harrison had told her. Now that she'd seen the bare bones of the operation for herself, her respect for silver miners grew even more. *And this is one of the bigger and better operations, Lord help them all.*

Feeling a bit claustrophobic, she allowed a little space under the bandana, loosening the knot in order to catch some fresh air. She started to speak, wanting to compliment Harrison on his dedication to his workers, and instead coughed and choked as she took in a stale breath.

Harrison frowned, then guided her from the narrower shaft into the wider opening leading to fresher, outside air. "Damn it, I shouldn't have brought you so far in." He curled an arm around her waist and almost carried her out.

Past the entrance, now standing on dry ground, he rubbed her back as she expelled the last of the dust she'd inhaled. Retta laid a hand on his chest to support herself, and straightened. "I'm all right, Harrison. Truly. I— It was my fault. I should have knotted the cloth better."

He cupped her cheek, watching her with concern filled eyes. "No. The fault lies with me. That's the last time you go anywhere near—"

She interrupted him. "How many hours a day do you and Frank spend in there? And how far down do you have to go?" She raised a hand to his face and stroked a finger along his cheek, coming up with a smudge of grime. "You were clean when we went in."

"You sure you're all right?"

"Yes. I'm fine." She rubbed her skin and held up her thumb to inspect the traces of dirt. "You breathe this in, day after day?"

"We never go in without bandanas over our faces. All my men are on one-hour shifts. Travel down, spend an hour digging or loading. Back to the surface, rest some before going back down. It's why our shifts are so long. Enough time to breathe clean air, get plenty to drink, eat something, wash off the worst of the ore dust, and then go back in." He chucked her under the chin. "Nothing to worry about, Retta. My men only work about seven hours total a day, all told."

Though she chafed at being treated like a tot Addie's age, Retta's respect for her husband's dedication to the wellbeing of his men outdistanced her impatience at his attempt to humor her. "Not all mine owners are like you," she guessed. When she met his honest, open gaze, she knew it for truth.

"No. They're not. Which is why my men work hard for me. I pay them well, give them a percentage of ownership in the smaller mines as long as the shaft produces enough. When I read of the pitfalls of working long, torturous hours in the California gold mines, I figured silver mining couldn't be much better. So I planned accordingly. I would never work any man nor beast to death just to pull minerals from the earth."

Impulsively, she slipped her arms around his waist and gave him a squeeze, sighing when she felt his answering embrace. "My husband is a very good man," she whispered against his neck.

"A man is only as good as the woman at his side." He held her close, and right in front of the mine where his men could see, Harrison kissed her.

Dimly, Retta registered a few whistles, a hoot or two, raspy laughter. And found it didn't bother her a single bit.

~ ~ ~

Addie spent the afternoon playing with Noodle. Harrison reckoned the odd name fit, especially when the floppy mutt slid over the floor, tiny nails scrabbling for purchase on the freshly beeswaxed surface, ending up in a heap of legs and paws against the hooked rug in the front room. With Addie screeching in joy at the pup's silly antics, and occupied for now, Harrison sauntered into the kitchen where Retta pared potatoes for stew.

Yep, he was growing right fond of his wife. Besides being easy on the eyes, she was sweet as spun sugar, a wonderful mother, and a damn good cook. Maybe he'd swipe one of the biscuits he'd spotted cooling on the table, before stealing a kiss.

Harrison managed the kiss first, but she smacked his hand before he could snatch a biscuit. He grabbed her around the waist and pressed himself to her backside, enjoying its rounded softness as she tried—none too strenuously, he noticed—to push him away.

His cock swelled, prodding into the curve of her back. Harrison had soon learned what pleased his bashful bride. What parts of her body were ticklish, and what parts liked to be stroked and kissed. Each night, she'd generously returned the favor. Her innocent enthusiasm had overcome any lack of experience.

But his patience was growing short, and he needed more of her. All of her. It was time Retta learned how a real man loved on a woman. With tenderness and care, her satisfaction always coming first. Always.

"You'll spoil your dinner," she scolded, laughing softly.

Tonight, I'll make her mine. A pang of guilt hit him when he thought of Jenny and the life they should have had. *But this is what Jenny wants,* he reminded himself.

Harrison pushed aside the unwanted emotion, focusing on the here and now. He buried his lips in her silky hair, gathered at her nape. "My dinner won't be spoiled if I nibble on you." He ran his tongue up the side of her neck and felt her tremble.

"Addie—"

"Is playing with Noodle. Silly name for a hound," he grumbled against her shoulder. Slipping his hand from her waist to her breast, Harrison groaned at the firmness he palmed. "I'm not hungry right now, Retta. At least not for food."

"Well, you're not getting anything else, Mister Carter, certainly not in the middle of the afternoon with our child running about." Even as she admonished him breathlessly, Retta crowded closer, resting her head on his shoulder and leaving her throat vulnerable to his mouth. Harrison gladly obliged, scattering more kisses over her soft skin and marveling at how she'd opened up like a flower to his affection.

As he turned her, determined to press every inch of her loveliness against his throbbing cock, Addie tore through the kitchen, with Noodle hot on her heels. High-pitched yips and squeals filled the air as pup and child rounded the table twice, then three times.

Moaning, Retta dropped her forehead against his chest. "Good Lord."

Harrison muffled his laugh in her hair. "Could be worse, you know. Frank might still take it upon himself to toss a kitten into the midst."

She slapped a hand over his mouth. "Don't even think it, much less say it."

He nipped at her palm before moving it aside. "I need to take care of a few things in my study—"

"You have a study?" Curiosity lit her sweet face.

"I do. Kind of a glorified office." He rubbed his nose against hers. "Want to see it?"

"Can I?"

"Sure."

Addie came running over, giggling, carrying Noodle in her arms like a baby. The inseparable pair had been playing together all afternoon.

Retta ruffled the top of her daughter's head. "It's time for Addie's nap. Let me lay her down first."

"Hungwy." Letting the puppy slide out of her grip, Addie eyed the biscuits. Then she looked over to Harrison as if sizing him up.

"Such feminine wiles." He chuckled. "Ask your mother."

"Mama," Addie beseeched. "Pease?"

"Yes, you may have one. Then it's off to bed."

Addie made a beeline for the pile of golden biscuits, Noodle bumping into the backs of her legs in his attempt to shadow her every move.

After the little tyke finished off two biscuits and a glass of milk, Harrison scooped her up and carried her down the hall to her room. Retta tucked her in, the pup curled into a furry ball beside her. Addie's eyes closed, sound asleep, before they'd made it out of the room. Taking Retta's hand, Harrison led her to his den. Fishing a key from his pocket, he unlocked the door and ushered her inside.

At her raised eyebrow, he said, "I used to keep the payroll in this room, until the bank was built. Guess I got so used to locking it, I just kept doing it." He paused at the untidy desk, tucked under the only window. "It's dusty in here."

Retta waved a hand in front of her face at the motes flying up from the ledger he poked at. "Calling it dusty might be an understatement, Harrison." She looked around the room, drawing a finger over the table where he kept his assessing maps and surveying equipment. She held it up, tsking under her breath. "I could clean in here, you know. Goodness knows someone should."

"I have been slightly distracted lately." A weak defense at best, but nevertheless the truth.

Retta's attention was caught by the ledger he had prodded. Silently she picked it up and carried it to the window, holding it to the waning afternoon light. Harrison started to speak, but she lifted a staying hand.

Almost a full minute went by as she stared at the ledger. Finally, she looked up from the numbers he had painstakingly entered two months or so ago. "Harrison, your arithmetic is incorrect."

"What?" He reached for the ledger, but she held it firmly and indicated the balance column.

"Here"—she pointed—"you subtracted in error. And here"—she tapped a deposit several lines further down—"you multiplied instead of adding."

"Where did you learn this?" He had never in his life met a woman who knew the kind of arithmetic required for keeping accounts and balances.

"My Aunt Millie taught both Jenny and me. From as early as I can remember. Aunty was a spinster, a schoolteacher. She went to university. Arithmetic was her special intellect."

Retta blinked back tears, before she stiffened her spine and offered a smile. "Harrison, I've been wondering how I might help you ease your burden at the mines." She gestured with the ledger. "If you and Frank didn't have to worry about the books, or the payroll . . . if I could do this for you, would it help?"

He sank onto the nearest chair, a rickety ladderback he should have broken up for firewood years ago. *Beautiful and smart.* What other secrets did his wife hold?

He glanced around the study. Truth to tell, he hated numbers and balances, accounts and dealing with finances. He did it because Frank was hopeless with sums and could barely add four and six. Of the two bankers currently toiling at Little Creede Commerce, only Elijah Lambert knew his way around keeping fairly accurate bank books. Jenkins, the other banker, Harrison trusted about as far as he could toss him.

In about a minute, Retta had located two errors he had made in the payroll ledger, and Harrison hadn't a clue if either or both errors were in his favor or not. He scrubbed his hands through his hair until it no doubt stood on end, then held out a hand for the ledger.

No sooner did she pass it to him than he tossed it onto the

desk, raising more dust, then snagged her arm and tumbled her into his lap.

"Harrison!" She wriggled to gain her feet, but he held her tighter and nuzzled the hollow of her throat until she stopped struggling and sighed against his shoulder.

"Retta, will you be my man, er, woman of accounts? I pay very well." He bounced her on his knee, and her tinkling laugh warmed his soul.

"Your woman of accounts, huh? How will you pay me? I already have all I need." Her eyes twinkled, and she fluttered her lashes.

Damn. He was lost.

With nimble fingers, he unfastened the first four buttons of her blouse and unlaced her chemise, baring her to the tops of her creamy breasts. He nudged away the fabric to reach silky flesh, then sucked one rosy nipple into his mouth, twirling his tongue around the turgid peak. When he cupped her other breast, her pulse jumped against his palm. "I have plans for the way I'll recompense you, Missus Carter."

Her breath unsteady, her blouse and chemise hanging loosely, Retta encircled his head with both arms as she held him against her.

Harrison stood, allowing her to slowly slide down his body until her toes touched the floor. Staring into her dazed eyes, he palmed her enticing bottom.

Aligning her soft center to his throbbing length, he rasped in her ear, "I have big plans, in fact."

Chapter 10

Retta's heart raced as Harrison swept her up in his arms and strode down the hall and into their bedroom. Given it was the middle of the afternoon, she found herself slightly scandalized at his actions. Her reaction to his touch left her with not a whimper of protest.

I want his hands on me.

Each night her husband introduced her to more delights of the marriage bed, though he'd never pushed beyond her limits. Without asking, he seemed to know what she wanted, and where she wasn't yet willing to go.

Her one experience left her with doubts, but she couldn't deny Harrison his right to her body forever. She didn't want to. The more she learned of this man, the more she wanted to share her life with him. In every way.

Harrison's easy laughter jerked her from her ponderings as he placed her on top of the covers. "You're thinking too deeply, Retta." He unbuckled his holster and belt before sitting on the edge of the bed. "I'd like to make love to my wife."

Retta's heart pounded harder when he reached for the ribbon holding back her hair, tugging until silky strands fell in disarray around her shoulders.

He let out a soft breath. "You're very beautiful." He cupped her face and tenderly swept his thumb across the curve of her cheek. "I want you badly, but I won't hurt you. You'll only know pleasure with me."

Even as her womanly center stirred at his sensual promise and the determined look in his eyes, she couldn't help but remember the searing pain when Cal had taken her so roughly. "Wh-What about Addie?"

His lips quirked at her halfhearted attempt to delay what was about to happen. "She's sleeping, and won't be awake for at least an hour." Harrison whispered against her lips, "A lot can happen in an hour, wife. Let me show you."

Her nod was barely perceptible, as Harrison took her mouth in a possessive kiss. Surrendering, she melted against him.

Sliding his hands under her hair, he held her head still, his lips thoroughly exploring her mouth. The feel of his tongue against hers curled her toes and made her breasts throb. She moaned, barely recognizing the impassioned sound as her own as she clutched him for support. If she let go, surely she'd float away.

Harrison broke the kiss with a groan and a raspy, "Open your eyes, Retta."

Slowly her lashes lifted, and she found him staring down at her like a hungry wolf. Trepidation fluttered in her belly. Retta wanted him, but there was a part of her that still resisted. Her chest heaving with her panting breaths, she forced that little voice to the back of her mind. This was Harrison. Her husband, and she trusted him.

"Lovely," he murmured, as he eased her blouse and chemise off completely. "So perfect." He tugged her up, lowering his head to cover her aching nipple with the heat of his mouth.

Retta arched her back as Harrison nipped the sensitive peak hard enough to sting, before caressing it gently with his tongue. The contrast of both pain and pleasure felt so good, her fingernails dug into his shoulders as he moved to her other breast and drew harder on her nipple, sending a sharp quiver over her. When he released her, she fell back against the mattress, unable to take her eyes off him as he stood and quickly disrobed. Her husband was all male. Handsome and rugged, devastating to her senses.

Her gaze dropped to his engorged penis, glistening wet at the tip, and suddenly she wanted to give him the same satisfaction he'd given her night after night. Yes, she'd used her hands on him, but even with her lack of experience she knew it wasn't the same.

Rolling off the bed, she fell to her knees before him, taking his thick shaft into her hands, glancing up at his startled face.

"Sweetheart, you don't have to do that."

She licked her lips, and glanced back down, wanting to taste him. "Let me. Please." Tonguing the very tip, she moaned at his musky flavor.

"All right. But we can stop anytime." His fingers threaded into her hair and he guided her close to his hard flesh. "Open your mouth, Retta."

Eager to please, Retta opened wide. As the velvety skin brushed her tongue, she took him in, bobbing forward until he hit the back of her throat. She abruptly choked.

"Easy now," Harrison murmured, tugging her head back slightly. "There's no rush."

Eyes watering, Retta managed to catch her breath. But when she looked up, he appeared anything but relaxed. Tension etched his face, and sweat dampened his brow. A delicious surge of feminine power filled her. She, mousy Retta Pierce, soiled dove and town outcast, held this man's desires in her hands, her mouth. For the first time in her life she knew what it felt like to be a woman in control. And she liked it.

A thrill shot through her heart as she kept her eyes focused on her husband and slowly moved her mouth down the length of him, taking more care this time. The same techniques she'd learned with her hand, she now attempted with her mouth. Using his passionate ministrations as her guide, she flicked her tongue along the throbbing vein, then swirled it around the broad tip.

Harrison groaned, tilting his head back, but his fingers, twined through her hair, did not force or push as she found and set a steady rhythm.

"That's it. Your mouth feels so good." His hips jerked with her movements, but not enough to cause her any discomfort.

At his praise, Retta grew more confident. Longing for this experience to be wonderful for him, she again took him deep inside her mouth, slower this time, until he touched the back of her throat. His deep groan sent tingles of delight through her. Gauging her movements by his reactions, she pressed her fingers into his hips and quickened her pace, concentrating solely on pleasing him.

Harrison's muscles went rigid, and his low guttural moan rent the air. His hands held her still. With one final pump of his hips, he filled her mouth with the warm rush of his release.

Satisfaction surged through her.

Then she froze when Harrison gave a hoarse shout in his last shudders. "*Goddamn*, Jenny."

~ ~ ~

Harrison felt Retta jerk away, and his eyes flew open. The look of horror in her tear-filled gaze had him replaying the last five minutes in his somewhat scrambled brain.

Then it hit him. What he'd said.

Retta's sweet mouth had been wrapped around him, draining him of his seed, yet his thoughts had gone to Jenny. And he'd fought off a tinge of guilt for having gotten over her so quickly. But it hadn't been his wife's name that he'd called out.

"Retta . . ."

Scrambling to her feet, she began to rapidly button her blouse, backing away from him. "I-I need to check on—"

Before she made it out the door, Harrison reached her side and pulled her into his arms. She struggled to get free. "Let me go, Harrison."

"I can't." Lifting her into his arms, he carried her back to their bed and laid her on the mattress. He had to make her listen to his apology and pray it'd be enough for her to forgive him.

"Don't move," he barked out, pointing a finger at her and feeling like the worst kind of bastard as her face lost all color.

Reaching for his trousers, he slipped them on, then sat on the bed to haul her onto his lap so that her head was cradled against his shoulder. Her slender body went rigid with hurt and defiance. "Retta. I'm sorry."

She didn't respond, but there was no missing the feel of her tears dropping onto his chest. He raked his fingers through his hair and sighed. He'd really stepped into it this time.

How can I make this right?

Harrison wasn't sure he could, but he had to try. "I loved your sister. You know that." He doubted she'd respond, and she didn't. He made soothing circular motions to her back, trying to ease the tension under his fingertips. "Even though I hadn't seen Jenny in years, I remained faithful to her, knowing one day she would be my bride. Every morning I would take out the tintype I had of her, so I'd never forget. The entire town knew I was holding out for my girl back home, much to their amusement. When you got off the stagecoach with that letter, all my dreams fell apart."

Retta buried her face into her palms and began to sob.

Harrison brought one hand up and held her head close to his heart as she cried. Damn. He was terrible at explaining.

With a deep breath, he continued, hoping to make her understand. "Then I brought you and Addie home and got to know you, and Jenny's memory dimmed a bit more each day. And each day I felt guiltier. But I pushed it to the back of my mind, because this is what Jenny asked of me. Of both of us. To marry, provide for Addie, and live a happy life."

Retta trembled in his arms, but not as she had when her body came alive against his. This time, he'd caused her pain. And that knowledge sent a wave of self-disgust through him. But at least she'd stopped crying, and he hoped she was listening.

Harrison pressed a kiss to the top of her head. "You're my wife, Retta, and I've grown very fond of you and Addie."

Head down, she kept her hands clenched in her lap.

"Retta, look at me."

She didn't move.

"Please." He was done ordering her around. He wanted her to submit to him because she desired it, not because he forced her to. So he waited patiently as his wife took a deep breath, before lifting her accusing stare to him.

Harrison kissed her pert nose.

Her lips firmed stubbornly.

He sighed again. "I know who was pleasuring me with her pretty little mouth. Not once did I imagine it was your sister."

She looked away and blinked rapidly, before returning those soulful eyes back on him. "Then why did you call out her name?"

"Guilt, Retta. At that moment, I realized I had the wife I wanted. Jenny's memories are close to four years old. Faded. Aged. Like a painting covered in dust, holding images from the past. But you're here with me, right now. You're beautiful and sweet, smart and sassy, with a precious daughter I already think of as my own."

He tipped her chin so he could see her face. "Don't give up on us, honey. Please. Give me a chance to make it right."

She stared at him for a long time, before a tired sigh left her lips. "Yes, Harrison. You're my husband. Of course I'll give you another chance." Retta swiped at her damp cheeks with fingers that trembled a bit. "How can I be jealous of Jenny? She's my sister and I love her with my whole heart."

Harrison hugged her close, resting his cheek on the top of her head. "Jenny will always hold a spot in our hearts. But you're my wife. My future. Addie is my daughter. I promise, you are the family I want. You are the wife I want."

She only nodded, relaxing against him. As he continued to hold her in silence, Harrison knew he hadn't won the battle, but at least they'd reached a peaceful draw.

He'd hurt her deeply, and he had some ground to make up with his new bride.

Chapter 11

Retta swiped the cloth a final time over the window in Harrison's study, trying her best, and failing, to ignore the tempting sight of her husband, his muscled forearms flexing as he finished replacing a loose board across the threshold. She had caught her petticoat on a splinter earlier that morning and torn out a chunk of lace trim.

When he abruptly stopped hammering and stared at her, she hurriedly lowered her regard and polished with more vigor.

I'm still angry at him.

In the corner of the study, Addie played quietly with a sock doll Retta had made from a pair of her old woolen hose that had seen better days. Yellow yarn for its hair and buttons for eyes gave the floppy toy a somber expression. Retta had dressed it in a sack gown fastened with a large hook and eye so Addie's tiny fingers could remove it easily. Noodle lay boneless at Addie's side, occasionally whimpering in his sleep.

Even her child and the family puppy had avoided her contrary mood this morning.

Retta gave herself a firm nod. *I've got every right to feel out of sorts.* Then she stole a peek at her husband, now examining other sections of the floor for loose boards, and sighed under her breath.

She didn't want to remain out of sorts with Harrison. For the first time she'd felt like a true wife to her husband, experiencing such pride in giving. The thought of what she had done—and how he'd reacted to her mouth, her hands—made her shiver in the light of day.

Then he'd ruined everything by calling out Jenny's name.

Retta swallowed back the urge to break into more tears. *Crying solves nothing.* Truthfully, when he'd revealed his heart to her and asked for her forgiveness, she'd understood his reasoning. She didn't like it one bit, but she understood.

"Mama, look." Addie's high, sweet voice brought Retta out of her doldrums, and she set down her cleaning rag to cross the room, kneeling at her daughter's side.

"What's Lulu Dolly doing, my angel?" Retta pointed to the half-dressed doll. Addie had managed to unhook the fastening, but the dress wouldn't pull down over the doll's rather lumpy hips.

Addie thrust the doll under Retta's nose. "Fix, pease?" The imp actually batted her lashes entreatingly. She'd already mastered the art of flirting. *Heaven help us all.*

"I surely will." Biting the inside of her cheek, Retta took the doll in hand, running her fingers over the seam she'd sewn up the back of the little sack gown, and ripped out several stitches. "There, now." She handed the doll back. "All fixed."

She watched Addie play with Lulu Dolly, easily pulling on the gown, then crowing happily when the soft fabric slipped down its legs and dropped to the floor. Jumping up, Addie flung herself into Retta's arms and smacked her cheek in a wet, noisy kiss. Retta pressed her face in her daughter's neck and breathed in the scent of sweet little girl.

When Retta raised her eyes, Addie still clinging to her as well as her doll, she spotted Harrison standing in the middle of the room, hammer dangling from one hand, and a look of such tenderness on his handsome face, it made her heart thump. In that single look Retta's resentment began to ease.

"Retta." Harrison's voice sounded thick in the quiet room, and he cleared his throat. "Would you come to town with me?"

Not quite what she had expected from him, but she remained quiet, waiting to see what else he said, and cocked her head inquiringly.

He gestured with the hammer, toward the pile of ledgers he'd shown her just a few days ago. "I want to talk to the folks at the bank."

"Why?" She snuggled Addie closer, feeling how her child's head drooped as she dozed off in her arms. "Addie needs a nap. And I already found—" An unwelcome thought came to her, and she rose unsteadily to her feet, Addie propped against her shoulder. "Don't you trust what I told you?" she snapped, her back ramrod straight. "Do you think I don't know what I'm talking about?"

As soon as the words left her lips, Retta wanted to take them back. She let loose a frustrated sigh. "Harrison, I didn't mean that."

"No, it's all right. And we can go after she wakes up. It's not your numbers, Retta. It's mine." Harrison gestured wearily with his free hand as he set the hammer on a corner of the cluttered desk. "Each month I go to the bank and deposit the vouchers I get for selling the ore. The vouchers are good for an exchange of money at the mercantile. I pay my men from those vouchers, and Frank draws on them, too. If I messed up my arithmetic, then how long have I made mistakes? How far back might it go? I need to go see Elijah Lambert. He's the bank president." He reached for Addie, tentatively, and with a sigh Retta relinquished her hold on her child, Addie snuggling into his arms easily.

As her grip loosened, Lulu Dolly fell to the floor, and Retta hastily snatched up the toy before the inquisitive Noodle could get his teeth into it. The pup had already proved himself a champion chewer.

Thwarted, the pup whined, sniffed himself a few times, and started chasing his own tail.

"Dumb dog," she muttered, then started as Harrison rumbled out a laugh. Retta glanced at him, feeling her own face breaking into a smile.

Maybe her husband really did desire her for something other than a hot meal, a clean house, and a warm presence in his bed. It went a long way toward making her feel better.

Crossing to the desk, she selected the ledger containing the mistakes she'd found before. "You know, the errors might also be on the side of the bank. Would it do any good to take this with us?"

He shrugged as he rocked Addie in his arms. "Might. But I don't think it matters. If you find errors in the account book the bank clerks keep for me, we'll have our answer." He regarded her somberly, his cheek pressed to Addie's soft curls. "Does this mean you'll go with me?"

"Yes, I'll go with you. After Addie's nap," she added, when it looked like Harrison might bolt for Copper right then and there.

~ ~ ~

The buckboard clattered to a stop several yards before the bank, and Harrison patted Copper on his rump. That last bit of road coming into town had been a teeth-rattler. He glanced over at Retta, one hand holding onto her hat and her opposite arm clutching Addie. "You all right over there?"

"Somebody ought to pull those rocks out of the road." Retta smoothed down her skirt. "Is there anything like a town council here? You must remember how Bolster voted on street repairs and such."

"This isn't Bolster." He shrugged. "If we want something done around here, we just do it ourselves." Harrison swung down from the seat and looped the side rope to the hitching post closest to the boardwalk. He strode around the back of the wagon and held up his hands for Addie, who fearlessly jumped into his arms, clinging to his shoulder like a monkey.

He met Retta's gaze over the little tot's head.

Retta pursed her lips and his britches grew tight, to think of how that lovely mouth had engulfed him so sweetly, before he'd crushed her spirit with his thoughtless outburst.

Gracefully accepting his free hand, she braced herself against his shoulder as he swung her off the seat and set her gently on the ground. At her retreat, he bit back his protest of losing her touch so quickly. *Small steps, Carter*, he told himself. She'd willingly come with him today. That had to count for something.

Hoisting Addie higher on his arm, he held out an elbow for Retta to clasp, and guided her into the interior of the clapboard building Little Creede called a bank.

It wasn't much to look at, just a square structure with two rooms, one set up as a vault and the other boasting a high counter and a few chairs scattered around a crudely built desk. Plans were already underway to expand into something bigger, more secure and more along the lines of the commerce bank in Silver Cache. But for now, this one served its purpose.

Harrison led Retta up to the counter and called out, "Mister Lambert, are you here?"

"He's not here. Just a moment." The gruff rejoinder belonged to Zeb Jenkins, Elijah Lambert's worthless assistant and the town's other bank teller. Harrison cursed under his breath. He didn't want to deal with the man, who was ignorant as well as offensive.

Jenkins' body odor preceded his rotund belly through the back door that led out to the necessary. He sidled inside, fumbling with his trousers and revealing a glimpse of the dingy union suit he wore beneath.

Harrison quickly pushed Retta behind him, shielding her. Too many of the men in this town had no care for a woman's sensibilities. He waited until Jenkins approached the counter, then brought Retta around to face him.

"Mister Jenkins, may I present my wife, Retta, and our daughter, Addie." Harrison chose not to react when the man's beady little eyes swept up and down Retta's body, lingering on her neatly-buttoned bodice, before offering a smile that bordered on a leer.

"Why, I'd heard you got hitched. How-do, Missus Carter. Welcome to our little town." Ignoring Addie completely, Jenkins spread his hands wide as if he'd been fully responsible for everything within twenty miles. His expansive gesture revealed dark stains under both arms. Harrison held in his revulsion. He never understood how Lambert had been impressed enough to hire the man in the first place.

"Mister Jenkins." His sharp voice got the man's attention away from Retta. Jenkins turned, his smile almost as objectionable as his stench. "I want to see my account book. Can you fetch that for me, right quick?"

"Well, now," Jenkins demurred, smoothing over his balding head with stubby, ink-stained fingers, "I don't know . . . Mister Lambert usually approves bringing out the account books."

"I have a right to see my books, Jenkins." Harrison kept his voice level, but his tone held plenty of threat.

Annoyance flashed across Jenkin's eyes, but he nodded. Fishing out a key from his trouser pocket, he threw open the vault, returning with the account book. Sweating profusely, he carried it to the desk and motioned for them to take seats.

Addie settled against her mother's shoulder, thumb in mouth, and smiled around the wet digit as he sat next to Retta. *Little flirt.* He gave her a wink and a grin, which faded as he pulled the book toward him and flipped open the pages.

"As you can see, everything is in order," Jenkins began importantly.

Ignoring him, Harrison spun the ledger toward Retta. "What do you think?"

She leaned forward, causing Addie to fidget. "Can you take her?" Retta dropped a kiss on her daughter's head, then murmured, "Go to Papa, angel."

Harrison's heart swelled, not only at how eagerly Addie crawled into his lap, but at his wife's usage of 'Papa.' For a moment he forgot about the very reason for visiting the bank, locking eyes with Retta over Addie's head as she reached for the open ledger.

"Harrumph," Jenkins broke in. "Why would you care what the wife says about anything?" He made a grab for the ledger.

Before Harrison had a chance to flatten the repugnant little man for his insult, Retta caught the edge of the book in a solid grip. "I beg your pardon, sir. My husband would like me to look at his accounts."

"Now see here, missy," Jenkins blustered, tugging at the ledger. "I'm a busy man." He glared at them. "A woman's got no business pokin' into a gent's affairs." Yanking it away, he held the ledger to his blubbery chest, then sent a pasty smile, bordering on a sneer, in Retta's direction. "Best you leave the intelligent-like matters to your husband, and take care of that little tot, there." His nod toward Addie, snuggled on Harrison's lap, held a palpable insult.

"*Enough.*" Harrison surged to the edge of his chair, hefting Addie over his shoulder. "I'd wager my wife has more book smarts than you or anyone else in this town." He pinned the man with a hard glare. "Give her the account book."

Harrison cradled Addie closer, rocking her when she squirmed in his hold. "Shh, sweetpea," he murmured into her hair, and she instantly settled, popping a thumb back into her mouth.

Jenkins tried one more bluster. "Mister Carter, I really do think—"

"*Now,* Jenkins."

Jenkins' mouth tightened, but he laid the book on the desk. Huffing out a gusty sigh that reeked of onions, he pushed the ledger closer to Retta.

Silently she flipped the pages until she reached the last few entries. Brow wrinkled in concentration, she ran a finger down the page, her eyes flickering over the neatly-jotted numbers as she mumbled softly beneath her breath. Then she looked up at Harrison with a frown.

"Half these entries are added incorrectly," she announced firmly.

Jenkins immediately bristled. "Just what are you accusin', missy?"

Retta straightened, her hand steady on the ledger when it looked as if Jenkins would make another grab for the book. "Sir, I've been settling accounts for years. I was taught by a brilliant teacher, and I say these numbers are wrong." She flipped a few pages back, stared at the columns of numbers, paused, and jabbed a finger halfway down the balances. "Here as well. Wrong."

Even as Harrison swelled with pride at her confidence, Jenkins stomped around the desk until he loomed over Retta. "You come into *my* bank and accuse me of bein' a liar?"

"Back away, Jenkins." Harrison rose to his feet, shifting Addie to his wife's arms as she, too, stood. Silently she took Addie and walked toward the dusty windows facing the street. Harrison tried and failed to curb his anger. How much of his accounts, his money, had been ruined by this ignorant cur?

As he grasped Jenkins by the collar and jerked him up on his toes, Retta's voice broke into his fury. "Harrison, don't."

She ventured closer, placing her free hand on his arm. "Let me dig a bit deeper, first. Please?"

Slowly, Harrison released Jenkins, watching as he plopped his flabby rump into the nearest chair, sagging as if all the air had just been sucked out of him. "All right. But I'm taking the book." He plucked it from the desk and placed it under his arm.

Jenkins raised a hand as if to stop him, but Harrison's low growl kept him from spouting any further protest. "Lambert won't like this," the fat bastard muttered.

"Lambert can come see me if he's bothered by anything." Harrison took Retta's elbow gently. "Come on, let's go."

~ ~ ~

Halfway to the wagon, Frank hailed them, hurrying across the rutted street from the mercantile, his boot heels clicking on the boardwalk.

Addie raised her head from Retta's shoulder. "Unca Fank." She held out eager arms.

"There's my girl." Frank swung her up, resting her little bottom on his shoulder, and she clutched his hair in two tiny fists.

"Um, she might be a bit wet, Uncle Frank," Retta cautioned, though she had a feeling he wouldn't care. The elder Carter had fallen hard for his niece, and a damp pair of bloomers didn't seem to bother him.

"Aww, she's fine," he assured her, before turning to his brother and lowering his voice. "Listen, that south shaft really doesn't look right. I sent Dub and Clem down to check deeper, and Clem'll stand guard tonight. Nell's got the boys digging sand."

"Sand?" Retta asked, puzzled.

"For sandbags. Never know when you might need some, and those Washburn runts think they're in hog heaven if they can muck around in sand. They're having a fine old time." Frank jiggled Addie up and down, making her shriek and hiccup in excitement. He slid her off his shoulder and onto one muscled arm, ignoring the faint splotch she left behind. Retta shook her head, glancing toward Harrison.

"Let's get her home so I can clean her up." She indicated Frank's shirt. "Sorry, I should have taken her to the necessary while we were in the bank."

"You went to the bank?"

She nodded as she took her daughter from Frank and propped her on a hip. "Harrison wanted me to examine the account ledger." At Frank's questioning brow, she continued, "We found, uh, maybe we should hurry, Harrison." She grimaced at the warm wetness Addie unleased on her poor skirt. "Addie just, well, you know." She stared beseechingly at both men, trying to hold her soggy-bottomed child away from the soaked garment.

"Right." Harrison took her arm and headed toward the wagon. "Frank, meet us at the ranch."

"Be there shortly." Frank strode across the street toward his tethered horse, as Retta settled herself and Addie next to Harrison on the wide seat. He took up the reins and clucked to Copper, sending the big horse into a jerking trot.

They made good time on the way back, arriving before Frank. "I bet he went to the main mine first," Harrison mused, as he guided Copper into the barn and jumped from the seat. He swung first Addie, then Retta, to the ground. "I've got to deal with the wagon." He pressed a swift kiss to Retta's cheek.

"I'll make coffee," she promised, guiding Addie toward the house. As she hurried her daughter to the kitchen to clean her up, Retta wondered if Frank would be as amenable to her taking over the accounts for Carter Mines, as Harrison.

~ ~ ~

A soft whimper jolted him awake, and Harrison sat up in bed, confused for a moment, rubbing sleep from his eyes. The pup, needing to go outside?

Another whimper. *No, that's Addie*. Probably a nightmare or a sour stomach, considering that third helping of apple crisp she'd gobbled down. Frank's donation of a half-dozen apples to the family meal had been made into the best dessert Harrison had ever eaten. His wife was a wonderful cook, something he felt so thankful for. Among other talents . . .

His lips curved in a smile.

Their evening had been tempered by Frank's presence and the antics of Noodle as he raced through the house and acted foolish as usual, alternately chasing and then being chased by Addie. Frank had slipped away early, claiming his intent to check on the mining perimeter before he retired for the night.

After letting Noodle run around outside and water every bit of scrub he could find, Harrison had joined Retta in Addie's room, settling both tot and pup under the blankets. Wondering if he'd be allowed to hold his wife while they slept, he'd followed Retta to their room, leaving the door open to listen for either Addie or Noodle. Removing his clothes down to his drawers, he climbed into bed. It was the first time since their wedding night that he'd worn anything to sleep in besides his skin.

To her credit, Retta seemed to have left her anger outside the bedroom, approaching her side of the mattress with a head held high, wearing a thin cotton gown and a blush. She had offered her cheek to kiss and a soft, "Goodnight, Harrison," then turned her back and didn't protest when he cuddled her close, an arm under her head and one over her narrow waist.

Harrison pressed his lips to her shoulder, bared by the unlaced neckline of her gown, and smiled in the darkness when she sighed and relaxed fully in his embrace. He would have pushed his advantage, but he held back, unwilling to coerce her for more.

The next thing he knew, Addie's cries had woken him.

Yawning, Harrison rose from his warm bed and strode silently down the hall to the child's room. He lit the candle sconce on the wall, affording enough light to see Addie sitting up in bed with tears running down her face and Noodle pressed into her side, snoring.

"Hi, sweetpea." Harrison sat next to her and opened his arms. "Want me to take you to the potty?"

She shook her head. Harrison felt carefully along her little bottom. She hadn't wet herself. "Does your tummy hurt?" he queried, nestling her in his lap.

Another headshake, accompanied by a whimper.

"Well then, how's about I rock you a little, and you see if you can fall back asleep?" At her nod, Harrison picked her up and crossed to the old wooden rocker in the corner nearest the window, settling her against his chest, her legs dangling on either side of the seat, the way he knew she liked to be cuddled best. Addie immediately buried her face in his neck and stuck a thumb in her mouth as he began to rock, humming softly in the quiet room.

He rubbed a hand over her back, skimming along her spine, brushing golden curls from her eyes so he could watch for signs of drowsiness. Addie sighed as if she carried the weight of the world, but her eyes remained half open, sucking on her thumb. Maybe she was still teething, though at two, he supposed she'd gotten them all. He sure wasn't about to rile her up by feeling in her mouth for any nubs under her gums. If he could just get her to sleep, then perhaps he could go back to bed himself and coax Retta to let him do more than simply hold her—

"Papa." The sleepy, childish mumble about stopped his heart, and Harrison glanced down at the precious weight in his lap. *Did she just call me—*

"Papa. I wove you." Raising her tousled head, Addie reached out with two fingers and ran them over his eyelashes. Her baby grin was so sweet, Harrison had to swallow back the emotion or else choke on it. Enchanted, he stared at his little girl.

I'm the luckiest damned fool in the world. He cupped Addie's head in one palm and cradled her close.

"I love you too, sweetpea," he whispered. Chest tight with emotion, he watched her doze off, every inch of her delicate frame surrendering to sleep as she finally went limp.

Rocking his daughter and enjoying the warm, still night, Harrison stared out the window, counting his blessings.

He abruptly straightened as a deep rumbling filtered inside the partially opened window, the floor vibrating under his feet. *What the—*

A black plume of smoke belched into the clear night sky.

"Son of a . . ." He leapt from the chair.

Addie woke with a startled cry and clung to him as he raced down the hall.

"Retta, wake up," he hollered, bursting into the room. She bolted up in the bed, wild-eyed and confused. Thrusting Addie into her arms, he grabbed his trousers off the bedpost.

"What? What's wrong?" She clutched their whimpering daughter against her chest.

"Stay here, I've gotta go." Harrison jerked up his suspenders. "There's been a mine explosion."

She recoiled, the look of horror in her eyes matching the fear in his gut. "Oh my God, Harrison. Frank!"

Jaw locked tight, Harrison nodded. Unable to voice the possibility that his brother could be injured, or worse, he dashed for the door.

Chapter 12

By the time Harrison reached the mine, a dozen miners were frantically hauling rubble out. Lanterns blazed around the opening, hung from nails pounded into the wooden frame. Several more torches had been shoved into the ground, then lit. Even from a distance he could see the extent of the structural damage.

Jumping off Copper, he raced over to join his men, while tying a bandana around his mouth to avoid breathing in the thick smoke and dust clogging the air.

Spotting Dub's nephew tossing rocks into an empty wheelbarrow, Harrison barked, "Robert, what happened?"

Robert looked grim. "Don't rightly know. We were coming out with a full cart, when there was an explosion near the south tunnel."

"Where's Frank?" Harrison asked, fearing he already knew the answer.

Dub climbed over his nephew and clapped Harrison's shoulder. "I'm sorry, boss, but Frank was working with Clem and his crew in the south tunnel."

"Dammit. Grab a lantern." Not waiting, Harrison entered the mine and strode toward the tunnel where his brother and men were trapped. "How many?"

"We figure seven, all told," Dub replied, hurrying ahead of him with the lantern held high to light their way. "Clem warned us about some timber damage. Thought it might be from upper stress. But Frank found places where the frame had been chipped, prob'ly on purpose. Couple of us off-shift said we'd go back in, and Frank went, too."

Dub hung the lantern on a nail driven into a support frame and rubbed his arm across his grimy face. "Boss, I coulda swore I saw someone who shouldn't be around the mine, watching from a distance a few days back. Sure looked like that bastard Brody Mills."

Harrison's shoulders bunched and his eyes teared up from the smoke and dust filling the narrow passage. Brody Mills was a hired gun, joined at the goddamn hip to Slim Morgan. "Not an accident, then."

"Don't believe so." Dub coughed a couple times behind his bandana then lifted the cloth and spat. "All I know, everything looked good on Monday. Not a lick of trouble in either tunnel."

They all moved to the side as one of the miners pushed past them with a wheelbarrow full of rocks. Rounding the second bend, Harrison spotted the debris blocking the south entrance. Four of his men were using pickaxes to tear away at the obstruction, while three more loaded a cart.

Joining them, Harrison went to work with his bare hands, yanking at stones as they were loosened by the pickaxes. Uncaring his fingers would soon be raw and bloody, he yelled, "Frank. Dammit, answer me."

No response.

"Shit." Harrison took up a shovel that had been propped against the crumbling rock wall, and attacked the clumps of rubble. The stale air worried him. Frank and the men were breathing God only knew what combination of poison, locked behind a wall of debris. Even with the cloth over his mouth, he had to stop every now and again to cough and hack up grayish spit, as did the other men.

It seemed like hours later when, sore and battered, they all pressed their shoulders against the weakened structure until, with cries of triumph, it tumbled down.

Ignoring the dust that exploded around him, Harrison pushed through, gagging on the foul air, until he stood in another narrow passage, staring at an even larger obstruction about twenty feet in front of him. "Ah, hell."

"Son of a—"

"For Christ's sake—"

"Damn it all . . ."

Swearing and muttering continued to ring in the settling dust, until everyone finally fell silent, despair like a live thing twisting throughout the cramped chamber. Harrison examined the solid wall of rock. How were they going to break through in time to save the men?

Fear overwhelmed him, and he rubbed his chest. Not for the first time since arriving at the mine, he wondered if Frank was still alive.

That's when he heard it. A muffled yell came from behind the pile of timbers and boulders blocking their way.

He barreled forward, the sound of the men's footsteps right behind him. "Frank," he shouted. Everyone fell silent again. "Frank, is that you?"

Please God, let it be him.

"No, this is Peter," came the muffled reply.

A fist squeezed his heart. "Where's Frank?"

"Frank's tending Clem. You've got to get us out of here. Clem's bleeding bad." There was a short pause, then, "Jacob and Sweeny are dead."

Relief that his brother was alive tempered the sadness of losing two of his men. They needed to get inside before they lost Clem, too. The man had a wife and six children who depended on him.

Robert spoke quietly from behind him. "It'll take more than pickaxes to get through that monstrosity."

"I'll run back for some dynamite." Dub took one of the lanterns, hightailing it back down the passage without waiting for an answer.

"Peter," Harrison yelled, "anyone else hurt?"

"I'm good, but I think Frank broke his shoulder. It's hanging down in the worst way. Pretty sure Johnson's leg is broken, and Will's head is laid open. Got hit with a couple rocks."

The fist squeezing Harrison's heart finally eased. Injured, but alive at least. Now he just needed to get his brother and everyone else out. Eyeing the stone, Harrison searched for a weak spot. Grabbing the pickaxe from Robert, he went to work on making a hole to nestle the dynamite inside.

Robert hollered, "Peter, get back. Get everyone as far back as possible, we're gonna blow it up."

"Just hurry."

Five minutes later, Dub was back with the dynamite. "Only got one. I hope this'll do it. We excavated a portion of the mine interior today."

"Who's got a matchstick?" Harrison asked.

Dub fished two out of his shirt pocket and handed them over.

"Everyone back," Harrison ordered, then waited until all the men were well out of the blast area. Kneeling, he thrust the dynamite deep inside the crevice he'd hollowed out. Sweat beaded on his forehead, and he wiped his upper arm across his face. Rising, he struck the matchstick on the heel of his boot and let it burn to get a good flame. Carefully, he lit the fuse. Waiting a scant second to make sure it took, he turned and ran as fast as his legs would carry him.

Retta's face flashed across his mind, and he prayed that he'd get to see her and Addie again.

Then the explosion blasted behind him, lifting him off the ground and flinging him forward. If not for Robert and Dub blocking him midflight, he would have been crushed against the stone wall, but instead they all tumbled to the ground as debris landed on and around them.

For one stunned moment, Harrison couldn't move, until one of the men he was slumped over pushed him to the side.

"Good God, Carter, what's the little woman feeding you? You weigh a ton." Dub rolled to his feet, and with a grin, held out his hand.

"Thanks." Harrison heard the tremor in his own voice as he gripped Dub's hand and let the man pull him up. The huge hole left from the blast was big enough for a man to crawl through.

The other men came running from further down the passageway, where'd they'd taken cover, just as Peter poked his head out, relief wreathing his blackened face. "Y'all are a sight for sore eyes."

Harrison scrambled inside to see Frank using his shirt to put pressure on Clem's leg, which was soaked in blood. Frank's collarbone, bruised and swollen, appeared to be sliding off his shoulder.

"'Bout time, little brother." Frank's smile didn't reach his eyes. "We gotta take Clem here to town. Gonna be tough to recover Jacob and Sweeny from the bottom of the hole so their families have something to bury." He pressed his ruined shirt harder on Clem's torn and busted limb. "He's not gonna lose the leg." Frank's red-rimmed eyes bore into Harrison's. "Nell would have both our hides—" He broke off, his Adam's apple moving convulsively as he swallowed.

Harrison cupped a hand over Frank's uninjured shoulder. "We'll take care of him. We'll take care of them all." He studied the gaping hole left behind. In his gut he knew this was no damned accident. "And then we'll find the bastard responsible."

~ ~ ~

It was afternoon when Retta glanced out of the front window for about the thousandth time that day, and spotted a cloud of dust from approaching horses. Exhilaration raced through her and she bolted for the door, then came to an abrupt halt.

What if it's not Harrison?

Slim Morgan's smug face flashed across her vision, followed by Sheriff Lang's worried expression when he'd rode up earlier that day to tell her Frank had been hurt in the mining accident. Imagining the danger Harrison must have faced rescuing his brother, Retta's stomach clenched. As upset as she was with her husband right now, there was no denying that she cared for him a great deal.

Raking her fingers through her loosened hair, she took a fortifying breath and glanced over at Addie, who, as if recognizing her mother's stress, had been subdued all day and was now quietly cuddling with Noodle on the rug in front of the fireplace.

Crossing over to her daughter, Retta knelt, giving Noodle a pat on the head. "Addie, don't go anywhere, Mama will be right back."

Addie looked up from playing with her ragdoll. "Yes, Mama."

"That's my good girl." She pressed a kiss to her daughter's forehead, then retrieved the rifle from the front entrance. Her nerves frazzled, pacing the porch, she waited until the two riders got close enough for her to recognize her husband and Frank.

Relief swept through her. She returned the rifle to its safe spot, out of Addie's reach, then lifted her skirts high enough so she could run out to meet them. Seeing her approach, Harrison jumped off his horse and opened his arms wide as she flew into them. He was dusty, his face was streaked with grime, and his hands were raw and bloodied, but she didn't care. When his strong arms closed around her, her nerves calmed, even as her breath hitched on a sob, hot tears flooding her eyes.

Harrison attempted to soothe her, his quiet, "Hush now. Don't cry," finally easing some of the fear that'd been tormenting her all day.

Clutching his shirt, she pressed her face against his chest. "I'm not crying." Then she gave a strangled laugh at her lie. "I've been horribly worried."

"I'm sorry I was gone so long. But everything's under control now." The tone of his voice indicated perhaps things might be under control, but they weren't all right. She lifted her face to his, not missing the hard lines bracketing his mouth or the hint of anger in his eyes that he couldn't quite hide.

Glancing over to Frank, she gasped. The man looked like he'd been trampled by a herd of wild stallions. His face was a mass of cuts and bruises, his clothes torn and stained, and his arm had been strapped in a sling made out of faded cotton. She could see how much his injured shoulder drooped.

Hadn't Doc Sheaton at least thought to sponge off the grime, before he set Frank's fracture?

Then she gave the makeshift sling another, closer study. And her irritation flared. "That's not anything the Doc would use, Frank. In fact, it sure looks a lot like the fabric from one of your shirts. You haven't been to town yet. Have you?"

Frank gave her what she assumed passed for a smile, but to her it looked more like a grimace due to the pain in his eyes. "I'm fine."

"Told you she'd notice." Harrison's voice held weariness as he caught her hand and gave it a tug to gain her attention. "Frank wouldn't leave the mine until the men were pulled from the debris. I gave up arguing with him, and Dub helped me bring Clem to town. Wasn't about to just leave him there, so Sheriff Lang volunteered to come out and let you know what happened."

"Yanked me out of the hole this morning," Frank said. "Kept telling 'em I was fine, but you know how damned stubborn your husband is—"

"I know how stubborn you *both* are." At Harrison's soft snort, she turned on him. "You think this is amusing?" Fresh tears threatened to brim, and she blinked hard to keep them from falling. This was no time for showing weakness; they'd ride roughshod right over her.

Her spine stiffened. "Harrison, bring Frank into the house. He's staying with us."

Chapter 13

Frank slid off his horse. "That's not necessary," he began, as Harrison sputtered, "What, live here?" Both wore identical looks of horror.

Retta's patience, already stretched thin, cracked. Maybe if she knocked their heads together, each might grow a bit of sense.

"That's right." She waved a hand in Frank's direction. "Look at him. He's a mess, and in pain." She jabbed her finger toward her brother-by-marriage who'd opened his mouth, no doubt ready to tell fibs about how he felt. "Yes, you are. You're just about cross-eyed from pain, not to mention stubborn as can be for not going to town and letting the Doc set your shoulder properly. You're going to lie down on the sofa." She paused, then brightened. "Better yet, I'm putting you in Addie's room."

"I'm not sleeping in a little girl's room," Frank grumbled.

Harrison covered his mouth with one grimy hand and smothered a cough.

"You can, and you will." Retta laid a gentle hand on Frank's good arm. Gazing up into his dirt-encrusted face, she spotted such weariness, beyond the bone-deep worry she knew plagued both brothers. She might not yet comprehend the extent of the damage the main mine suffered, but Sheriff Lang had revealed enough when he visited for her to understand that more than one miner had perished in the explosion. Their deaths would weigh heavily.

"Please, Frank." She took his hand and squeezed it. "Ease my mind and stay here, let me help you heal. I know you don't want him to, but Doc Sheaton still needs to come out and examine you." She frowned as she eyed the swollen, discolored skin under his neck and down his shoulder, where the sling held his arm in place. "At the very least, you've got a break in your shoulder. Maybe your collarbone, too. That's pretty serious."

"I can't lay around, doing nothing," he cut in, then jerked his chin toward Harrison. "We got too much work to do."

"And you're not going to be the one doing it," Harrison rasped, "you stubborn jackass. Retta's right. Not until your bones set." He moved to his brother's side, and Retta released Frank's hand as Harrison curved a supporting arm around his back. "Let's go. Addie can move into our room for a while." He urged Frank toward the front door.

"I'm not gonna sleep in some little baby bed." He hobbled through the kitchen toward the hall.

Harrison steered Frank inside the room. "It's not a baby bed, and stop whining. That bed's as big as the one Retta and I sleep in. You'll be fine."

Retta hurried before them to clear off the few toys scattered over the mattress, including a favorite blanket of Addie's.

With a ragged sigh, Frank slumped on the edge of the bed, then stared down at himself. He struggled to stand. "I'm filthy. Let me up, I gotta go wash."

Harrison pushed him down. "No, you don't. Clean up later. Sleep now." At Frank's growl, he released a hard breath. "Frank, I'm weary to the bone and so are you. All I want to do is sleep a couple hours, then figure out what to do next. Stop goddamn fighting me for once." He rubbed a grimy palm over his sweat-stiffened hair.

Retta's heart clutched for them, two big, tough men laid low by this disaster. Wiping at her stinging eyes, this time her fingers came away wet. This would never do. She straightened, clearing her throat. "I'll heat some water and bring in washrags for both of you. Some hot stew and biscuits would be easy to—"

"Unca Fank." Addie tumbled through the doorway with Noodle in pursuit. Before Retta or Harrison could stop her, she'd leapt onto the far side of the bed and scampered on all fours. Even as Frank put out his good arm to block her, Addie's pinafore tangled in her legs and she flopped on her face. With a giggle, she gained her knees, lurched toward Frank, then stopped, her mouth in a rounded *O*.

"Huwt." She reached out a pudgy hand and touched an ugly bruise on his shoulder. "Ouch." Leaning in sweetly, she pressed her mouth to the darkened mass in a smacking, wet kiss that probably did more harm than good on Frank's torn up skin. "All bedda." Curling on the mattress next to him, she batted her lashes outrageously.

Frank blinked a few times, then caught Retta's eye with such a manly, yet helpless look on his face, it was all she could do not to either laugh at his panic, or choke back emotion at Addie's endearing attempts to nurse her beloved Uncle Frank back to health.

"Well, Frank, I do believe the doctor here knows best." Crooking a finger at Addie, Retta coaxed her daughter off the bed and pushed her out of the room with a pat to her bloomer-clad bottom. "Go on and play with Noodle. You can torture your poor uncle when he's rested and feeling better."

She returned to Frank's bedside and caught the beginning of a grin on Harrison's blackened face as he struggled to his feet, swaying a bit.

Retta lightly touched his shoulder. "Harrison, you have to get some sleep."

"Yeah, I'm about to fall over if I don't." Harrison brushed a kiss over her mouth. His lips tasted of smoke and bitter minerals, but at least he was alive.

Slowly she eased back, and pinned a smile on her face as he staggered to the door. As soon as she heard his boot heels clomping down the hall, her backside hit the mattress and she covered her mouth to hold back a sob.

The bed shifted, and dimly she registered the feel of a wide palm on her head, patting her hair as if she were a child. "Gonna be all right, little sister." Frank's voice was thick with exhaustion. His hand dropped away and landed with a thud on his chest, disturbing the sling that held his other arm immobile. "Damn it all to hell and back," he seethed.

When she looked up, alarmed, and turned toward him, he waved her concern away. "I'd sure like some of those biscuits you talked about. Got any?"

"I know what you're trying to do." She huffed, exasperated at the stubbornness of men in general. "Sidetracking me won't work, Frank Carter. I've got a bit of laudanum I brought from Bolster, and you're going to take some for the pain. If I have to pour it down your throat myself."

With that, Retta bounced off the bed and strode toward the door, ignoring his raspy, "Damned ornery woman."

~ ~ ~

A short nap hadn't done much to improve Harrison's mood, any more than a fast scrub in tepid well water. If he'd had more time, he'd have taken a towel and a bar of soap to Bonney Creek and washed up there. But he wasn't about to leave the ranch, not with Frank helpless inside and his wife and child in danger. Not until they knew exactly what had happened at the mine. He had his suspicions.

Proving them might not be so easy.

Shrugging into a fresh shirt, he dug a clean pair of dungarees from the folded pile Retta had left earlier, hurriedly buttoning up and shoving in his shirttails. He'd burn the clothes he'd been wearing at the mine. Torn and bloody, they were too far gone to repair.

Delicious smells wafted from the kitchen, and he remembered Retta had promised stew and biscuits. Famished, Harrison slicked back his wet hair, and followed his nose down the hall to the kitchen.

The room was empty, the biscuits stacked on a plate near the stove, all golden brown and fat, just begging him to snatch one. Maybe he'd grab two, and see if Frank was awake for a pre-dinner sampling.

A knock at the back door had him dropping the biscuit back on the pile. Who would come to the back when they could use the front like civilized folk? Striding down the hall, Harrison whipped the door open.

And stared at Cat Purdue—the last person he expected to see at the ranch—standing on the stoop with her customary half-smile curving her mouth. "Cat? What are you doing here?"

When she raised a slender, arched brow, he waved her forward. "Come on inside." Glancing around the backyard to see if anyone else came with her, he spotted one of the horses usually stabled at the Lucky Lady. "Did you ride out here alone? Not a smart thing for a woman to do."

"Nobody bothers me, Harrison." Lifting the hem of her plum riding skirt, she revealed the knife strapped to her ankle, right above her leather half-boot. "I know how to use this and I've got good aim."

"Still doesn't explain what you're doing here." Harrison gestured toward the kitchen, waiting until she'd reached the table and settled gracefully on one of the chairs. He took the seat across from her, noting her polished appearance, not a hair out of place.

Had she come to see Frank? "My brother is all right," he began.

"Why should I care about that fool? I merely stopped by to deliver a package." She produced a frilly bag and fished a bottle from its depths, setting it on the table with a thump. "Here. Laudanum. Your wife might already have some. With the pain I know Frank's in, an extra bottle might come in handy. Bet he won't take any of it." She relaxed against the chair, smoothing her riding gloves over her hands.

Harrison wasn't mollified by her casual demeanor one bit. Fingering the bottle, he picked it up and studied it. "Where did you get this from, Cat?"

"Oh, you'd be surprised what the girls at the Lucky Lady receive as payment, sometimes." At his raised brows, she hastily amended, "Not me, of course. I only serve the drinks and sing for my supper." Cat fussed with the jaunty hat she wore, playing with the purple plume curling along its crown, then straightening the satin frogs decorating her short-waist jacket. "Not that your rude brother would believe it. He likes to think the worst of me."

Behind her lovely, slanted green eyes lay a sadness even Harrison could spot. Sighing, he set down the bottle of medicine and propped his elbows on the table. "Do you want me to say anything to him?" God knew how stubborn Frank could be, especially in matters of the heart. And for all Cat's supposed indifference, she seemed just as stubborn.

But Cat waved a dismissing hand. "No. He can think what he likes." She rose, shaking out her skirt. "Just make him swallow some of that laudanum. You might have to pinch his nose and wait until he opens his mouth to breathe. That's the way children are made to take their medicine."

Harrison followed her as she glided to the back door. "You can stay a while, if you want. Maybe meet my wife, Retta. She's in the parlor with our daughter."

"I've no wish to intrude on your happy family, Harrison. Another time, perhaps." Cat paused at the door, her hand on the latch, and turned. The smile she offered was genuine, as was the concern in her eyes. "I hope Frank heals, and I hope you find answers regarding what caused the explosion at your mine. I'm heading to the Washburn place next. Thought I'd help with Clem's leg."

She opened the door, then added as an afterthought, "I was apprenticing with a doctor back East when my, well, that's another story entirely. If I can assist Doc Sheaton when he makes his rounds, I will have done my civic duty."

She strode to her horse and swung into the saddle with the ease of years of practice. Harrison stood on the stoop and watched as she turned her horse toward the mine, and the cluster of miners' cottages there.

"She's not what I expected at all." Retta's soft voice gave him a start, and Harrison glanced over his shoulder. She stood in the doorway, Noodle in her arms, his tongue lolling out the side of his mouth. She nodded toward the disappearing flume of dust as Cat galloped away. "I listened a bit," she confided breezily, though she blushed at the confession. "I figured she might want to ask you about Frank. Maybe I'm wrong, but I sense some feelings between them."

Harrison rubbed his chin thoughtfully. "Yeah. Hard ones, I think. Frank doesn't say much, and Cat's pretty tight-lipped." He slipped an arm about Retta's shoulder, relieved when she left it there as they headed for the kitchen.

As she broke away to set the pup on the floor, then stirred the stew, Harrison leaned against the pantry and watched his lovely wife tend to their meal. No malice, no judgement, not a single speck of resentment shone in her eyes or on her face at knowing Cat Purdue, a reputed saloon woman with loose morals, had come into her home. Anywhere else, Harrison knew the scandal would have thrown Retta's reputation into question.

He had a feeling Retta took everyone at face value, assigning no blame to lives gone awry or circumstances beyond someone's control.

To get his mind off the sweet temptation of her shapely curves and fresh-faced beauty, he asked, "Has Frank woke up at all?"

One corner of her mouth curled in a smile. "Funny you should ask. Currently your brother is asleep, while your daughter has decided he'll look quite dashing with his beard plaited."

"*What*?" Harrison bolted for Addie's room. "This, I've got to see."

"Don't you dare wake him." Retta caught hold of his arm and tugged him away from the door. "It was hard to get him comfortable so he'd actually doze off. Right now Addie's happy and Frank is sleeping like the dead. Time enough to see how he reacts when he wakes up, but Addie thinks she's 'healing' Unca Fank. I'm sure not going to interfere."

Chapter 14

The next morning, Retta peeked around the door of Addie's room, smiling to see Frank slouched on the edge of the mattress. When he lifted his head, she spotted Addie's handiwork on his beard, entwined into twisted tufts that vaguely resembled braids. Behind her, Harrison snorted.

Hearing them, Frank squinted one eye and glared.

"Can you two keep it down?" Groaning, he shifted. "I feel like I've been kicked by a mule." He carefully straightened, slapping both hands on his spine.

Retta bit her lip to hold back her mirth. Harrison wasn't as polite and began laughing uproariously.

"Gonna let me in on the joke?" Frank asked, confused. He reached up to tug at his beard, as he so often did when in contemplation, halting when he felt the loose plaits. One brow, puffy over his swollen eye, quirked in amusement. "Addie?"

"Yep."

"Little stinker." Frank ran his fingers through his beard to untangle it as he rose stiffly from the bed. "I'll be ready to leave when you are."

Retta leaned in threateningly. "Lie back down, Frank. You need another day's rest, at least. Doc Sheaton's orders. Breakfast is on the table, but after you eat it's back to bed with you."

"The hell," Frank muttered. "I've got shit to do, woman. Like finding out who sabotaged the mine."

"I have a pretty good idea." Harrison's amusement at his brother's expense had vanished. "But Retta's right. You're no good to me in this condition. Get some rest. Tomorrow I'll check around town and see what I can find, collect some solid proof before making any accusations."

Frank grudgingly conceded. His eyes flashed dangerously. "We lost two damn good men in that explosion, Harrison. Almost lost Clem, too. Someone's going to pay."

"But not today." Retta was adamant. "Harrison, help your brother to the table so he can eat. He can't take laudanum on an empty stomach."

When Harrison crossed to the bed to help him stand, Frank shot her a defiant frown, his sullen expression so much like a child's, she nearly laughed.

"I ain't taking any of that snake oil. It makes my brain fuzzy."

"Don't waste your breath, Frank. Once my wife sets her mind to something, it's best to just give in gracefully."

As the men took a seat at the table, Retta hurried to the parlor and scooped her daughter off the nest she'd made with her blanket and Noodle's backside. Carrying her to the kitchen, she plopped her in the chair next to Frank.

Addie beamed. "Unca Fank all bedda?"

Frank grinned down at her, ruffling the top of her head. "All better, shortcake."

"Lemon dop?" She held out a small, imperious hand for the candy Frank had gotten into the habit of keeping in his pockets just for her.

Chuckling, he patted his shirt, then his trouser pockets. "She's got a nose like a bloodhound." Frank produced a piece and held it out. Bright-eyed, Addie snatched it up.

After breakfast, Harrison headed out for the mine, and Frank took a dose of laudanum without too much argument before promptly falling asleep on the sofa, despite Retta's protests that he should rest in an actual bed. His long legs hanging off one end of the cushions, he looked tough and fragile at the same time, the bruises starkly purple on his sun-weathered face.

Tiptoeing from the parlor, Retta busied herself straightening up the kitchen, and checking supplies for their next few meals. Both Frank and Harrison ate enormous amounts of food, so it was no surprise to find her cupboards and cellar larder running low. She'd take the wagon to town and stock up. Extra medical items wouldn't hurt, either.

She glanced over at Frank snoring on the sofa, trying to figure out how mad the men would be if she left on her own. Surely she was perfectly capable of making the short trip to town. Nodding decisively, Retta entered Harrison's cluttered office, retrieving a piece of paper and the stub of a pencil. She would prop a note on the kitchen table. Harrison and Frank had their hands full with the mine, and she wouldn't bother them with these little chores.

Collecting her bonnet, her daughter, and one of Harrison's rifles, for good measure, Retta hitched up the wagon and headed out.

~ ~ ~

From the shadow of an alleyway between the bank and the barbershop, Slim Morgan watched speculatively as Retta Carter's wagon approached the general store. *Without a male escort, I see. My, my.*

She stepped down, gracefully lifting her skirt out of the way and displaying a slender ankle. Saliva pooled in his mouth at the sight. Then his upper lip curled with distaste as she turned back to pluck her daughter off the seat before entering the store. The damned brat was going to be a nuisance.

He found it hard to believe Carter allowed his wife to travel the distance to town by herself. Then again, the woman had a defiant streak a mile long, and it was obvious Carter couldn't control her. *High time a real man shows her who's boss.* And *he* was just the man to do it.

Silently, he crossed the dusty street toward the general store, casually peering inside, pretending to window-shop, as he tracked her movements. With one of those ratty baskets over her arm, she gathered supplies, chatting with the old harridan who owned the store. The graceful sway of Retta's hips made his cock throb, imagining what that rounded perfection would feel like, rubbing up against him—

Brody's sudden reflection in the glass, as he appeared at Slim's side, put an end to his lascivious thoughts, and Slim cursed under his breath.

"What did you find out?" Slim never took his eyes off the prize, watching as Retta grasped her daughter's hand and walked her over to the penny candy. His ears twitched in irritation at the girl's high-pitched squeal when she pointed at the display.

Brody tipped back his Stetson with grubby fingers. "Carter headed for his mine early this mornin'. It'll take 'em days to clear out all that damage from the blast. Not sure what they lost, though. You'll have to ask Jenkins how much it'll hit 'em in the purse. But they're down three men."

Slim rubbed his chin thoughtfully. "Only three men? Not enough to hinder his operation, Mills. Especially if they didn't have to close down that main mine." He paced along the window, his eyes still locked on Retta. "The idea was to make the Carters sell—"

He broke off as Retta stopped to look closely at a display case, bending over with her backside in the air. Slim adjusted himself in his drawers to obtain some relief.

God*damn*, the woman was delectable.

Brody bumped him from behind when he crowded closer to the window. His gaze caught on Retta, still bent over a display. "Ain't that the Carter woman? If you're wantin' to poke that skirt, I'd get started today."

"Button your lip and just tell me about the brother."

"Word is, he's lickin' his wounds at Carter's ranch. Sounds like he'll be out for a couple days anyway."

They both backed into the alley when Retta exited the mercantile. While Loman stacked her purchases in the bed of the wagon, she swung the little girl onto the seat and climbed up after, showing more leg this time. Slim couldn't take his eyes off her as she settled herself and picked up the reins. Clucking her tongue at the horse, she released the wheel brake. The wagon rolled smoothly down the rutted street out of town.

Inhaling a deep breath, Slim turned to Brody. "Keep an eye on things for me."

"Sure thing, boss."

Dismissing his employee, Slim waited until Brody ambled off in the direction of the saloon, before returning his attention to the wagon wheels churning up dust on the narrow road out of town.

A ten-minute head start should do it.

The sun was high, a warm breeze blowing across the prairie as he followed her trail. Lust roiled through him, his cock already hard at the thought of taking her in the back of her wagon. Too bad she had the girl with her, but it was never too soon for the brat to learn a woman's place.

Staying back far enough so she didn't spot him, he waited until they passed the fork between her ranch and the Carter mines before making his presence known. Maybe if she pleased him, he'd keep her for a while in one of those back rooms at the Silver Cache Inn, so they could continue their fun in private. If not, he'd slit her throat here and make it look like an Indian attack. He didn't care what happened to the girl. She was too young to say anything. He'd leave her further out where the coyotes could deal with her.

Urging his horse into a gallop, he noted the instant Retta realized she wasn't alone. Glancing over her shoulder, her eyes widened when she saw him. She snapped the crop, urging the horse faster, but it was too late. With ease, Slim closed the remaining distance and grabbed the reins.

"What's your hurry, Missus Carter?" Bringing the wagon to a halt, he dismounted his horse, dropping the reins to the ground as he approached her.

She stared down at him with wide eyes. "What do you want, Mister Morgan?"

"Why, I spotted you in town, my dear, and thought we could finish the conversation your husband so rudely interrupted the other day."

Retta's eyes flicked to the floor of the wagon, but before she could go for the rifle propped near the seat, he reached in and grabbed it.

"I don't think you'll be needing this." He unchambered the bullets and let them drop to the ground. "Nice repeater." He fondled the barrel suggestively. "I'll just keep this. Otherwise, you might hurt yourself." He set it aside in a patch of nearby scrub.

Nudging back his hat, he squinted through the blinding sun at her. "Now, are you going to come down here and talk to me, or do I have to come up there?" He lifted a brow, nodding toward the little brat sitting next to her.

Retta's cheeks went chalky-white. "No. No." She turned to the girl, stroking her hair. "Stay here, Mama will be right back." Retta plucked the old ragdoll off the seat and gave the ugly thing to her.

"Yes, Mama." She began playing with her doll.

Retta swung around, glaring at him, before scooting to the edge of the high seat. When he didn't step back, she lifted an imperious brow. "Move please, Mister Morgan."

Slim held up one hand. "What kind of gentleman would I be if I didn't help a lady down?"

Anger filled her eyes, but he could also see her fear.

Satisfaction surged through him. Considering how the little bitch had held a rifle on him . . .

Oh, he was going to make her sorry for that.

She hesitantly stretched out her hand. Impatiently, he grabbed her fingers, and with a sharp tug he pulled her from the wagon. Retta tumbled against him, her breasts flattening against his chest, and he slid an arm around her waist, crushing her to him. His cock surged to attention, and he pushed her back against one of the wheels, pressing his hard length against her.

Slim groaned, lowering his head to nuzzle her ear. Retta pushed against his chest with both hands. Ignoring her struggles, he caught the edge of her ear in his teeth and bit down, forcing a yelp from her throat.

"Mama?"

Cursing, Slim released Retta's lobe and glanced at her child. The little brat played with her doll but stared at her mother. "Tell her everything is fine," he muttered harshly.

Quivering in his arms, Retta quietly pleaded, "Please, let me go."

"You don't mean that, Retta. I saw the way you looked at me that first day we met. Admit it. You want me."

"I *don't*." She pushed ineffectually at his shoulders, and hissed, "Get off me."

He stared into her pretty blue eyes, snapping with fury. A hunger, like nothing he'd ever felt for a woman before, clawed at him. There was no denying her beauty, and he had to have her. Twisting a long golden curl around his finger, he lowered his head, his mouth a scant inch from hers. "One kiss, and I'll think about it."

Liar. You have no intention of releasing her. You're so hard for her that in two seconds you're going to toss her into the back of that wagon and fuck her. Once she had a taste of what he could give her, she'd never want another man.

Judging from her reaction, he knew she could read his lusty intention in his eyes. The frantic beat of her heart against his chest gave away her fear. No matter how hard she tried to hide it, she was frightened.

Power swept over him at her reaction to his advances.

Women were weak. Submissive. Good for only one thing. And Slim loved to show them exactly how weak and submissive they were meant to be. The ones that'd tried to deny him, thinking they were better than him, quickly learned their mistake.

He swooped in to take the kiss he'd wanted since the first day he'd set eyes on her—

Sudden pain exploded between his legs where her knee connected hard. He released her, bending over to shield his injured groin, and snarled at the agony.

She stumbled toward the back of the wagon, trying to escape.

One hand still cupping his throbbing cock, Slim cursed and lunged for her, managing to get hold of her skirt.

With a cry, she tripped and her face smacked the side of the wagon wheel.

"Did that hurt, *sugar*? Wait till I take when I want from that body of yours," he grunted, looming over her. "You're gonna know plenty of hurt."

Once, he might have been gentle with her, but no more. Retta Carter would soon learn her place in this world, right before she left it.

As he reached for her, she flipped onto her back, holding her bloodied cheek. Stark terror now shone in her eyes, firing his lust.

A sudden gunshot rent the stillness and he whirled around, spotting a horse and rider fast approaching. Shading his eyes against the blazing sun, Slim recognized one of the miners, a pistol clutched in one hand, aimed straight at him.

"Goddammit!" Deprived of his prey, he jumped to his feet. Then his glare swung to the child, and for a split-second he itched to snap her scrawny little neck, just out of spite. But such an act would get him lynched.

For now, he needed to escape. Slim rushed to his horse and mounted.

They'd have to finish this another day.

~ ~ ~

Retta stood unsteadily, cradling the side of her face, blood dripping between her fingers. Fear pounded through her with debilitating force . . . not for her own safety, but for Addie's. She stumbled around the wagon and climbed up to tug her daughter on her lap, her eyes burning with unshed tears. The sound of hoofbeats as Slim Morgan galloped away eased her panic, but there'd been a moment when she knew the bastard intended to harm her daughter.

"Mama," Addie sobbed, staring at Retta's face. "Huwt." Her wailing increased.

"It's all right. I'm all right." She rocked Addie, trying to calm her down as she pressed her uninjured cheek to her child's sweaty curls.

Retta raised her head and stared as another man approached on foot from the opposite direction, leading his horse. Recognizing Peter, she slumped with relief.

If he hadn't come along right when he did . . . Unable to keep her own emotions at bay any longer, she burst into tears, hugging Addie.

"Missus Carter, are you all right?" Peter reached into his shirt pocket and pulled out a clean handkerchief, handing it to her. Catching the end of Slim Morgan's dust trail, he turned back and eyed her worriedly. "Did he hit you?"

Weary, Retta held the handkerchief against her throbbing cheek. "I fell on one of the wheels. Can you follow me home, please?"

"Of course, Missus Carter."

Minutes later, almost to the ranch house, another horse approached, this one carrying her angry brother-by-marriage. Still favoring his shoulder, Frank snapped, "What happened, Peter?"

Retta bit her lips to keep them from quivering, helpless to staunch the tears stinging her wounded cheek under the handkerchief. She shouldn't have gone into town. She'd put not only herself in danger, but also her innocent child. She'd only wanted to help.

"Not sure, Frank. But I came upon Missus Carter bleeding, and that weasel Slim Morgan galloping away."

Rage darkened Frank's face. "Did he touch you or Addie?"

"He— I—" Retta felt a shudder sweep through her body. "It was an accident. I fell."

Frank eased his horse closer, eyeing Addie, who'd fallen asleep, her face still flushed from crying. He reached out and lightly stroked the top of her head, a look of relief flashing across his features. When he carefully pulled Retta's hand away and studied the damage to her cheek, his eyes turned as hard as flint.

"Peter," Frank gritted out, "ride back to the mine and send Harrison home."

"No, Frank." Retta crumpled the stained linen in trembling fingers, stretching out her free hand to grasp his arm. Beneath her palm his muscles were like stone. "Please don't say anything." She tugged until she regained his attention. "Harrison will go after Morgan. You know he will. And if he does, think of what could happen—"

"Retta, we believe Morgan's responsible for the disaster at the mine. Because of him, we lost several good men. Clem'll probably lose a leg. I'm not hiding this from my brother."

"And if he runs off in a lather, looking for blood? What then?" Retta propped her sleeping daughter on her shoulder, rubbing her back as Addie roused and whimpered. "I agree, if Slim Morgan committed a crime then he's got to pay, but do it the right way. Send for the sheriff."

"If you think your husband's gonna let this go, little sister . . ." Frank removed his hat and slapped it against his thigh, dislodging a cloud of dust, before dropping it back on his head. "You should know better by now."

Chapter 15

Harrison dug his heels into Lightning's sides and the black and white stallion leapt forward, tearing up the narrow trail leading to the ranch. He'd left Peter's gelding, Boomer, in the dust, struggling to keep up.

With each pounding hoof, Harrison vowed to find that bastard Morgan and end his life for daring to lay his filthy hands on Retta. Adding that crime to the mine explosion was like pouring kerosene on flames.

I'll flay his rotten hide and string him up for the buzzards to finish off. Harrison spurred Lightning on harder.

Peter said her face was bloody and swollen.

Don't think about it. He'd probably half-kill his horse trying to force the poor beast into flat-out racing over a path rutted with gopher holes and rocks. If Lightning twisted a leg, he'd have to put him down. It cost Harrison mightily, but he eased up on the reins, encouraging the horse to slow.

Rounding the final bend, his ranch house visible up ahead, Harrison fought to swallow his fury. If he confronted Retta in this condition, he'd say things he'd later regret. Or worse, spank the shit out of her rounded little backside, until she promised never to leave the ranch again—

He reached the barn and jumped from the saddle before Lightning stopped completely. Landing on one knee and ignoring the pain shooting up his shin, Harrison bolted down the lane and across the yard, stomping the patch of daisies Retta had been nurturing all month into the dirt as he leapt over all five steps of the porch.

"Retta!" He pushed at the door, fumbling with the latch, finally getting it open and flinging both halves of heavy wood so hard, they crashed into the wall. Uncaring his muddy boots left clumps on the floors Retta polished religiously, he strode into the kitchen, desperate to hold his wife and kiss her. Check on his daughter, too.

He halted in the doorway, his focus locked on the sight of Retta, slumped at the table. Knotted hair hanging over one shoulder, a tear in her blouse and a rent in her skirt, she looked exhausted and in pain judging by the way she cupped her face. From across the room he could see the bruises her dirt-stained hand failed to hide. Next to her, Frank clutched a mug of coffee no doubt left over from breakfast. Addie slumped in his lap, sucking on her thumb, half-asleep. Under the table, Noodle lay curled in a snug ball, dozing.

Harrison advanced slowly when all he wanted to do was rush to his wife's side and scoop her up, then lock her away somewhere so she wouldn't put herself in danger again. Lord knew he didn't mean to scare her, but the injuries to her face made him crazy.

He squatted in front of her and raised her chin gently. "Let me see."

Obediently she lowered her hand and tilted her head. Harrison sucked in a breath at the damage. Dark bruises, a gash already split open high on her cheek, the eye on that side puffy and black-rimmed. A damp dishtowel streaked with dirt lay on the table, but blood still crusted her nose and the corner of her mouth. She'd clearly cried many tears, her lids red-rimmed, lashes spiky and damp.

As furious as Harrison found himself, he couldn't do anything other than hold out his arms, clasping them around her shivering frame when she launched off the chair into his embrace. She sobbed against his neck.

"Mama huwt," Addie whimpered around the thumb jammed in her mouth.

"Shh, shortcake. She's just tired." Frank met Harrison's frown as he stroked Addie's hair. Sighing, she settled instantly, closing her eyes. "She was in the wagon playing with her doll," Frank murmured. "I don't think she saw much."

"Jesus." Harrison's grip tightened on Retta. She didn't protest, but her fingers dug into his muscled arms. He set her away until he could look in her eyes. "He hit you."

"No, he grabbed my skirt and it ripped. I got off-balance. Smacked my face on the wheel." Retta patted his chest, as if such a simple gesture might hold Harrison back from his rage.

His jaw rippled with tension. Thoughts of all the things that could have happened to her and Addie, traveling unprotected, made something snap inside him. The feral emotions he'd managed to keep at bay, during the short ride from the mine, burst to the surface.

"Retta, you let yourself get into a situation where the bastard had a chance to go after you." Harrison gave her arms a shake. "Going to town, alone . . . What was so necessary, you couldn't wait until I got back?"

"I had the rifle, Harrison. I'm not a complete ninny." She tried to push away from his grip, but he wasn't having any of that.

Instead, Harrison turned to Frank. "Where's the Winchester?"

Frank shrugged. "Well, let's see. I found six bullets in the dirt near the wagon, and the rifle on the ground. Would appear to me Morgan got hold of your fine weapon and unarmed your wife."

Retta shot him an annoyed stare. "You're *not* helping matters."

Frank scowled back. "You dodged a passel of trouble, in case you haven't figured it out. If Peter hadn't come along when he did, what do you think would've have happened?"

At her sharp inhale, he gave a nod. "Yeah. I see you got it sorted out." He snuggled Addie closer, cradling her as if she were made of spun glass.

The entire mess was taking a toll on Frank, his face drawn tight from pain. Addie's head lay against his bad shoulder and broken collarbone, yet he hadn't moved her aside, love for his niece glaringly obvious.

Harrison's heart hurt at the thought of the precious child being hurt or traumatized in any way. Which got him hotter under the collar at Retta's foolish actions. Abruptly, he straightened and deposited her on the chair. He had to *do* something even if only to pace the room and kick the furniture.

His boot connected with the far wall, making Retta scramble to her feet. Slapping her hands on her hips, she stormed over to him. "Stop that. You'll break your toe and then I'll have two surly, injured men to deal with."

"I'm not surly," Frank protested.

She rounded on him. "Oh, yes you are. You've been lecturing me since we got back to the ranch. I'm not some child you have to nursemaid."

"Don't yell at my brother. He cares what happens to you, Retta. If you'd goddamn waited for me to get home, we wouldn't be having this little discussion."

"Is that what you call this bullying?"

Harrison jabbed a finger in her direction. "Did you even thank him? I'll bet you didn't. Probably didn't thank Peter, either."

"Stop it!"

"You're not leaving this ranch until Morgan's caught and in jail." Harrison folded his arms decisively over his chest.

Retta's cheeks flushed deep red and her hands fisted as if she'd like to bury one or both in his gut. If he wasn't so angry, he'd have found amusement in her orneriness and even pleasure that she wasn't frightened of him any longer.

But this wasn't a laughing matter. Retta had to understand how serious it had become.

Frank shot Harrison a disbelieving look. "Now you've done it. Don't you know women at all, brother?"

"Stay out of it, Frank." Harrison broke off as Retta advanced. Eyes burning a hot blue, she flattened her pretty mouth in irritation. He wasn't sure if he wanted to rattle the stubborn right out of her or kiss her until neither of them could think straight.

Probably both.

"You listen to me, Harrison Carter." She shoved a fist in his face. "I had your rifle. I know how to shoot it. There's no reason I can't go to town as part of my household chores. Other wives go by themselves. You think I'm going to stay inside all day, every day, and wait for you to come home and escort me? We'd all starve to death."

"Other wives don't have Slim Morgan sniffing around them like a damned rabid dog. For Christ's sake, woman, the bastard's dangerous. Peter said when he rode up he saw you on the ground and Morgan hanging over you, ready to pounce." Harrison shoved his hands into his hair and yanked hard, trying to dislodge the image his own words invoked, but it didn't work. He did his best to speak reasonably and rationally, but instead shouted, "You're forbidden to go into Little Creede until I say differently."

At a sudden yowl, he turned. Noodle cowered under the table, head flung back, baying and shivering. Before Harrison could grab for him, the pup peed on the floor.

"Son of a bitch," he began, only to whirl at the sound of Addie's sob.

"Damn it, are you both happy now?" Frank brought Addie to his shoulder and rubbed her back. He jostled her gently, until she quieted. "I'm taking her to my ranch. I think you two better hash this out. *Alone.* I'm taking the dog, too." He whistled sharply, and Noodle slunk out from beneath the table with his tail between his legs, still whining. Before Harrison or Retta could react, Frank strode from the kitchen, Addie huddled in his arms and the pup following.

Thick, tense silence formed as they stared each other down in the kitchen, while twilight descended outside the open window. In the other room a few drawers slammed, Noodle woofed softly, Addie released a high-pitched, wordless chirp, and over both was the sound of Frank's deep voice. A few minutes later, he trooped back into the kitchen, carrying Addie, a partially-filled pillowcase clutched in his free hand.

"I've got a change of clothes, her blanket, that ragdoll she drags everywhere, and some diapers for tonight." Frank hitched Addie higher on his shoulder. Harrison wisely didn't approach. Instead, he blew his daughter a kiss and mugged a silly face, making her giggle. Taking her cue from him, Retta managed a smile and a pat to Addie's head. Their daughter was too busy playing with her Uncle Frank's eyelashes to pay any mind to leaving for the night.

"Frank?" Retta called hesitantly. When he turned, she offered a faint smile. "Thank you for taking care of Addie. And for protecting me."

His stern expression softened a bit, and he nodded once before heading for the front door. "See you both tomorrow afternoon."

"But—"

"Wait—" Harrison and Retta both spoke at once.

Frank kept on walking. "Better yet," he called over his shoulder, "one of you come get me when you're all up and around." The door slammed behind him.

Harrison remained facing the empty foyer, at a loss. Behind him, the scrape of a chair across the wood plank floor indicated Retta had taken a seat. He peered over his shoulder as she sank her head into her palms, her elbows on the table, the very picture of dejection.

Which only made him angrier. *So fragile. So delicate.* How could she think to keep herself safe enough, traveling the road to town alone, rifle or not? Before he could rein in his temper, Harrison found himself hovering over her. "You promise me, Retta." When she didn't raise her head, he slapped both palms on the table surface and loomed. "Did you hear me? I want your promise you'll obey me and stay away from town."

For uncounted seconds, he waited for her to look him in the eye, to speak, nod. *Something* that would indicate she'd heard him.

Nothing.

"Retta, answer me."

She suddenly lurched to her feet so fast, her head made contact with his chin and he almost bit his tongue in half. Chest heaving in agitation, she confronted him, the tips of her breasts brushing his untucked shirt. Jutting her chin out in defiance, her lips came within an inch of his own.

Her usually soft voice had grown to an enraged snarl. "You don't *own* me, *Mister* Carter."

Meeting her accusing glare, the lingering bit of control he'd been desperately hoarding, afraid he would put his hands on her in the heat of anger, vanished. Now, a different kind of heat took control, and he could no more have stopped his reaction than sprouted wings and flown.

Days of trying to court her, slowly entice her to accept him, their marriage. Their lifelong commitment to make a life for Addie, keep a promise to a young woman he could barely recall any longer.

Nights of sharing a bed, blankets, and body heat. Telling himself she wasn't ready for more, pretending he didn't want her under him, over him, every second of every night, that it was vital he give her time for their attraction to grow—

It all went up in a blistering flare.

Her lips parted to speak, probably to rail at him some more about how she wasn't chattel to be owned in holy matrimony, or some such nonsense. But before she could draw breath, he clamped his arms around her, one hand cupping her backside as he wound rough fingers through her hair and gripped, hard.

Lifting her at the waist, he carted her over to the kneading counter next to the sink and sat her on its edge, then pushed between her thighs and plundered her sweet mouth.

Deep and sure. Hard, passionate . . . He poured frustration, worry, need all into a kiss that might be too bruising for her lips, but he couldn't stop. Couldn't even ease up the slightest speck, though he was careful not to put pressure on her injured cheek.

She was his wife, and he'd never hurt her. But it was his responsibility to make sure she and Addie stayed safe. Today, she'd put herself in danger. Tonight, he'd be laying his claim, and by the time he was through making love to her, there'd be no doubt in her mind that she belonged to him. As her husband, he'd be damn certain she never acted so foolishly again, even if he had to keep her too exhausted from his loving to venture into town.

For frozen moments, Retta remained passive under his demanding onslaught, her limbs trembling, her breathing erratic and her heart thumping against his. Even her inability to respond wasn't enough to make him stop. He only kissed her deeper.

Then she kissed him back. Arching into him, elegantly slender hands clutched him, nails digging through his shirt to score his arms.

"Retta." Her name left his throat on a thick edge of want as he buried his lips in her neck and nipped the soft, tempting curve.

Chapter 16

Retta trembled as Harrison pressed seeking lips along her throat. The feel of his tongue licking the fluttering pulse under her skin elicited a burn deep within. A sensation she'd come to recognize since that first night he'd touched her.

So, so good. She melted against him.

Even as anger and desire thrummed through her in equal measure, she knew there'd be no stopping this time. She wanted to feel Harrison moving inside her, wanted to truly be his wife in every possible way.

"Harrison, please."

He lifted his head, pinning her with eyes that burned molten hot. "Please what?"

The only sound in the room was their panting breaths.

"Make love to me." Even now, she couldn't quite keep the anger from her voice.

Harrison's lips quirked, though his eyes remained hard. "Is that a plea or a demand?"

Emotion flooded her with dizzying force. Anguish over Jenny's illness. Fury at Cal, and his disregard for her feelings, but gratitude for her daughter. Uncertainty, warring with a determination to stand up for herself . . . and desire.

So much desire.

It all rolled together into one big knot of need.

Desire surpassed every other emotion. Clenching her fingers into his hair, she tugged his face close to hers, flicking her tongue against his lips. "Demand."

Harrison chuckled, but there was no amusement in his tone as he fisted her skirt and lifted it to her waist, then slid his hand to the part of her that burned for him. "Tonight, I won't be stopping, Retta."

"I didn't ask you to," she retorted. She could feel the heat of his palm clear to her womb.

He took her mouth in an unyielding kiss, thrusting his tongue past her lips the same way he probed the slit of her pantalets and pushed two fingers inside her. She panted into his mouth. Harrison eased her back onto the wide counter, and all sane thought fled as he delved deeper.

A moan filled the air. Hers? His? Retta was too lost to the ecstasy coursing through her to care.

Harrison edged closer, spreading her legs wider as his fingers stroked a spot that sent a shudder of delight through her. Then his mouth covered her breast through the cotton material of her blouse, nipping its taut peak just enough to cause a jolt that quickly dissolved into a throbbing ache as his fingers twisted inside her, sending her over the edge.

Her back bowed and a scream tore from her at the intensity of her release. She was barely aware of Harrison's hoarse groan, when his weight lifted and she felt his tongue at the juncture of her thighs, thrusting inside her body where tiny shudders of bliss still pulsed.

"Oh God, Harrison," she pleaded, pressing one hand to the top of his head, "I don't . . . I can't take any more."

A groan was all the answer she got, before he cupped her bottom and lifted her up to bring her weeping center tight against his mouth. Flinging her arms along the counter, Retta scrabbled for purchase but could find none on the smooth wooden surface.

She struggled for breath as Harrison nipped her womanhood, sliding a finger back inside her and reaching for the spot she knew would throw her into another sea-storm of ecstasy, unlike anything she had ever envisioned happening between a man and woman.

And that was her last coherent thought as Harrison sucked the tiny bud at her entrance into his mouth, running his tongue around it, his throaty growl ringing in her ears as she flew apart.

By the time she came back to her senses, Harrison was carrying her into the bedroom. He placed her gently on the bed, then stripped off his clothes. His darkened gaze raked over her. "Tonight, wife, you become mine in every possible way."

Too sated to move, all she could do was nod. How much time had they spent in the kitchen? The first faint beams from the moon shone through the window, giving her a wonderful view of her husband, hard and lean.

Harrison Carter was no dandy, but all male, with solid muscles that only came from hard labor, toiling in the mines. Her eyes lowered to his cock, pointing at her like a divining rod. She licked her lips, recalling the salty taste of him, thirsty for more.

"Retta," he said, "keep looking at me like that and this will be over far too soon." Moisture gleaming at the tip, his thick shaft bobbed.

With a sigh, Retta lifted her eyes to meet his. The tense lines on his face eased, as he leaned over her.

He caressed her undamaged cheek with his knuckles. "I need you naked, now, sweetheart. My restraint has cracked." Not waiting for an answer, he quickly stripped her, tossing her dress and camisole, her pantalets, to the floor. His heat pressed her into the mattress.

He nudged her legs wider with his knee, positioning his shaft at her entrance. With a gentle thrust of his hips, his hard length slid across the moisture at her cleft. "I want you too badly."

For an instant Retta froze as Cal's face, etched with the same look of lust, flashed across her mind. She choked, panicked.

Harrison stilled, then his fingers stroked lightly down her cheek. "Stay with me, Retta. Right here, in this bed, with your husband." He kissed her, tearing her away from unpleasant thoughts.

As fast as it'd come, the memory faded, replaced with an overwhelming affection for this man, who'd married a stranger and welcomed her into his life, claimed her daughter as his own, and even now took time to care for her comfort.

"You're the only man I see, Harrison." Her vow came out a mere whisper but she meant every word.

His hand trembled as he caressed her face. "I'm sorry," he said gently. "I can't wait any longer." With a groan, he thrust, filling her completely.

The feel of him moving inside her, oh so slowly, tenderly, then hard and deep, was unlike anything she even knew existed. Unable to keep her eyes open, she whispered his name and quivered.

Harrison jerked her hips high and plunged deeper, gritting out, "Wrap your legs around me."

Eyes squeezed shut, she did as he bade, a low keen escaping her throat as the new position allowed him to reach to the very heart of her. Holding her in place, he drove into her again and again, the mounting pleasure so intense, Retta wasn't sure she would survive.

Then her body erupted, and all she could do was cling as he shouted her name against her neck, convulsing above her.

The warmth of his seed filled her for endless moments, making her womb clench, and she shuddered through another round of rapture, until her mind spun away completely.

She came back to awareness slowly, as Harrison rolled their bodies to the side, sharing her pillow, still intimately joined with her. He stared into her eyes for a long, silent moment before smoothing a palm over her hip, his thumb drawing a caress there. Her lips parted on a soft exclamation at the feel of him, hardening inside her.

"Again?" She laughed breathlessly. "Let's give me at least a minute here to regain my strength, Mister Carter."

"I suppose so, Missus Carter." His slumberous gaze swept over her nakedness, lingering here and there. As he slid from inside her, his smile faded. Lifting his hand, he carefully grasped her chin, studying her cheek. "Does it hurt?"

It did, but she wouldn't tell him so. "Not really. I'm fine."

He didn't look like he believed her. "I'm sorry I yelled. Sorry I frightened Addie."

"And the puppy," she reminded him.

He grinned, the frown line between his thick brows easing. "Right. And Noodle. I'll make it up to them both tomorrow." He fingered one of her breasts, rubbing his thumb over the still-sensitive peak. "It makes me crazy to think of what could have happened."

Trying to ignore how wonderful his hand felt, Retta forced herself to concentrate on the concern in his voice. As much as his overbearing attitude irritated her, her heart broke to think she'd put Addie in danger. Worry over the evil way Slim Morgan regarded their daughter sent a shiver of terror through her.

Harrison's hand stilled. "What?"

She shook her head to dispel the images of the many ways the man could have hurt her sweet little girl. "Nothing. It's just . . ."

He brought his hand to her face and cupped her injured cheek. "It's what? Tell me, Retta." Though his expression remained neutral, the urgency in his tone gave away his concern.

She licked her dry lips. "After I kicked him between the legs, Peter galloped down the trail. Morgan became incensed. The way he looked at Addie, it was like he wanted to hurt her."

Harrison's face hardened, and she could read Slim Morgan's death in his eyes.

Fresh worry gnawed at her. "He didn't actually touch her. Maybe I'm wrong."

"No, you're not. Morgan is an extremely dangerous man who likes to hurt women. I don't doubt he could easily harm a little girl if he's angry enough. You have to promise you'll never travel alone like that again." He curled her into his arms, up against his chest. One palm smoothed over her hair. "I've already lost Jenny, I would never be able to bear losing you too. Promise me. Promise you'll never travel anywhere again without me or Frank along. Or at least one of our men there to guard you and Addie."

Reluctantly acknowledging he was right, *this time*, Retta gave in as gracefully as she could. "I promise."

He kissed the top of her head, murmuring, "Thank you."

Then, rolling her beneath him again, and with great tenderness and attention to her needs, Harrison made love to her, until hours later she fell asleep, exhausted and content in her husband's arms.

Chapter 17

Tossing the reins onto the seat, Harrison jumped down from the wagon. Accustomed to the wider buckboard bridle, Copper wouldn't budge. Patting his stallion on the rump, he strode to the other side, eyeing Frank as he climbed stiffly from the seat.

Stubborn jackass.

There'd been no use trying to talk Frank into staying at the ranch with Retta. Instead, he'd rode to the miners' cabins and rousted Peter for guard duty. Retta didn't like it, but that was too damned bad. He wouldn't leave her alone after what'd happened with Morgan.

He nodded toward Frank, who used Copper's wide flank to balance himself. "You all right?"

"Yeah. Quit fussing over me, dammit." Frank swiped his dusty Stetson from his head and slapped it on his knee, wincing as he dropped it back in place. "Shit." He gingerly rotated his injured shoulder.

"Hurts?" Harrison edged closer, ready to offer a helping hand, whether his idiot brother asked or not.

Scowling, Frank awkwardly sidestepped around Copper. "I'll live. Let's get this done." He started toward the two-room log cabin that served as Little Creede's temporary jail.

A few of the town's founding fathers had drawn up plans for a larger building. In the meantime, the cramped enclosure held a desk in one room. Another contained a single cell, made from nice, thick iron bars. Harrison would like nothing better than to see Morgan rotting in it.

He followed his brother through the door.

A picture of relaxed contentment, Sheriff Joshua Lang sat back in his chair, fingers laced over his chest and his spurs propped on the battered desk. A Stetson rested over his eyes as he lightly snored.

Harrison swept an arm toward Lang's boots and knocked his feet off the desk.

Joshua snapped forward in his teetering chair, hat flying off sideways, cursing, "Goddamn-the-hell—"

Frank slammed a hand down on the desk, swaying, unsteady on his feet. "Why aren't you out digging in the muck for Morgan?"

"Jesus." Harrison dragged a beat-up wooden stool from against the wall and positioned it under his brother's backside, pushing on Frank's good shoulder. "Sit down before you fall over."

Frank slumped on the stool, holding his arm and grumbling under his breath.

Harrison yanked off his hat and scrubbed a hand over his face. "Mornin', Sheriff. Now that the niceties are over, why aren't you going after Slim Morgan?"

Joshua regarded Harrison for a few, drawn-out seconds, before rasping, "Charges?"

"You know damned well the charges." Frank punched a fist into his open palm. "Try setting our mine with explosives, trespassing on Carter land, and threatening our females. I bet there's a half-dozen barmaids between the Lucky Lady and that bordello in Spiketown who'd give you an earful of the pain he's put them through."

Scooping his hat off the grimy floor, Joshua fingered the rim. He brushed at a streak of dirt, then plopped the once-pristine Stetson back on his head. "Y'all crudded up my goin'-to-Sunday-Sermon hat, boys. Oughta make you buy me a new one."

When Frank bristled, Joshua waved him off. "Settle down, Frank. I'm only funnin'."

Joshua's deep-blue eyes settled on Harrison. "Tell me about your womenfolk. I'm assuming you mean your wife and that sweet gal of hers. Addie, right?" He rubbed at his chin. "She's just a babe. What happened?"

Harrison propped a hip on the corner of the desk. "Morgan came sniffing around after I brought Retta and *our* daughter to the ranch. He frightened my wife. Then, a few days ago, he followed her back from town and accosted her on the road to the mine." His back teeth ground together just thinking about it.

Joshua's face hardened. "He tried to force—"

"You heard right. Didn't succeed thanks to one of our men running him off. According to Retta, Morgan also made threats toward Addie." Harrison leaned in so the sheriff didn't miss his next words. "Either you do something, or I will."

Joshua sighed. "All right, simmer down." He tugged on a desk drawer and fumbled around, unearthing a pencil broken in half and a piece of grit-stained paper. "Tell me everything you know."

~ ~ ~

The second the jail door slammed behind them, Frank growled, "*Not enough evidence.* That's pure horseshit."

"Then we'll find some evidence." Harrison didn't like it any more than Frank, but he couldn't blame the sheriff. "Without a witness, it's Retta's word against Morgan's. A woman's word doesn't hold much sway against a man's. And Peter really didn't see anything."

"Well, it ain't right."

Harrison nodded. "Fair or not, that's how it is."

Frank pulled his bandana from around his neck and mopped his face. "Let's head to the mine. More than one of the men must've seen Brody sneaking around. I'm thinking Mills might bend under the right kind of pressure."

Harrison rubbed his shirtsleeve across his forehead, catching the sweat before it dripped into his eyes. The thought of spending the rest of the day in the miserable suffocation of the mines didn't hold a speck of appeal. Worth it, though, if they got hold of the witness Sheriff Lang required.

Maybe then he could go home to Retta. A cool bath sure as shit sounded good. Then falling into bed with his lovely bride. His cock pulsed at the image of Retta, naked and smiling up at him from a tub of water.

Except Retta's still sore at me.

He turned to consider the girth of the wagon bed. Probably wide enough for one of those fancy washtubs he'd spotted at the mercantile. The old basin they'd been using wasn't fit to bathe in any longer.

In his mind's eye, Harrison could visualize the pleased smile on his wife's face when he presented her with such a gift.

Reaching Copper, Harrison gave the stallion a scratch behind the ears, and waited for his brother to catch up. Finally, Frank settled onto the seat, releasing a string of colorful curses as he tried to find a comfortable spot.

As Harrison grasped the bench bar to heft himself up, a husky, feminine voice called out, "Mister Carter."

Easing back to the ground, Harrison watched as Cat Purdue picked her way across the rutted street. In the bright sun her bronze hair gleamed, piled high on her head, a silly excuse for a hat clinging to her curls. The woman had fine taste in clothes. Even Harrison could spot quality when he saw it. Despite Cat's chosen profession, she could easily dress the part of a lady when she wanted to.

Holding her skirts high enough to reveal her laced-up leather boots, Cat paused near Copper's head, crooning softly. She offered her free hand and the smitten horse dropped his nose into her palm, snuffling, his eyes closed as if ecstatic.

Harrison watched in amazement. "You know, Copper doesn't cotton to women much."

"Yes, I can see that." Cat gave him a wink, but her smile faded when she spotted Frank.

His ornery brother returned her annoyed stare, looking like he was sucking on a sour lemon. Just because the jackass couldn't admit his attraction to the winsome Cat, didn't mean Harrison would snub her.

He gave her a welcoming smile. "Miss Purdue, you look lovely as always. Other than making my horse melt like butter, is there a reason you've graced us with your presence?" Had she heard something? Cat knew a great deal of what went on in this town. She sang for her supper at the popular Lucky Lady, but she also listened subtly and well.

"Might I trouble you for a ride, Harrison? And the other *Mister* Carter, of course." She nodded toward Frank, who grunted and turned away as if finding the front buckboard wheel fascinating.

"Well, sure. As soon as I'm done over at the mercantile. Where can we take you?" Harrison placed his hands on Cat's tightly corseted waist and lifted her to the bench. *How the hell a woman can breathe in a contraption like that is beyond me.* No wonder Retta refused to wear one most of the time.

Cat settled herself gracefully on the wide seat. Harrison took note of the inches she managed to put between her pale green skirts and Frank's leg. Snorting, he jumped up to the foot rest and plopped down next to Cat, catching the reins. "Miss Purdue? Destination?"

"Now, you know you can call me Cat. I promised Nell Washburn I'd stop by for a bit." She held up her arm. A frilly, beaded bag swung from her elbow. "I've got medicine for Clem. I wanted to look at his leg, too. Doc Sheaton can't get out to the miners' village until this evening, but I can change Clem's bandages and get some of this pain medicine down the stubborn man's gullet."

Frank tossed her a dismissive stare. "Laudanum, you mean. That stuff is rotgut. And when did you become a nurse?" His upper lip curled. "Then again, guess you've got plenty of drunken men at the saloon to practice on."

Harrison frowned at his brother's lack of manners. "Frank, shut up."

"No, it's all right." With a haughty sniff, Cat ignored Frank and instead gave Harrison a sweet smile. "I apprenticed in Boston, with a well-known surgeon who maintained a small private school of nursing. Until my family decided my education cost too much, and made me come home."

She tilted her head toward Frank. "Is that acceptable to you, Mister Carter?" When he refused to answer, she abruptly presented her back to him and locked gazes with Harrison. "I heard something last night. Brody Mills sat at the bar, skunk-drunk and bragging about doing a job for Slim Morgan. I could have sworn he mumbled something about a mine."

Harrison frowned as he snapped the reins for Copper. The buckboard jerked forward and Cat grabbed the nearest arm—Frank's—to steady herself. For once, his brother wasn't complaining.

A few yards from the mercantile, Harrison brought Copper to a halt.

Frank snapped, "Now what?"

Harrison hopped down. "I'm gonna ask Lang to bring Brody in, see what he knows."

~ ~ ~

A commotion at the front door had Retta hurrying from the kitchen to the parlor, where she stopped and gaped at what sat, perched on its side, halfway over the threshold.

"Harrison, what on earth . . .? Is that a washtub?" She ventured closer, stretching out a hand toward the shiny copper surface. The metal felt warm against her fingertips.

His head popped up over the riveted edge, damp tendrils clinging to his perspiring brow, eyes bright as they met hers across the wide expanse. "We needed a new one. That rusted heap of metal we've been using is going out to the barn for the horses as soon as possible."

"This is bigger than any washtub I've ever seen. It must have cost a fortune." She studied the tub as Harrison rolled it through the parlor. It was fancy with a hammered surface and brass handles. She followed her husband, watching him maneuver the tub into a corner of the kitchen a few feet away from the cellar door.

Settling it into place, Harrison dusted his hands off and stood back. "Last winter I did some work for Silas Loman. Told him someday I'd swap for a household item of equal value. When this tub came in a few days ago, I knew I wanted it." He shot her a quick grin as he caught her close. "Probably big enough for two," he whispered enticingly.

Retta shivered at the brush of his lips against her ear. Although she hadn't worked through all of her frustration and ire where his high-handedness was concerned, she couldn't deny his muscular frame, so warm next to hers, sent prickles over her skin every place their bodies touched.

Today's decision, dragging the still-recuperating Frank into town and leaving Peter as her personal guardian, rankled. Yet at moments like this, when Harrison showed her such sweetness and consideration, she was hard-pressed to dwell on the ways he could get her dander up.

Regretfully she eased away, fussing with her blouse. A sideways glance almost became her undoing, noting the hot glow in his eyes. Retta swallowed and mumbled, "Addie is in the parlor. Behave yourself, Mister Carter."

"Maybe I will," Harrison drawled, a teasing glint in his eyes.

As she moved toward the tub, he slapped her on the bottom.

She whirled on her heel, firing him a glare.

He winked at her. "Then again, maybe I won't."

"Well, make an effort," she suggested sternly, even as her belly fluttered like clean sheets in the wind.

Peering inside the wide tub, Retta found it all too easy to imagine a wet, delightful frolic in warm water . . . with Harrison and his roaming, talented hands. It was hard to hold on to her pique when her body craved his touch. "I hope you know, filling that tub will drain the well."

"We've got a very deep well." Harrison ran a hand along the rolled edge, then nodded toward the shiny interior. Invitation shone brightly from his heated gaze.

Resolutely she turned toward the pantry. "I'm starting supper. Unless you want to pluck a chicken, I recommend you make yourself scarce."

She let loose with a breathless squeak when he grabbed her around the waist and bent her over his arm. To her dismay, her heart raced in anticipation. "Harrison, let *go*."

"Give me a kiss and I'll think about it." He swooped, his mouth within a breath of hers. Those stormy gray eyes, gazing into hers. Those full lips, so temptingly close. Helpless to resist, Retta curved a hand behind his head and sighed when the kiss he gave her spun from gentle and easy to moist and passionate.

It didn't matter that she was still at odds with him, or they were in the kitchen with Addie playing in the next room. Or that the front door stood half-open, where anyone could peer around the corner, getting themselves an eyeful. She craved his touch, his hands stroking her ever so gently as his mouth stole her last bit of resistance.

Retta kissed him back with all the passion rioting inside her.

An eternity later, Noodle's high-pitched yips brought Retta to her senses, and she pushed against Harrison's chest until he released her. Her face felt boiling hot, and his quiet laugh confirmed her state of disarray as he set her on her feet and straightened her blouse.

Somehow, he'd managed to unbutton her from neck to mid-bodice. Looking down, she blinked at the sight of her left breast, exposed almost to the nipple. Wresting away, she frantically tucked and fastened just as Addie bounced into the kitchen followed by Noodle, as usual tripping over his own clumsy paws.

"Harrison, good grief. How many hands do you have?" she grumbled, as he swung Addie onto his shoulder, making her shriek with glee.

He offered a wickedly smoldering grin. "More than enough to get the job done, wife. More than enough."

~ ~ ~

Retta poured another kettle of hot water into the washtub. She tested it with her elbow. "It's pretty hot. Ready?"

Turning, she caught the sight of her unclothed husband in the dimly-lit kitchen. Fully aroused.

Yes, I'd say plenty ready. Mercy.

She bit back a moan, eyeing Harrison shamelessly as he approached the tub and climbed in. *Think of other things. Cow-pies. That chicken you beheaded for supper. Garden muck.*

Wasn't working. And by the way his mouth formed a wide smile, Harrison clearly knew it.

Blasted man.

He held out a hand. "Want to join me? It'll be a close fit, but we can snuggle up." He waggled his brows suggestively.

"Addie just fell asleep." Even as she spoke, Retta drifted closer, unable to resist touching her husband. Her fingers stroked over his shoulder, glistening with bathwater. Warm, wet, smooth, browned from the sun. She uttered a sigh saturated in longing, quivering when he pulled her hand to his lips and pressed a kiss into her palm.

"Harrison . . . we can't." But she allowed him to tug on her hand and bring her within a few inches of his mouth. Eyes hooded, he waited, until with a low cry, she lowered her lips to his.

Oh, his mouth. The way he kissed her, so deep, hard one moment and tender the next. Her last bit of defiance faded. Never had she imagined a man would give so much of himself, send her to the edge of heaven with a simple touch of mouth upon mouth.

When he tumbled her into the tub, still dressed in her skirt and blouse—and apron, for pity's sake—she didn't protest, but nipped playfully at his tongue. Between their four hands, they managed to divest her of her sopping garments, until she straddled him, their hips aligned so perfectly and her breasts one nibble away from his teeth.

"Retta," he groaned, urging her down on his hardened flesh. His mouth took possession, opening over her aching peaks, pulling at one after the other, until her cry of need echoed around the kitchen.

Thoughts of their child waking, possibly interrupting them, flared once, then disappeared. The entire population of Little Creede could have stomped through the house and it wouldn't have yanked her from this single, heated moment.

Retta wound her arms around Harrison's neck and buried her fingers in his hair as he arched beneath her and filled her to bursting. Shudders wracking her, she rose and fell over him, uncaring that her knees scraped the floor of the tub with each bounce of her hips. His mouth roamed her neck and the arch of her throat, wet from the slippery soap bubbles, and she keened in response, clutching his head, her sopping curls clinging to her back.

Bathwater sloshed over the side of the tub as they made love in the overly warm, dim kitchen.

Chapter 18

Slim studied the numbers before slamming the ledger shut. "Shit."

The Lucky Lady Saloon was bleeding money faster than his girls could spread their legs. If he hadn't lost so much in a poker game last month, he wouldn't have had to ask Lambert for an extension of credit.

And since Harrison and his bitch of a wife raised suspicions, Slim couldn't get the sniveling Jenkins to skim what was needed to pay the bank note coming due. He'd be lucky to have enough cash on hand to resupply the liquor for the next month.

At the thought of all he stood to lose, he slammed his fist on top of his desk. This was Harrison Carter's fault. The man should've accepted his offer to buy one of the mines. After an unusually high-winning hand, he'd actually had enough to pay a fair price. He could be raking in the ore this very moment, collecting enough valuable minerals to replace all he'd lost, and more. Instead he'd been impulsive enough to think another hand of five-card stud would double his winnings, and he'd lost every cent he'd set aside to fork over for a Carter Mine.

Hate and jealousy crawled through him. The Carter brothers had it all. Wealth, with their steadily producing mines. And women, too.

Harrison possessed the wife Slim craved. And all Frank had to do was walk into the saloon—*my saloon, for Christ's sake*—and the whores couldn't offer themselves up fast enough. Except for Cat, probably the only woman in the

Lucky Lady the man hadn't bedded.

Much to Slim's annoyance, Cat considered herself too good to entertain the men upstairs. Even the threat of violence hadn't convinced her. If not for her singing voice drawing in crowds, he would have put her in her place long ago. Didn't matter to her that he owned her, right along with the Lucky Lady. The woman was far too bold.

He stroked his mustache, plotting. Maybe if he sweetened the deal by offering her too, Frank would reconsider and talk Harrison into selling. *Except now I don't have the goddamn money.* He couldn't afford an extra chamber pot to piss in. And after Brody's inept fumbling at the Carter mine, Cat rode out there each day, nursing those wounded men, instead of doing her job at the saloon. Another reason his profits were down.

He'd tried to remind her once, how she belonged to him and the Lucky Lady. Slim's fingers moved from his mustache to the scar that ran from behind his ear to the edge of his starched collar. She'd almost slit his throat with that damned knife she kept strapped to her leg. "I do as I please, Morgan," she'd spat, flashing the knife—stained with his blood—right in his face.

The slut has disrespected me for the last time.

Slim ground his back teeth together. It was time to rid himself of her, for good. *Think, damn it.* How could he get what he wanted? What were the Carter Brothers' weaknesses?

Then it hit him. Both men had a soft spot for women. Frank had once stopped him from berating Cat for spilling a drink in a patron's lap. Not that she appreciated any man's chivalry. Frustrated, Slim discarded the idea. He didn't believe Frank cared enough about the songbird to meet any demands. But Harrison with Retta? That was a different matter.

As a plan formed in his mind, Brody burst through the door to his office. "Boss, we got trouble."

Annoyed at the interruption, Slim snapped, "What?"

"Them Carter boys visited Sheriff Lang the other mornin'. Got the sheriff riled up and askin' around about the explosion. Seems one of their men spotted me scoutin' out the mine."

"There's nothing against the law about that. Just keep your mouth shut and you'll be fine."

Brody frowned, reaching into his pocket to pull out his tobacco pouch. "Dunno, the sheriff's like a bird dog when he's on the trail." Shoving a hefty chaw in his cheek, he tied off the leather pouch.

"Where are the Carters now?"

Brody grinned, tobacco juice leaking from one corner of his mouth. "Still diggin' out rubble at the mine. And lookin' for you on account you sniffed after Harrison's wife."

A commotion from the saloon sounded through the door. Angry voices, breaking furniture. A woman's scream. The sound of fist hitting flesh.

"Check on that for me," Slim ordered. "I don't have time to settle a bar brawl."

Brody spun on his oversized clodhoppers, dropping the pouch as he reached for his holster. The bag landed on the dirty carpet as he lurched toward the door, gun in hand.

Ignoring the noise, Slim got to his feet and scooped up the pouch, examining it thoughtfully before shoving it inside his waistcoat. The smelly thing might prove useful.

He paced his office. Maybe if he grabbed Harrison's lovely bride while the man was distracted . . .

And finish what they'd started. Slim's loins throbbed in anticipation.

Then he'd ransom her and collect the money needed to pay off his debts. *Not that anyone will ever see Missus Carter alive again.* He'd make sure of it.

Whistling, he plopped his favorite black Slouch on his head and strode out the back door.

Somebody'd take the fall for murdering poor Retta, but it wouldn't be him.

~ ~ ~

"I'm sorry, Missus Carter, but I can't leave you alone." Peter twirled his battered hat in his hands, nervously shuffling his feet in the dirt outside of Clem's cabin. "I promised Harrison I'd escort you back to the ranch. He'd have my hide if anything happened to you or your little one."

Juggling her cranky daughter in one arm, Retta worried her bottom lip. "I won't be alone. Clem and Nell are both here."

"Clem can't walk," Peter said, frowning.

"But his shooting arm is fine. I'll be perfectly safe. It'll take most of the day to help Nell with the wash and cooking. And with her children down with chickenpox, she needs my help more than ever."

"I don't know." He shifted again, looking uncomfortable. "How 'bout I stay outside with the youngin' until you're ready to leave?"

"Addie can't stay. My sister Jenny had chickenpox as a child and it nearly killed her. I've been exposed to it but Addie never has." Retta stroked a hand over her daughter's silky head. "Please, Peter. I promise I'll stay put. I won't leave until someone comes for me."

Peter released a gusty breath, then nodded. He plastered on a smile and held out his hands for Addie, who was still fussing. "All right, little one. I bet that puppy of yours is missing you 'bout now."

"Noodle," Addie whined, rubbing at her eyes.

"Yep, that's the one." Peter hefted her onto one beefy arm.

~ ~ ~

Slim wiped at his sweaty brow, growing impatient. He'd been camped out near Harrison Carter's ranch for hours, with no signs of Retta anywhere. The curtains were drawn, the wagon missing from the barn. When at home, the woman liked to have the house opened up, and often left half the damned door flung wide. A fact he was very aware of since he'd spent several afternoons watching her as she'd gone about her day.

More than once, he'd considered going in to take what he wanted. If he thought he could've gotten away with it, he would have done it. The time had never been right.

Now, Slim had no such reservations. He was a desperate man. Ransoming her for the money to save his business was his top concern. Finally getting under her skirt only served to sweeten the deal.

Hearing an approaching wagon, he eased out of sight behind the barn. He'd left his horse out some distance in the rocks, to avoid being tracked. A burst of anger shot through him when he spotted one of Harrison's men, and the Carter brat.

Retta wasn't with them.

"Son of a bitch," he muttered as his brain recalculated his options. He was running out of time. The bank wouldn't wait much longer. He'd have to take the girl instead. From what he could tell, Harrison had claimed her as his own. It should still get him what he wanted, though he'd never killed a child before.

I'll have Brody do it.

With that problem solved, he watched as the buckboard stopped in front of the ranch house. The man, one of the older miners Slim recalled was named Peter, hopped down and began to lead the horse into the barn. Curled up on the bench seat, the child appeared sound asleep.

Rifle cocked and ready, Slim slunk from his hiding spot,

aimed, and fired, a kill shot through the heart. Peter flew back and lay sprawled in the dirt.

The girl slept right through it.

He walked over and kicked the fallen miner in the side to make sure he was dead, not that he had any doubts. A Smith & Wesson made quite an impact.

Heading into the barn, he found a length of rope, and strode out, toward the wide boxelder in the side yard. He formed a makeshift noose with one end, then flung the other over the lowest branch he could reach. Dragging Peter's carcass toward the trunk was backbreaking work, but Slim finally yanked him into a sitting position. He slipped the noose around the man's neck and hauled him up until he dangled, tying the rope off on another branch.

"I want Harrison Carter to know I'm dead serious." He smirked at his own pun.

How to make a clear point to the Carter Brothers? Slim thought a moment, then sprinted to the front door of the ranch and kicked it open. Rummaging through the rooms, he found Harrison's study, which yielded a few blank ledger papers and a pencil stub. Quickly he scrawled on the paper, then crowed aloud to see a silver letter opener shaped like a dagger.

Perfect. He snatched it up and headed for the door.

Back outside, Slim heard the girl fussing. *Mouthy, like all females.* Giving the buckboard a wide berth, he slid the note onto the pointed end of the letter opener, then embedded the tip into the miner's chest.

As he admired his handiwork, the brat's caterwauling increased. Anger flared inside him. Slim loved the sound of a woman crying as he'd administered his own form of punishment to them, but the sound of a whining child was irritating as hell.

Doing his best to ignore her, he searched for a good spot to leave the evidence in his pocket. He finally decided on a hedge near the barn and carefully tucked the leather pouch underneath the needles where it would be found.

Eventually.

The best plans take a bit of time to properly mature, don't they? And I know how to make things go my way. He dusted off his hands.

This plan was foolproof. When everything fell into place, he would be in the clear.

Crossing to the buckboard, Slim yanked the girl off the wagon seat. Her whining turned into sobs, and she began flailing her skinny arms and legs around, screeching for her mama.

"Shut up," he snarled, giving her a hard shake.

She stilled, her big brown eyes widening and overflowing with tears, her cheeks bright red. But at least she'd quieted. Tucking her under one arm, Slim made haste toward his horse and mounted up.

~ ~ ~

Harrison studied the sky, enjoying the vibrant colors of the setting sun. It'd been a hard day at the mine, clearing out rubble from the explosion, and even their horses were worn out.

"I'm starving," Frank said, giving his horse a scratch behind the ear. Beauty, a Paint with more white than brown markings, softly whinnied her appreciation at the attention. "Think Retta will have enough grub for me to join you for supper?"

The hole in Harrison's stomach stretched clear to his spine. Thinking of Retta's cooking made his mouth water. "Don't worry, Retta prepares extra food just in case you drop in."

"Really?"

"Yep. Shortly after your first meeting, she told me family meant everything." His heart hurt to think back on the sadness in his wife's voice. "Said since she'd never see her sister again, she was adopting you as a big brother. Believe her exact words were, '*There will always be a plate for Frank at our table.*'"

Frank's eyes took on a glassy sheen before he looked away, mumbling, "That's one sweet little woman you got."

"Can't argue there." Harrison understood Frank's reaction. They'd been out West without any family. Having Retta here felt like home.

Frank turned back to him. "You're one lucky bastard."

Harrison scowled. "If you'd quit dallying with the barmaids at the Lucky Lady and spend a little time looking for a proper wife, you could have it too."

"Nah." Frank tugged at the reins, guiding Beauty to the left as they neared the fork leading to the ranch. "Nobody here appeals to me."

"Now I don't believe that, Frank. I've seen how you look at Cat Purdue. And if I'm not mistaken, she's just as interested."

Frank snorted. "Cat's not exactly wife material, Harrison. I don't want to settle down with a woman who's bedded half the town."

"You don't know that for certain. You're assuming."

"She works at the Lucky Lady Saloon, doesn't she?"

Harrison's lips twitched at the hard note in Frank's voice. His brother's anger gave away his interest in Cat, even if he was unwilling to admit it. "Well, maybe you should find out—"

They rounded the barn and the words died in his throat as they both spotted Peter strung up on the old boxelder in front of the cabin.

"Son of a bitch," Frank shouted. They spurred their horses forward.

"Retta," Harrison yelled, nearing the front porch. He jumped off Copper and raced inside, frantically searching each room, finding nothing amiss except for the splintered wood where someone had kicked the door open.

Running back outside, he found Frank lowering Peter to the ground, his chest ripped open from a gunshot wound. And if that hadn't killed him, the letter opener jammed into the open wound, straight into his heart, would have.

Jerking the bloodied piece of paper from the sharp blade, Harrison ground out, "Retta and Addie are missing."

Frank paced furiously. "We've got to find Slim Morgan."

After reading the note, Harrison crumpled it into a ball. Rage filled him, and he quaked from the force of it. "We're to drop off ten thousand dollars near the well on the abandoned Johnston ranch, or he'll kill Addie. We have until sunrise."

Frank spun and punched the tree, then pulled his arm back and punched it again. He turned eyes hard as steel toward Harrison. "If Slim harms one hair on that child's head I'm going to skin him alive and feed his carcass to the wolves."

Harrison glanced at Peter's bloodied body. Shoving aside his grief at the man's death took almost everything he had. He would mourn his friend later, after Retta and their daughter returned home safe. "I took them to the Washburn's cabin this morning on the way to the mine. Retta wanted to help out with Nell's chores." He smoothed out the crinkled paper in his hand. "There's no mention of Retta."

"Think she's still at the cabin?"

"She's fiercely protective of Addie. It doesn't make any sense she'd let Peter take our child anywhere alone."

They both turned and strode back to their horses. As Harrison grabbed the reins, Noodle trotted over to them carrying something in his mouth. Harrison crouched down and scooped him up with one hand, then tugged what looked like a piece of leather from his tiny jaws. One of the pup's milk teeth came loose as Harrison freed the worn leather.

"Look at this." He held the object aloft. It stank of cheap tobacco and one side boasted a tarnished chunk of silver, shaped like a 'B.'

Frank cursed again, snatching the pouch from Harrison. "That belongs to Brody."

Chapter 19

Retta sat back on her heels and wiped the perspiration from her forehead. Piecing together oilcloth wasn't a pleasant task, and she'd stabbed her finger several times with the thick, sharp needle. It was worth the sweaty effort, in the name of greater family comfort.

In each crowded bedroom of the Washburns' cabin, a few of the younger miners had finished cutting into the walls, and were now sanding them smooth. Another miner pounded together frames. By evening Clem and Nell would have four extra—and necessary—windows, one in each bedroom plus the front room. Harrison had already placed an order for glass. In the meantime, the oilcloth would help keep out the bugs at night, and could be rolled up easily enough to let in air during the day.

"Nell, I'm done here. I'll get the biscuits going, all right?" she called, rising and stretching out her stiff legs. When no answer came, Retta slapped a hand to her lower back and stumbled to the tiny kitchen, where a pot bubbled on a cast-iron stove that'd seen better days.

On the corner table Nell's daughters laid out bowls and spoons for the beef and potato stew Retta had tossed together earlier in the day. One of the girls, ten-year-old Lizzie, scratched absently at her arm, and Retta winced to see the pimply rash forming. Blast it, another child affected by chickenpox.

Thankful she had sent Addie back to the ranch with Peter, Retta crossed the room and gently took the remainder of the spoons from the child's hand. "Lizzie, stop scratching. Fetch a rag and go outside to the creek, splash some water on you. All right?"

"Yes, Missus Carter," Lizzie replied, clearly miserable.

Retta laid the back of her hand against the child's temple, sighing in relief to find her skin sticky but cool.

"No fever, thank heavens. That's a good sign." She patted Lizzie's thin shoulder reassuringly. "Rose," she addressed the other girl, a scant year younger, "go with your sister and rinse off. Just in case."

As both girls scampered out the door and it creaked shut behind them, Retta started the biscuits, mixing flour and Rumford together. The baking powder didn't look too potent, and she made a mental note to purchase extra when she visited the mercantile. Fresh beef lard left over from breakfast would help disguise any stale taste, and the Washburn children would crumble their biscuits in their stew anyway. How she wished she could do more for these families, with their small dwellings and sketchy necessities. The men worked so hard, and their womenfolk kept producing more mouths to feed.

A shout from outside startled her and she dropped the mixing spoon in the flour. Retta tossed a discarded dishtowel over the bowl to thwart the flies she'd spotted in the kitchen. What on earth was it now? She hurried to the front room and out onto the sloping porch just as Harrison and Frank tore up the trail.

Harrison leapt off Copper before the beast even stopped moving, striding to her and yanking her into his arms. Retta automatically huddled into his embrace as he nestled his face into her neck. She could feel the tremor in his big frame as he gripped the back of her head, holding on too hard.

She winced. "Ow." He'd caught her hair in his fingers. She pushed him away until she could study his face, pale and drawn. Was he sick? Had he caught the chickenpox, too? "Harrison, what is it?"

"I . . ." He swallowed, his Adam's apple a knot against the open neck of his work shirt. Turning, she shielded her eyes against the high afternoon sun, spotting Frank, reins in hand while his and Harrison's horses grazed in the grassy scrub along the front of the cabin.

Several miners stood nearby, listening to Frank as he spoke low. Whatever he told them had anger forming on their weathered faces, and more than one man had made fists from tensed, windburnt fingers. Retta spun toward her husband. "You're frightening me, Harrison." Inexplicable tears burned in her eyes as her worry mounted.

"It's Peter. He's—" Harrison held her close, as if worried she'd collapse. "He's dead. We're certain Brody Mills killed him." At her shocked cry, his fingers curled in a painful grip. "There's more."

"No, oh no."

Sagging in his hold, Retta clapped a hand over her mouth, but a scream escaped as Harrison uttered the most agonizingly terrible words. "Brody's got Addie."

~ ~ ~

The snick of the lock caught Slim's attention, and he brought the cocked revolver up, holding it steady. On the old settee in the corner, the Carter girl slept, whimpering now and then. He'd crammed some laudanum down her scrawny little gullet an hour ago, anything to avoid listening to her sniveling. Bringing her to the saloon hadn't been the smartest idea. At least he'd thought to hide her in the old office. Nobody came back here.

"Boss?" Brody's harsh whisper echoed in the shabby room.

"Over here." Slim motioned with the weapon. "Keep your voice down."

Brody edged closer in the dim room, pausing when he spotted the sleeping girl. "What's she doin' here?"

"Change of plans." Slim uncocked his revolver and pointed toward the sagging chair across from him, waiting until Brody took a seat. He leaned in. "Listen carefully. Hide the girl. I've got some dealings in the works and I want her out of the way."

"Where? Those Carters are gonna tear this town apart lookin' for her." Brody cast a glance toward the curled-up lump on the settee.

"I don't give a damn where. Use your sad excuse for a brain and figure it out."

"How long do I hide her?" Brody's incessant questions grated on Slim's dwindling patience.

Idjit's not worth a thimbleful of horseshit. Slim flung himself back in his chair, his temper spiking. Every time he solved one problem, two more cropped up. Like that slimy worm Jenkins, who'd not only started hinting about being owed money for keeping his fat lips buttoned shut, but had threatened to tell Lambert all about Slim's bank dealings.

Slim bit out, "Until I tell you to kill her." He only needed the piss-soaked little runt alive long enough to collect the ransom he'd written down and left embedded in a hanging man's chest. Once he had the money in hand, the girl could rot for all he cared.

He'd regret the loss of Retta, but ten thousand dollars would go a long way toward consoling him. A smile slid across his face as he took amused note of the distasteful frown on Brody's face when he looked over at the Carter girl.

"What's the matter, Mills?" Slim taunted, low and ugly. "Never been around children before?" He rose slowly to his feet and advanced until he towered over the sleeping lump on the sofa. "Never killed one either, I suppose."

Brody snorted, though he eyed Slim with caution. "Ain't got a problem killin' no one."

Slim toyed with the revolver he'd re-holstered. "I'm giving you a very important job, Mills. You better tell me now if you're not equipped to follow a few simple orders. I might have to rethink my investment in your *employment*, if you understand my meaning."

Brody held his ground even when Slim drew his revolver from its holster and hooked it over his index finger, spinning it by the trigger. Watching Brody's bewhiskered face for any sign of weakness, Slim abruptly stopped the spinning motion and the gun barrel jerked into place an inch from the man's left eye.

An audible swallow was his only reaction.

"Can I count on you, Mills?" Slim's voice was soft, gentle. Lethal.

"Yessir."

Deftly holstering his revolver, he patted Brody on one tense shoulder. "Well, now, that's mighty fine."

Slim offered a wide grin. Lifting his hat from a side table, he settled it on his head, then strode to the door. Turning briefly, he jerked a thumb toward the sleeping child. "Find a place to stash the brat, then meet me in town. Oh, and take this."

Fishing the bottle of laudanum from his coat pocket, he tossed it to Brody, who caught it neatly. "If she gets mouthy, dose her. I don't care where you put her."

"How long we gonna keep her alive?"

Setting his hat to a jauntier angle, Slim smoothed his brocaded lapels. "Until she's no longer useful."

~ ~ ~

Harrison scrubbed both hands over his burning eyes as he paced outside Clem Washburn's cabin. Someone, probably Dub, had slapped oilcloth over the holes in the walls. And why in hell he noticed something so unimportant, while his family fell apart . . . Pausing near the open door, he was grateful to see Nell and a few of the other wives surrounding Retta, offering comfort. She'd sobbed so hard in his arms earlier, the collar and front of his shirt remained soaked. Never had he felt so helpless.

Every instinct screamed at him to burst into town with both barrels gunning for Brody Mills. Wouldn't solve anything if he did. A cool head was vital.

As if reading his thoughts, Frank walked over and grasped his shoulder. "You all right?" He released a low curse. "Stupid question, sorry." He nodded toward the men gathered in a circle, waiting. "Got five for a posse. Ten more volunteered, but I chose the ones who can handle themselves the best."

"Thanks." Harrison registered names and marital status as he looked the men over. Young, strong. Single, probably most important of all. God only knew what they'd find in town, or beyond in the hills if they found Brody'd gone on the run. Besides, he wouldn't wish this kind of worry and pain on anyone with a family. Bad enough these men risked themselves, though Harrison would be forever grateful.

"I'd better spend a few minutes with Retta."

Frank's hand dropped from his shoulder as Harrison entered the cabin where his wife stood.

She flew into his arms, and he cradled her slight frame. Harrison stroked her hair, pressing his mouth against her neck, uncaring of who might be watching. Drawing back, he cupped her cheek, thumb brushing her lower lip. It trembled, then firmed, even as her eyes brimmed in tears.

"I want you to stay with Nell," he began, but she was already shaking her head furiously. "You can't stay by yourself right now. Be reasonable." He gripped her upper arms when she tried to pull away. "Retta, please—"

She twisted out of his hands and faced him, her braid coming undone, her dress wrinkled and stained. Even with red-rimmed eyes, she looked so lovely, his heart splintered.

Harrison reached for her and she darted sideways, out the door, her mouth thinned into a stubborn line.

"I'm not going back to the ranch and I won't just wait here. I'm going to town with you." She untied her apron and tossed it to Nell, who'd ventured out onto the porch and stood with her mouth agape. The apron landed at her feet and she stared at it for a moment before bending to pick it up.

Harrison strove to contain his temper. "You can't go, Retta. This is a posse, not an outing to town."

"I know perfectly well what it is." She jabbed her index finger toward the cluster of men and horses. "I know who you're looking for, and there isn't a chance I'd stay behind. You can't ask me nor can you stop me." Her cheeks had flushed red, bright slashes in her weary face. If he tried to hold her back, she'd likely filch his Bowie right out of its sheath and stab him with it.

Frank had come up behind her, and at his touch on her arm she wrenched away. "Not one word, Frank. I'm going."

"Goddammit all, sister." Frank rubbed at his injured shoulder. Harrison suspected it bothered him more than he let on. "You can't go." Frank looked as worried and pissed as Harrison felt. "We're hunting a criminal, armed and dangerous. Once we get him we're gonna do whatever it takes to make him tell us where Addie is. Ain't no place for a woman to be."

"*I'm going.*" Retta included both of them in those two firm words. "She's my daughter. I want a horse and a gun." She folded her arms decisively.

"Jesus Lord, woman! No horse. And no gun." Harrison had heard enough. He strode forward and yanked her to his chest, ignoring the fist she landed on his shoulder. She struggled, surprising him with her sudden strength. Harrison silently held tight. Finding it pointless to say anything else, he waited her out.

Finally, she quieted and stared up at him with such wounded eyes, he actually flinched. Slowly she relaxed her fingers, then slipped her palm up and cradled his jaw. The change from furious hurt to sad acceptance defeated him. In this small war, she'd won.

Harrison crushed her close, meeting Frank's scowl over her head. Bending, he placed his mouth close to her ear. "You ride with me. You stay with Betsey in the mercantile, and you don't get a gun. Deal?"

He slapped a hand over the hot retort that threatened to burst from her lips. "Take it or leave it."

She stiffened, but he felt her lips purse against his palm. He waited until she nodded, before he removed his hand. Rising up on her toes, she kissed his cheek. "Thank you, Harrison," she whispered.

As Harrison turned her toward the horses, Frank called, "Mount up."

Chapter 20

"At the first sign of trouble, I want you to run and hide." Harrison shot a quick glance over his shoulder at Retta, where she clung to him on Copper's back. His jaw ticked at the sight of her tearstained face. "I promise, we'll get her back."

"Damn right we will," Frank growled, urging Beauty to go faster. "Then Brody's a dead man."

Retta buried her face against his back and nodded. "Just find her." The break in her voice felt like a hot branding iron shoved into his gut.

"Brody's mine," Harrison bit out. His brain nearly exploded with rage each time he thought of Addie frightened, without her mother, and in the hands of a lowlife like Mills.

"Don't you worry, Missus Carter." Dub guided his mare closer, keeping pace a short distance away. "We'll get your youngin' back. Brody might be a dirty snake, but he ain't ever hurt a child."

From Harrison's other side, Joe piped in, "I don't believe the man's smart enough to figure out something like this on his own."

Harrison nodded as the town came into sight. "My money's on Morgan."

"Agreed," Frank replied.

As they entered Little Creede, Harrison headed straight for the Lucky Lady. "Dub, go get the sheriff." Without waiting for a reply, he cantered up to the front of the saloon. Dismounting, he hitched Copper's reins, then turned and gripped Retta's slim waist to swing her down.

Stark fear shone from her eyes though her lips formed a brave smile. "I'm all right, Harrison." She gave him a little push. "Go. Find Addie."

Harrison cupped her face in his palms, brushing his thumbs across her damp cheeks as he stared into her eyes. Not believing for a minute that she'd run to safety if trouble started, he called to his brother, dismounting nearby. "Take care of her, Frank."

Frank gave him a curt nod. "If he's in there, Harrison, you drag his carcass out here so we can all get a whack at him until he tells us where Addie is."

With a grim smile, Harrison leapt onto the slatted sidewalk in front of the Lucky Lady and plowed through the swinging doors. He had no intention of sharing this showdown with anyone else. If the son of a cur had taken his daughter, Harrison would get the truth out of him, one way or the other. Then he'd make Brody beg for death.

When he entered, Cat Purdue glanced up from across the room. One look at him and her friendly smile dropped off her face. As if sensing danger, those closest to the entrance swiveled their heads in his direction. Harrison spotted Brody slamming back a shot at a corner table and strode toward him across the warped wooden floor.

Soft murmurs began, as smart folks got out of Harrison's way.

Pouring himself another drink, Brody lifted the glass halfway to his mouth before he spotted Harrison and froze.

Suddenly, Cat was standing between him and his target, a Colt steady in both hands. "Hang on there, Harrison. We don't want any trouble here."

Brody slowly lowered his shot to the table with a clunk. A bead of sweat slid down his forehead and dripped off his nose. His gaze darted toward the door.

"Addie's missing," Harrison stated bluntly. The urge

to put his gun to the man's temple and pull the trigger was strong. But he needed information first.

A flurry of murmurs went through the crowd. Cat's eyes narrowed to fierce slits.

She tilted her head toward Brody. "Think he's got something to do with it?"

"Yep." Harrison jerked his thumb toward the swinging doors. "Retta's outside, Cat. She sure could use a woman's comfort right now."

Lowering her weapon, Cat nodded, and without another word she pushed through the crowd to the door.

Brody slowly got to his feet, hands raised in the air. "I ain't got nothin' to do with nothin'."

Harrison never took his eyes off Brody, as the man grew more and more agitated. Edging toward the door, he looked ready to bolt.

"Where's my daughter, Mills?" Harrison managed evenly, though he was anything but calm. The rage bubbling inside him had taken on a life of its own.

Brody was obviously too dumb to understand how close he was to having his head blown off, because he had the audacity to shrug. "I don't know nothin' about your daughter."

Harrison narrowed his eyes. "Wrong answer."

Whipping his arm out, Harrison fisted Brody's collar and yanked him across the table, flinging him into the middle of the room. Shattering glass and breaking wood mingled with the sound of disgruntled gamblers as they quickly snatched up their winnings and moved out of the way.

Two long strides brought him to where Brody lay sprawled on his back. Gripping his shirt in one fist, Harrison jerked him up, punched him in the face, repeatedly, as he demanded, "*Where*." Punch. "*Is*." Punch. "*My*." Punch. "*Daughter*?"

Punch.

Punch.

Dub's voice broke through his fury, as he caught hold of Harrison's shoulder. "Carter, dead men can't talk."

Breathing heavily, Harrison forced his fist to relax as he let go of Brody, uncaring when the barely conscious man slid to the floor with a groan. His bloodied face had already begun to discolor and swell, one eye puffy, his nose smashed. Bending, Harrison relieved Brody of his gun, shoving it toward the barkeep. "Put this behind the bar."

As the man silently obeyed, Harrison turned to his foreman. "Wait outside."

Dub exited out onto the sidewalk, the swinging doors creaking behind him. Harrison glanced around, spotting a beer tankard that hadn't ended up on the floor. Finding it almost full, he grabbed it, stepping over strewn cards and broken glass, then flung its contents into Brody's face. "Wake up, Mills. We're not through."

Sputtering, Brody blinked away foam as he opened his eyes. When he spotted Harrison standing over him, he swore and rolled to his feet. Before anyone could stop him, he bolted from the saloon.

Harrison sighed. With his brother and the other miners waiting in the street, Brody wouldn't get far.

Dub poked his head through the door. "Sheriff's not in town, boss."

"Yeah." Wiping his knuckles on his trousers, Harrison stomped outside. As he'd expected, Frank and half a dozen of his men had their guns leveled on Brody, who swayed unsteadily in the middle of the street, unarmed, hands in the air.

Near the mercantile, Cat stood with her arm wrapped protectively around Retta. Betsey hovered on the other side, a hand pressed against his wife's stomach as though to hold her back. Briefly meeting Retta's eyes, Harrison spotted desperation along with anger. *I know how you feel, honey.*

He wanted to kill the dirty skunk with his bare hands. Hell, he had to hold himself back as it was.

More townsfolk were lined up and down the street. Some called out encouragement, others retribution.

"Punch his face in, Harrison, he'll tell ya."

"Hang him!"

"What kind of monster hurts a child?"

From the corner of his eye, Harrison saw how Retta shifted against Betsey's hold. Raising a hand, he pointed his finger at her and mouthed, "Stay put." If she actually heeded his command, he'd be surprised. She jerked up her chin in defiance and even from a distance he could see her chest heave as she sucked in a deep breath, but then she gave a curt bob of her head. Cat spoke to her, and Retta's tense posture eased.

Thankful his wife was out of the line of fire, he turned back to Brody who hadn't moved, and studied him. The man had taken a beating in the saloon and hadn't broken. Maybe more extreme measures were necessary. His mind flashed to the sight of Peter hanging from the tree. Unclenching his jaw, he called out, "Anyone got some rope?"

Brody gulped, but remained still. Smart move, considering there were half a dozen guns aimed at him, cocked and ready.

Ben, who'd been in the saloon earlier, came forward. The wiry young cowpoke worked for them at the mines when cattle driving slowed down. He nodded to Harrison. "I got rope." Crossing to his gelding, Ben threw back the saddlebag, returning with a thick coil. "There's a tall tree near the church that'll work real fine."

"Thanks." Accepting the rope, Harrison stalked toward Brody, whose panicked eyes darted back and forth, searching for a chance to escape.

There was no way out for him. Not until Harrison knew where he could find Addie. And maybe not even then.

"I'll ask you again, Brody, real nice like." Harrison cracked his knuckles. "Where is Addie?"

More shouts sounded behind him. "Hang him high, Harrison!"

"Shoot him in the legs!"

"Cut off his man parts, bet that'll make him talk," a woman muttered loudly.

Every second that passed put his precious girl in more danger. All the ways she might already be hurt, ran through his mind like a never-ending nightmare.

Brody's nervous gaze flicked across the street where folks were still shouting. "I told you, Carter. I don't know nothin'."

Stopping directly in front of the coward, Harrison loomed threateningly. "Wrong damn answer. Again." He turned to Frank and Dub. "Bring him."

Harrison's long strides ate up the rough ground between the saloon and the church, its large sugar maple shading the front entrance. Clomping feet and disgruntled muttering told him the townsfolk followed behind, along with the rest of the miners he'd gathered as a posse. The mob undoubtedly included Retta and Cat, too.

Coming to a stop under a low-hanging branch, he tied off the rope securely, then tossed the length over a higher limb. Brody fought against Frank and Dub, each holding an arm to keep him from escaping.

Harrison let the rope slide along his hands, finding grim amusement in the way Brody eyed it as if it were a slithering snake. "Final chance, Mills. Where's my daughter?"

"Go to hell," Brody spat, struggling to get free.

Gathering the end of the rope looped over the branch, Harrison began crafting a hangman's noose. Everyone fell silent as he worked, the only sound Brody's curses as he fought against Frank and Dub.

The sound of a door creaking open indicated certain interference by a higher authority, but damned if he'd stop now. Still, Harrison cringed a bit when Reverend Matias asked, "What's going on, Mister Carter?"

Finishing his task, he met Matias's steady gaze. "Nothing that concerns you, Reverend."

Retta surged forward, breaking through the safety line of his men. "This man stole our daughter." She pointed a finger at Brody, who sneered and rasped out a few more curses.

Frank cuffed Brody upside the head with the barrel of his gun, then aimed it at his ear. "Don't even look at her."

"Is that true, Harrison?" Reverend Matias asked.

As if sensing an ally, Brody wrenched toward the Reverend and pleaded, "I already told them I got no idea where the girl is."

"He's a killer, Reverend. And killers lie." Harrison reached into his pocket and tossed the tobacco pouch at Brody's feet. "Your chaw bag was found near Peter. You remember Peter, the man you shot and hung from a tree?"

Staring at his pouch, Brody mumbled, "That dirty, no-account, sumbitchin' . . ."

Harrison turned to Matias. "I think it'd be best if you went back into the church."

At the Reverend's conflicted expression, Harrison prodded him. "Every passing moment is a moment our daughter is in danger. We've got to hurry this along."

"Please," Retta whispered brokenly.

Matias's demeanor softened as he took in Retta's tear-ravaged face. Then his mouth firmed, and he nodded. "Don't be wrong, Harrison."

"No, sir, Reverend." It took everything inside Harrison to keep the fury off his face and at least appear calm and sane. But time was running out and Brody still hadn't confessed anything concerning Addie's location. Harrison wasn't a murderer, didn't plan on actually hanging the bastard. *Not yet, anyway.* He only wanted to scare the information from him. But if his daughter had been harmed, all bets were off.

With an acknowledging nod, the Reverend turned and walked back inside the church.

Frank lowered his gun as Harrison loomed over Brody. "One more opportunity to do the right thing, Mills. Where's Addie?"

"I ain't tellin' you shit."

"If that's how you want it." As the afternoon sun beat down on them, Harrison dropped the noose over Brody's head, then pulled the rope taut around his neck, until the man was forced onto the tips of his boots in order to breathe.

Harrison met the bastard's frantic, rounded eyes. "Last chance."

He tugged the rope until Brody's toes left the ground.

At the sound of Retta crying softly behind him, Harrison ground his back teeth together. She had been so brave. So strong, until now. He couldn't comfort her, not until Brody confessed Addie's whereabouts.

Fear coiled inside him at the thought of losing the child he'd grown to love as his own. Harrison gave the rope a vicious jerk.

"Abandoned mine, outside Animas Forks," Brody choked out. "P-Please—"

The garbled words sent a rush of thankfulness through Harrison, and a chorus of relieved sighs surrounded him as he let go of the rope. Brody sank to his knees, gagging. Slowly he flopped around, finally struggling to his feet as Ben stood guard, pistol in hand.

Harrison barked, "Let's head out," sending his men running for their horses. Pulling Retta into his arms, he gave her a hard, swift kiss, then set her aside. "I need to go."

"Hurry." Hope shone from her eyes.

In the next instant, a child broke loose from her mother and darted into the fray as she chased a butterfly, drawing a collective gasp from the crowd.

"Melanie," her mother cried out, rushing forward to scoop her up as all eyes turned on them.

Using the moment to his advantage, Brody swung around and knocked Ben off balance. At the same time he reached into his boot and pulled a knife. Eyes locked on Harrison, he drew back an arm to fling the double-honed blade. Before he had the chance, Frank whipped out both Colts and shot him.

As Ben jumped to his feet, Frank strode up and kicked the knife out of Brody's reach.

Blood bubbled up from Brody's mouth as he clutched his chest. Amidst shouting and confusion, his hate-filled eyes glazed over. "I lied, you sumbitch."

Retta cried out in anguish at his rasping words.

And Harrison felt his heart plummet when the dying man wheezed, "You'll never . . . find . . . her."

Chapter 21

Cat sank down on the wooden pew and laid a hand on Retta's shoulder. "Please let one of the men escort you home," she began, pausing when Retta gave an emphatic shake of her head.

"No. Harrison will bring her to town. She ought to see Doc Sheaton." Scalding tears flooded Retta's eyes; she scrubbed them away, but more followed. Her breath hitched once, twice. When she tried to swallow, her throat felt drier than a bone.

"Oh, come here. Lean on me," Cat encouraged, and Retta couldn't remain brave and stoic a second longer. She turned her face into Cat's perfumed neck and sobbed.

Silently, Cat rocked her. In the musty church Retta's crying echoed up and down the narrow aisle, bouncing off the crude glass in the windows the Little Creede township wanted to replace with something prettier. As if it mattered what hung in the windows.

Her precious girl was still missing. Worse, the only man who'd known her whereabouts lay dead in the middle of the street, his final words a vindictive garble. Trying to imagine how anyone could steal a child, hide them away, seal their fate in a lie . . . it was plain evil. It was the work of a monster.

"She was only wearing a thin little dress. Not even a pinafore. Summer bloomers, because she wanted to use the p-potty like a b-big g-girl." Retta slapped a hand over her mouth to hold in her mounting scream. "I can't stay here, I've got to look for her."

"Young lady, stop right this minute." Betsey's firm voice and tight grip prevented Retta from tearing up the aisle like a madwoman. She kept her hand on Retta's shoulder as she admonished, "Trust your husband and trust Frank. All the other men, too. They'll find your little girl." With a bump of one ample hip, Betsey nudged until Retta had to either sit back down or risk falling over.

She sat, Betsey plopping down right next to her.

Retta tried to ease in the other direction, but Cat wouldn't budge. Trapped, she fidgeted, twisting her fingers into sore knots, as both women took turns patting her arms and rubbing her back. She knew they wanted to help, but it wasn't working. Nothing could shut off her brain or stop her memory from replaying the last few hours.

Hours her Addie suffered, all alone and frightened, cold. Maybe worse.

Only when Betsey slapped a hand on her knee, did Retta realize she had been bouncing her foot up and down, faster and faster. Her eyes met Betsey's sympathetic regard, and more tears blinded her, sudden and scalding.

"Shh," Betsey soothed. "Why don't you lie down for a bit, try to rest? You can use this for a pillow." She patted her stomach. "Goodness knows I've plenty of padding."

"I couldn't sleep."

"Perhaps not. But you can rest," Cat urged, pressing on Retta's arm until she relented. A few seconds later, she lay on her side, with her head in Betsey's lap and her legs stretched over Cat's expensive watered silk walking dress. Releasing a shuddery sigh, Retta managed a broken, "Thank you."

Cat smoothed out the wrinkles in Retta's skirt. "You know, once I had this horse. Ran off in the middle of the night."

Lost in her own tortuous thoughts, it took a bit for Cat's remark to sink in. Retta turned to look at her, sitting so properly in a church pew with someone else's legs and feet in her lap. Cat didn't seem to care about the mud and heaven knew what else that clung to the soles of Retta's riding boots.

With a half-smile curling one side of her mouth, Cat continued to straighten Retta's crumpled clothing. "Want me to tell you about it?"

"Um," Retta replied slowly. "All right."

Vaguely she registered Betsey's fingers, gently winnowing through her hopelessly matted hair. It felt so soothing.

Cat's voice took on a dreamlike quality. "Her name was Priscilla. Her left foreleg had suffered an arrow wound, and she cantered unevenly. She ran away in a storm, right after I purchased her from my weasel of a landlord." Cat reached for one of Retta's hands and held it. "I cried for hours. Got plenty angry, too. A couple of days passed. Then one night at the Lucky Lady, Frank Carter happened to mention he could find Priscilla for me, on account of the heavy rains in the area, and the way my sweet mare limped."

She tugged on Retta's hand until her weary eyes opened and she struggled past the fog surrounding her brain. "Cat, I don't understand what—"

"Think about this." Cat gave her fingers a squeeze. "Frank's a tracker. I had no idea how good he was, since we don't much like each other and up until then hadn't exchanged more than maybe four insults. But he found Priscilla for me. Said he appreciated fine horseflesh too much to see one lost in the hills."

Retta blinked as she processed what Cat was saying. Frank, a tracker? She sat up, pushing her hair off her face. "He tracks horses?"

"And men, and deer, elk, bear. If it leaves a print on the trail, Frank can follow. Listen to me, now." Cat grasped Retta's chin, urging her to pay attention. "The men examined Brody's horse. They removed his boots, too. You understand? They're going to find Addie." She gave Retta's chin a little pinch. "Whether she was taken away on foot or on a horse. You've got to trust and believe."

~ ~ ~

"Goddammit," Frank said as he straightened. "Dead end here." He pointed to a spot on the ground.

Harrison couldn't tell much difference between the mud pattern over the ground or anything else that might have crawled, hopped, or slithered by. "You sure?" He pulled the damp bandana from his neck and used it to wipe the sweat off his forehead. Squinting at where Frank indicated made no difference, but he trusted his brother implicitly when it came to tracking. He sat back on his heels, weary and heartsick. "Now what?"

Dusk had come to the lower mountain range to shroud it. Ben had brought lanterns and a few of the miners had borrowed some of the oil to fashion makeshift torches, tearing strips from a shirt one of the younger men volunteered. The oil wouldn't burn for more than a few hours.

Please, Lord, let us find her soon. He nodded to the men. "Light up. Keep your ears open. Noises out here should echo. If anything cries or screams, we follow."

"Harrison, sometimes animals sound almost human."

Cutting Ben off with a slashing gesture, Harrison stressed, "We follow." He waited until Ben gave a brief grunt.

Digging in his pocket, Harrison produced a handful of matchsticks and passed them around.

Frank held out a lantern for him to light and trimmed the wick until the flame steadied.

Harrison took it from his brother. "Let's go."

Frank paused, searching his face in the glow, then clapped him on the shoulder. "We're *going* to find her."

"Yeah." Harrison held the lantern high as he trailed behind Frank. Anger and fear burned hot in his gut, thinking of the dangers his precious little girl might be facing at this very moment, while they stumbled around in the dark.

It hadn't taken long to figure out which road from town Brody had used. Excitement and anticipation, hopefulness, pushed them forward. Ben walked alongside Harrison, as Dub and two other men followed on horseback at a distance, leading Beauty and Copper, pausing when Frank held up a staying hand, then moving forward at his all-clear. It made for slow progress.

Too slow.

Harrison ground his back teeth in frustration as he kept the lantern raised, enough for Frank's experienced eyes to track the hoofprints of Brody's horse, with its cracked and gouged, right rear shoe. Ordinarily, Harrison's fury would have boiled up at such disregard for a horse's safety, if not for that single shoe offering more of a chance. In the dirt of the trail, even over some of the scrub, Frank could track that distinctive print. After they discerned how a faulty shoe could affect the horse's canter, hope had grown to the certainty the prints would lead them straight to Addie.

Rain and muck on the trail, blurring everything, had killed that hope. They'd lost the prints several times already, and even with the lantern and torches, frustration had set in.

Now, a rutted section loomed before them, as if a stampede of critters had blundered through.

Frank cursed again, one long streak of oaths, as he stopped on the trail. In the torchlight, Harrison spotted the despair on his brother's face, and his heart dropped sickeningly. Frank held out a hand for the lantern, and Harrison passed it over, fighting to remain calm, more desperate with each wasted second.

Minutes went by with Frank on his knees, searching for the tiniest clue, the merest disturbance. Studying the ground, then moving the lantern carefully, keeping the flame as close as he could, Frank examined a growing swath of churned-up earth.

Finally, he sat back on his heels. "Nothing." He turned and met Harrison's eyes. "Too much here." He indicated the scrub and grasses, the mud that hadn't completely dried up. "This is a natural crossing for wildlife. One print scratches out another."

Ben brought over a torch, squatting down even with Frank. "Gonna lose the light soon, unless I snuff this out and add more cloth, soak it well. What d'ya want to do?"

Harrison squinted into the deepening shadows. Another half hour and it'd be full dark. Hopelessness clung to him like painful burrs, almost dropping him to his knees as he tried to fight it off. Turning in a circle gave him nothing to lock onto other than stunted cottonwood and rough pasture.

The foothills of Cascade Mountain loomed in the distance. Jagged rocks and caves he and Frank had explored only once or twice since they'd moved here.

The caves.

He grabbed on to Frank's sleeve and yanked him to his feet. "What if Brody took her to one of the caves?"

His brother tensed, his eyes hardening with the same knowledge flooding Harrison. What chance did a child have, abandoned? Bile rose up his throat at the thought of how terrified Addie would be. Then panic weakened his knees as he visualized a four-legged predator stumbling across her in search of its meal.

"Don't think about it." Frank tugged off his shirt and threw it to Dub. "Rip it up." He snuffed out the lantern and started unfastening its bottom latch, while Harrison removed his own shirt and sliced it in half, wadding a piece around one of the burned-out limbs they'd used for torches. He waited impatiently while Frank bound it with the torn strips Dub handed over, then poured lantern oil over it.

Less than a minute later, they had two brightly burning

torches that would illuminate a cave better than a puny lantern with barely any wick left. Mounting Copper, Harrison hefted the torch and took off toward the caves, leaving Frank and the rest of the men to follow.

They had to find her, alive. He couldn't even begin to contemplate anything less. Retta would never survive the loss of her child. Blinking hard to clear out the sting from torch smoke—and his own cloying emotion—Harrison urged Copper into a full-out gallop, arriving at the caves first then kicking free of the stirrups and leaping to the ground.

"Addie, where are you, sweetpea? It's Papa. Addie?" He rushed into the first cave, turning this way and that, searching for boot prints, little-girl prints, anything . . .

The soft snarl of something cat-like sounded from the back of the cave, and his heart broke anew. "Addie, answer me!"

"Harrison, over here," Frank yelled, waving his torch from a cave opening that looked bigger than most of the others. "Footprints, maybe boots."

Finding footprints shaped like boots had to be a good sign. "Go in, hurry," Harrison snapped, sprinting across the short distance. Sending up prayer after prayer, he raced to the cave, stumbling over rocks, dodging boulders and thick scrub.

Panting, he held the torch in front of him, following the glow up ahead where Frank searched. Small, jagged stones thrust up from the cave floor, and the smell of bat droppings was heavy in the dank air.

When he heard the rush of water, he paused.

The cave split into two passageways.

"Jesus Lord," he groaned. Which way to go? With torchlight already flickering down the left passageway, Harrison chose the right, toward the water, venturing deeper.

Then he saw the huddled form and dropped to his knees. "Oh, God. Addie." Tossing his torch a safe distance away,

Harrison scooped his little angel into his arms. "I found her," he shouted.

Pressing his lips to her forehead, fresh panic assailed him at how still and cold she was. Shallow breaths lifted her thin little chest, and she shivered violently. In the dim torchlight Harrison spotted blood encrusted on her forehead, over her left eye. Bruises, too. "Frank, get over here."

A few seconds later Frank knelt next to him, one hand reaching out to touch Addie's dirt-encrusted hair. "She open her eyes?" At Harrison's headshake, Frank motioned for Dub. "Give me your duster."

Frank took the stiff garment Dub handed him. "Lay her in this." When Harrison only clutched her closer, he added, "You got to let her go for a minute. We need to get her warmer, then you can carry her out."

Sucking in a shuddering breath, Harrison waited until Frank spread out the duster, and he laid Addie on it, immediately cocooning her as much as he could before he scooped her up again. "I'm not letting go, dammit. You'll have to lead Copper."

"Yeah, I figured as much." Frank urged Harrison to his feet. "Let's go. We'll take her straight to Doc Sheaton."

~ ~ ~

All during the longest night of her life, Retta had knelt in front of the altar and prayed for Addie's safe return, promising to be a better mother and wife, and give to charity when she could. She'd never say a cross word about anyone ever again, if only God would bring her baby back to her.

Her heart lurched when a shout came from outside the church. She leapt from the pew and tore down the aisle.

Retta darted into the street along with half the townsfolk, relief flooding her as Dub and Ben rounded the corner of the blacksmith shop. Frank appeared behind them on Beauty, his fist grasping Copper's reins.

And Harrison sat in the stallion's saddle, his knees pressing into Copper's sides.

Her hopeful gaze fixed on her husband, Retta swayed on trembling legs when she spied the bundle in his arms. Relief flooded her and her legs went weak. If not for Cat's steadying grip on her, Retta would have fallen to the ground.

Cat squeezed her arms firmly. "Didn't I tell you the Carter brothers would bring back your little girl? Good men, both of them." She laughed. "Even if one of them is a hard-headed, stubborn braying ass who jumps to conclusions about situations he knows nothing about."

She gave Retta a gentle nudge. "Go on now."

Nodding, Retta lifted her skirts and ran down the street to meet Harrison, dodging smiling women and whooping miners.

As she drew near, the worry in his eyes had her expelling a strangled cry. Stumbling to a stop, she trembled and fell to her knees. Her focus riveted on the still form of her daughter clutched to his chest.

Agony burned through her, and she clapped a hand over her mouth as a wail rushed out.

Harrison's lips moved, but it was as if she'd gone deaf, unable to comprehend what he said as her vision blurred and the earth shook underneath her.

In the next instant, her husband was kneeling in the dirt with her, settling Addie into her arms. "She's alive, Retta." He cupped her cheek, tipping her face up. "Do you hear me? Alive."

Retta peered down at the still form of her child, looking so pale and bruised. "Alive?"

As she cradled Addie, he lifted her to her feet. "Yes. But we have to take her to the doc, right now."

~ ~ ~

Retta managed a faint smile of thanks for the tumbler of water Cat placed on the bedside table. "Anything else I can get you, just give a holler, all right? There's chicken stewing in the pot, enough to feed everyone." Cat brushed a tender finger over Addie's cheek. "Still too pale, poor thing, though her breathing sounds better."

"I'm not resting easy until she opens her eyes." Retta held her daughter closer. She hadn't left the bed since Harrison first laid Addie down. Swaddled in her favorite blanket with Lulu Dolly tucked against her shoulder, Addie slept peacefully, an occasional shiver or cough her only outward signs of distress.

She pressed yet another kiss to Addie's forehead, noting it felt a lot cooler now that she had broken her fever. Poor mite had been burning up by the time Doc Sheaton examined her. A lukewarm bath had helped, though Addie slept right through it, and Retta cleansed most of the dirt and blood from her head, revealing additional cuts and bumps. More worrisome to Retta was the child's inability to waken. Doc Sheaton had explained it was a normal occurrence for head-bumps, and Retta did her best to hold on to that promise.

"How is she?" Frank whispered from the door.

Retta motioned him in, and he entered slowly, eyes locking on his sleeping niece. The frown he'd been wearing changed to a look of such tenderness, it actually hurt Retta's heart. In that instant she knew her brother-by-marriage would lay down his life for Addie.

Frank perched on the edge of the bed, one large hand stretched out to cover Addie's curled-up legs, still wrapped in the blanket. "I ain't never been so scared." His throat rippled as he swallowed, hard.

Retta looked away, feeling tears gathering behind her lids at the emotion this big, rough miner showed. For a time, quiet ruled the room, the faint ticking of the clock in the parlor the only sound.

"Doc says she'll be fine," Retta murmured. "She's got a few bites on her legs and under her arms. Spider bites, most likely." When Frank's hand fisted, she hastened to reassure him. "Frank, she probably slept right through it. God willing, Addie won't remember a thing. She is safe, thanks to you." Retta gulped against the emotion that instantly suffocated her. Blindly she reached out, and felt his roughened palm close around hers. "If you hadn't tracked—"

"No. It's nothing I did. I lost the prints, damn my own hide. I missed the trail. We'd have found her hours sooner." Frank pulled away and got to his feet, agitated.

"You did save her, Frank." Harrison appeared in the doorway with dark circles under his eyes and new lines of worry bracketing his mouth. His hair stuck up all over. He must have just crawled out of bed. It had taken all of her persuasion to get him to rest in the first place, and he hadn't slept nearly long enough.

He dropped a kiss on her temple, then another on Addie's hair, before confronting his obstinate brother. "Don't you think for a second you didn't do anything, you hear me? Jesus . . ." Words seemed to fail Harrison, and they glared at each other in equal measure, before Harrison's hand shot out and grasped Frank's arm, yanking him close enough to slap him on the back. Then he simply caught hold, hung on, an embrace when mere words would no longer do.

Watching them, Retta's throat burned with cloying emotion.

With a final cuff to Harrison's arm that would probably fell a weaker man, Frank propped himself against the wall. "Sheriff's coming by in the morning, Ben says. I sent him to town for any information on Morgan. Nobody's seen the bastard. Lang caught up with Ben and told him he wants to check on Addie." Frank frowned. "Man'd better not be scaring her."

"Do you think she could tell him anything?" Retta asked, stroking her child's hair. Addie released a soft sigh, but didn't awaken. Retta took the little huff as a hopeful sign.

"It's possible, but we already know Brody took her. If you're thinking she might help catch Morgan, I can't figure Addie's old enough to verify much." Harrison rounded the bed and sat on the other side, slipping an arm around Retta, encompassing their daughter. "We don't know what the hell she's been through other than Doc Sheaton mentioning her breath smelled of laudanum." He took a whiff close to Addie's face as she exhaled. "I don't smell anything. If that cur Brody poured laudanum down her throat to keep her quiet, he could have killed her."

"I'd like to bring him back to life just to shoot holes in him again," Frank growled.

Retta started to agree, when a piercingly high series of yips preceded Noodle down the hall. Spying Retta, he made a beeline for the bed, jumping on the mattress, all wagging tail and lolling tongue. Before Retta could think to stop him, he'd plopped his rump on Addie and was enthusiastically licking her face.

"Noodle, stop. No," Retta scolded, trying to push the devoted pup away. Noodle's backside pinwheeled harder.

Harrison made a grab for him but Noodle darted away playfully, then rushed back in and administered a few more licks. "Stupid dog."

"Noo-doh," a sleepy little voice squeaked, as Addie wriggled against Retta's hold. With a gasp, she looked down at their precious daughter struggling to push away her dolly and the blanket in a bid to coax Noodle closer.

Biting back a protest as well as more tears, Retta clapped a hand over her mouth as Addie cuddled the puppy. Noodle flopped on his back, stuck all four legs in the air, and whined ecstatically as Addie passed her hand over his exposed tummy.

"There's the shortcake," Frank said gruffly, sinking down on the edge of the bed. He looked as monumentally relieved as Retta felt. Addie was behaving so normally.

Addie's face broke into a wide grin. "Unca Fank." As Retta and Harrison looked on, their little girl batted her lashes and pointed a tiny finger at the shirt he'd run home earlier to grab. "You got lemon dops?"

"You bet." Frank opened his arms for Addie to climb into. She cuddled against his shoulder, one hand going right for his shirt pocket, crowing aloud when she unearthed a piece of the candy he was never without. "Lemon dops, just for you. And something else." He stood, gently dislodging Addie's arms, grinning at her pout. "You just sit tight, shortcake, and I'll be right back." He slipped out the door, leaving Retta to deal with their daughter's ire at losing her uncle's attention.

"What's he up to?" she whispered to Harrison as she tried to distract Addie with Lulu Dolly.

He shrugged. "Don't know."

Just then a plaintive mewl echoed in the hall outside Addie's room, and Retta groaned, "Oh, Lord, please tell me that's not a—"

"Kitten!" Addie squirmed in Retta's grip, until with a resigned sigh she let go. The ecstatic tot erupted out of her covers, crawling toward the edge of her bed where Frank stood, holding a tiny orange scrap of adorableness. In his big hands the kitten looked fragile and helpless, blinking big green eyes. Until it stretched, dug minuscule claws into his palm, then latched on to his thumb with ferocious kittenish fangs.

"Yowch, dammit. Let go, you little devil." Frank pried the kitten off his fingers as Addie reached him. Sensing an ally, the kitten made a dash for her nightgown and hid beneath it, meowing and hissing.

Addie beamed at her uncle. "Mine?"

"Yours." He tousled her hair and tickled her under one ear. "A little girl kitty. Whatcha gonna name her?"

She considered his question at length, one hand reaching under her gown for the now-calm bundle of fur. She held it up and tilted her head, then announced, "Dop."

"Dop?" Retta asked. "What kind of a kitten name is Dop?"

The kitten *was* sweet, and if it brought such joy to her daughter, then she'd reconcile having more mayhem in the house.

I'll deal with Frank later.

Addie stuck out her tongue, showing Retta the dissolving lemon drop. The candy was just a bit lighter than the purring machine currently climbing up her child's arm and nosing into her hair.

"See? It's Dop. Doppy." She sighed with happiness, then flung her little body, kitten and all, into Frank's arms, peppering his beard with kisses. "I wove you, Unca Fank."

Chapter 22

Retta stuck her head into Addie's room to let Harrison know the sheriff had arrived. She took a moment to appreciate the sight of him lying on the floor, gently tossing their giggling daughter into the air.

Her heart swelled with contentment, swiftly followed by a bone deep sadness that Jenny would never know the same satisfaction. She prayed her sister received the letter they'd written her, letting her know how happy she and Addie were, how much they loved and missed her, how they adored Harrison and Uncle Frank.

Harrison had included a private note at the bottom of the letter for Jenny. Retta didn't read it. She just sealed up the envelope and had him deliver it to the stage mail office in Little Creede. The letter could take months to reach Bolster, and Retta prayed Jenny received it in time.

"Again, Papa," her darling child squealed.

Chuckling, Harrison tossed her back up, then caught her and brought her to his chest to blow a kiss against her neck, causing more childish shrieks.

After Addie's initial alertness the day before, she'd slept for almost sixteen hours. Doc Sheaton said it was most likely the laudanum. Since she'd woken once and seemed fine, there was no need to worry. Not that it'd stopped everyone from doing that very thing. Besides the insect bites that were still slightly red and the cut to her forehead, nobody would have known she'd recently been dumped into a cave with all sorts of dangers.

Addie's smile remained bright and carefree, and her laughter as sweet and innocent as before the terrifying kidnapping. Retta had no doubt the new kitten—Doppy—helped, not to mention Noodle's crazy antics when he discovered there was a tiny, hissing plaything to chase around.

"Hate to break up the fun," Retta said, "but Sheriff Lang's here."

Harrison's concerned gaze cut to her. He knew she didn't like the sheriff questioning Addie on her ordeal. But he'd convinced her of the need to know if Brody acted alone.

Rolling to his feet, Addie tucked securely in one arm, he said, "It'll be all right, Retta."

He strode over in two long strides and tugged her close to his side as they went outside to meet with Sherriff Lang. Addie wrapped her arms around Harrison's neck and snuggled into him.

We're a family. For a brief moment, Retta was happier than she'd ever been in her entire life. Until they rounded the corner and it all came crashing down on her again.

Her daughter had been traumatized, and Peter murdered. *Why take Addie in the first place?* It made no sense.

"Hey, Joshua." Harrison released her to shake the sheriff's hand, then slid his arm back around her as they all stepped inside. "Go easy, she's been through enough."

The sheriff offered a short nod, removing his hat. Dressed informally today, he still wore his oilcloth duster, though his badge wasn't pinned to his chest.

Retta fretfully wrung her hands. "She's just little, I doubt she'll be of much help."

"I'll be careful." He studied Addie, who was watching him with curious eyes. "How's she doing?"

Harrison set Addie on the floor in front of the fireplace. "Children must heal pretty quick. She woke up smiling this morning and hasn't stopped since." He plucked her doll off the sofa and handed it to her.

She beamed up at him. "Tank you, Papa."

He ruffled the top of her hair. "Welcome, Addie girl."

Noodle plopped down next to her and licked her arm. Addie patted the pup's head with one hand, making her Lulu Dolly bounce up and down with the other.

"Let's step into the kitchen," Harrison said, leading the way. "We can still keep an eye on Addie in here."

"Would you like a cup of coffee, Sheriff?" Retta asked.

"No thanks, Missus Carter. And please, call me Joshua." Twirling his Stetson in his fingers, Sheriff Lang gave her a smile that changed his stoic appearance into a handsome devil-may-care cowboy who'd have most women swooning.

Retta blinked, a bit dazzled by that smile, then her gaze drifted to Harrison, who was pouring himself a cup of coffee.

He wore a blue pinstriped shirt, its white-banded collar left unfastened, and his favorite pair of pants. The dark denim covered a posterior she knew looked even better naked. Her breath caught, remembering how she'd had her hands full of that very same posterior last night, as he'd put it, *helping* to relieve her stress.

She smiled softly. How well it had worked.

There was no denying Sheriff Lang's appeal, but he didn't hold a candle to her husband.

Harrison turned toward her at that moment. His lips curved, as if he knew her thoughts. Then he winked at her, before addressing Joshua. "What have you learned?"

"Not much. Brody was last seen going into the Lucky Lady Saloon right before Addie was taken. But that doesn't prove Morgan had anything to do with it."

"I feel it in my gut, Joshua," Harrison said. "Brody wouldn't have the courage nor the smarts to do something like this on his own. He was in cahoots with someone, and Morgan would be my guess."

"Hmm." The sheriff tugged at his hair, then shoved the long mass of brown behind his ear. "What makes you think that?"

"Brody hung around the mine exterior before the explosion. One of my men recognized him. And we already know he was thick as thieves with Morgan. The man didn't take a shit without running it past Morgan first. I can't believe he'd have stolen Addie without Morgan telling him to do it."

Joshua set his hat on the table and crossed to the wide doorway to study Addie. "*If* he was the one who did it." He met Retta's gaze. "I promise I'll be gentle, but your daughter may remember something that could help."

She bit her bottom lip. "I don't want her upset."

Harrison tipped her face up and pressed a quick kiss to her lips. Right there in front of the sheriff. Even as her cheeks flamed at the impropriety, her lashes fluttered closed from the lovely tribute. It took her a moment to gain her senses after he broke the kiss. She finally opened her eyes to find her husband smiling down at her. "It'll be fine. Joshua would never do anything to upset our girl."

She turned to find the sheriff watching their exchange with open amusement. But his voice was sincere when he promised, "I won't scare her, ma'am."

Yes, she believed that. Smiling, she acquiesced. "Call me Retta, please." Not waiting for a response, she waved her hand toward Addie. "Let's get this over with."

They returned to the parlor, and Joshua knelt next to Addie, while Retta stood nearby with Harrison.

"Hi, Addie. I'm Joshua. It's very nice to meet you."

Addie glanced up, her eyes wide and uncertain.

Retta's heart stuttered, and she was prepared to intervene if necessary. Harrison engulfed her hand with his, squeezing lightly.

Joshua scratched Noodle behind the ear. "Is this your pup?"

Addie nodded so hard her curls bounced. "Noodle."

Noodle opened one lazy eye to stare at the sheriff, then promptly fell back asleep.

"And is this your doll?"

"Lulu Dolly." She held it up for him to get a better view. "I got Doppy, too."

"Doppy?"

"Kitty cat," Addie affirmed.

"Ah. Kittens are awfully sweet. But I bet she's not as sweet as you."

Their little flirt preened at the compliment.

"You and Lulu Dolly had a bad day, right?"

Addie's lower lip quivered into a pout. "Nasty man."

Joshua reached into his pocket and pulled out a fancy-wrapped butterscotch that Retta recognized from the mercantile's candy jar. "Yes, a nasty man."

He handed her the treat. Addie promptly abandoned Lulu to the carpet and unwrapped the butterscotch with nimble little fingers, popping it into her mouth. The sheriff continued to carefully extract information from her, enough to at least answer a few questions.

It soon became clear only one man took her from the ranch. She didn't recall much else. When Addie mentioned 'stinky spit,' they figured that was probably Brody's chaw.

Later, gathered around the kitchen table while Addie napped on the rug with Noodle, Joshua addressed Harrison. "Let's assume Morgan and Mills are both in on this. Why take her?"

Harrison looked grim, his gaze resting on Joshua. "Think about it. What does Morgan value most in life?"

The sheriff stared thoughtfully at Harrison, then muttered in disgust, "Money."

"Money?" Retta said, confused. "How is taking Addie going to get them money?"

"A note I found." There was no missing the fury in Harrison's voice. "They were going to ransom her."

Joshua nodded grimly. "It's the one thing that makes sense."

"Only a desperate man would kidnap a child for money. Mister Morgan is a rich man, why would he do such a thing?"

"Maybe not so rich," Joshua mused. "Elijah thinks Zeb is up to no good."

"Who?" Retta spun toward Harrison.

"Elijah Lambert, the banker at Little Creede Commerce. Remember, we stopped in and spoke with Zeb about that discrepancy in the payroll ledger you found."

"Yes, that's right. But with everything that's been happening, I haven't had the chance to look into it any further."

She rose to go get the book, when Harrison stopped her. "Hold on."

Retta eyed him quizzically. "What?" She followed his gaze into the front room, where Addie was now awake and playing with her new kitten.

Humming.

That was odd. She'd never heard her daughter hum before.

Joshua stood, his eyes locked on Addie, too, as the notes came together to form something childishly off-tune but familiar enough to recall lyrics.

"'. . . *Camptown ladies sing this song, Doo-da, Doo-da, Camptown racetrack's five miles long—*'"

"'Oh, doo-da day,'" Retta sang softly. Then she remembered the last time she'd heard that tune . . .

While standing in the general store, listening to Slim Morgan whistling.

Chapter 23

Slim edged toward the back entrance of the bank. Though early in the day, the sun beat down, and the outside privy stank to high heaven. He breathed shallowly through his mouth as he reached for the door, easing it open to slip into the narrow hallway between the bank lobby and the cramped vault room.

He peered inside the lobby. Lambert's desk stood unused. Moving soundlessly, Slim entered the vault area and reached for the brass handle, expecting it to be unlocked as Jenkins had promised.

Locked.

That son-of-a-bitch.

If Jenkins had run off, he'd eat lead, courtesy of Slim's Colt. He drew his weapon and cocked the barrel, sidling along the wall to the door, backing into the hallway toward the lobby. He had to find Jenkins before the dumb cur spilled his guts.

Low voices coming from the lobby indicated the bank had already opened for the business day.

What the—?

Slim pulled out his pocketwatch and verified the time. He should've had twenty-five more minutes. If this had gone to plan, he'd already be jumping on his horse, headed away from Little Creede. Thirty minutes before opening and then ten minutes after closing, the damned vault was unlocked. Lambert or Jenkins stood guard outside the front, twice a day.

Jenkins assured him nobody used the back door except during bank hours. He'd leave it unlocked and Slim could slip right in. The vault, too. Nobody would know. By the time Lambert arrived to open for the day, they'd both be long gone.

Jenkins, heading for Mexico. Slim, paying off his debtors and halfway to Silver Cache to catch an eastbound stage, with plenty left over to start new.

Ransoming the brat hadn't worked, though most everyone blamed Brody. *Except the Carters*. The stubborn bastards wouldn't rest until they dug up enough dirt to hang him from the highest tree. Fortunately for him, without Brody's collaboration, they'd have a hard time charging him with the murder.

But Slim wasn't going to wait around, just in case. Ten thousand dollars would've solved his immediate problems, but the load of silver and coins in the vault could make him a very rich man.

He ventured closer to the lobby door, peering through a crack in the frame. Hannah Penderson stood behind the counter Jenkins usually worked.

He silently cursed.

The simpleton was the town's nosiest busybody. Slim wagered she'd know where Jenkins was.

Slipping out the door leading to the privy, he holstered his gun and took the short trail bisecting the town's pathetic excuse for a business district. Not wanting to draw suspicion, Slim strolled along whistling his favorite tune, like he did every day.

He entered the bank and paused, acting surprised to see Hannah behind the counter.

She glanced up from jotting in a ledger. "Hi there, Mister Morgan. What can I do for you on this fine, sunny day?"

"Why, Miss Penderson, is that a new shawl? Most

flattering." Slim poured on the charm as he approached the counter.

The dried-up old spinster tittered like a schoolgirl. "Oh, lawd, sir. What a rascal you are." She fanned herself with a ledger, cheeks bright red.

Slim kept his smile pinned in place, though her shrill voice grated on his last nerve.

Finally, the woman regained her composure. "Ahem. Now, what can I do for you?"

You can open the goddamn vault and look the other way while I clean it out, you stupid cow. Aloud, he replied suavely, "Perhaps you could fetch Mister Zeb for me."

Her expression clouded briefly. "Mister Morgan, Zeb Jenkins is no longer employed by Mister Lambert. I heard them arguing, day before yesterday. I couldn't help but overhear a bit of their altercation." She waved in the direction of the vault room. "Such thin walls, you know."

Most likely she had her ear *and* a glass pressed up against it, too. Barely holding on to his patience, he extended a hand, patting her arm and causing fresh blushes over her sunken cheeks. "How distressing for you. Is Mister Lambert available then?"

"Mister Lambert is away from his office, on business." She clutched her shawl until it verged on strangling her. "Though I cannot help but be concerned."

He wanted to grab her by her bony shoulders and shake her until she got to the point. Instead, he dragged in a calming breath. "Hannah, if I might call you by your first name, what causes you such concern? You must allow me to help."

Casting a dramatic look toward the front door, Hannah beckoned him closer.

"Mister Lambert took all of the business ledgers. Said he needed to go over them in private. The mercantile. The smithy. The barbershop and Doc Sheaton's."

Hannah drew back. She brought a hand up to cover a flat breast and whispered conspiratorially, "Mister Morgan, he took the Lucky Lady's, too."

~ ~ ~

The boardinghouse Elijah Lambert called home was a depressing dwelling inside and out. Slim approached from the west, squinting into the morning sun, too infuriated to care if anyone spotted him striding down the street.

All that money and silver, locked away from him. Zeb Jenkins' fault, because the man was too stupid to keep his fat mouth shut. Slim would have liked to track Zeb down and make him pay for the state of poverty he now suffered. His debtors were not patient men, and his time was fast running out.

He'd find Lambert and *persuade* him to return to the bank. Make him understand it would be in his best interests to open the vault. Beyond that plan, Slim hadn't much plotted.

One thing at a time.

He eased down the shadowy hallway, the smell of onions and venison strong in the air, and examined each door until he came to number three, which Hannah Penderson had so eagerly assured was Elijah Lambert's room. Placing his ear to the door, Slim heard nothing from within. He knocked once, sharply.

The door opened a crack and Lambert peered out.

Slim forced his way inside.

Stumbling back, Lambert fell against an occasional table and crashed to the scuffed planked floor. Before he could gain his feet, Slim had his Colt drawn and aimed at Elijah's temple.

He cocked the barrel. "I wouldn't make any sudden moves if I were you, Lambert."

"Wh-What do you want?"

Slim pressed the muzzle harder into his pasty skin.

"I want us to take a little stroll to the bank. We walk arm in arm like the best of friends, and you will instruct Hannah to go have her lunch. Then you'll unlock that vault for me."

Sweat beaded on Lambert's forehead. "You plan on robbing my bank in broad daylight?"

"Something like that." Slim eased back, waving his gun toward the door. "Up."

Lambert slowly stood. "You'll never get away with this."

"Shut up, and move." Slim forced him through the parlor, to the front door.

"Let me go and I won't report you to Sheriff Lang—"

He yanked Lambert close and shoved the Colt under his chin. "You're not going to say anything to anybody."

Elijah tried to jerk away. "You'll have to shoot me, Morgan. Then you'll hang. That money doesn't belong to you."

Slim spun the man around and pinned him to the door, face-first, jamming the muzzle against the back of Lambert's neck. "One shot, and you're dead. Want to risk it? Now, *open the goddamn door.*"

"Ho there, what're you doing?" a voice called out.

Slim looked back over his shoulder and spotted several townsfolk in various stages of dress, crowding into the parlor from the hallway. One he recognized as Sarah, the young woman Lambert often stepped out with. Pale and on the scrawny side, she wore a shabby dressing gown and no slippers, her hands clapped over her mouth.

The elderly woman who'd spoken—Maude Adams, the boardinghouse owner—glared with rheumy eyes as she brandished a carving knife in one gnarled hand. Beside her, Buck Adams yanked a wrinkled shirt over his faded union suit.

Shit. He couldn't gun them all down.

"Mister Lambert and I have some unfinished business," he called out, then put his mouth against Lambert's ear and spoke quietly. "Now move, or I'll shoot that horse-faced stick you consider your intended." Slim jerked his chin toward the hapless Sarah.

Lambert yelled, "No."

Sarah screamed, "Don't hurt him," and clumsily leapt forward.

Slim didn't hesitate. He spun, brought his arm up, and fired.

She dropped like a stone.

Maude screeched.

Moaning, Elijah doubled over as if he'd been stabbed.

With a bellow, Buck lurched forward.

Slim shifted his weapon, leveling it on Buck. There really was no choice now. He had to kill them all.

The door flung open behind him, catching his shoulder and knocking him to the side. Slim landed in a heap several feet from Joshua Lang, who had both pistols cocked and aimed straight at his heart.

"Drop it, Morgan," Lang shouted. "You're under arrest."

Chapter 24

Retta snuggled Addie securely on her lap. Often rambunctious when riding in the buckboard, at least this time their child was content to sit quietly.

"You know, we could have let Nell or one of the other women come to the ranch and watch Addie," Harrison commented, as he guided Copper over a deep rut in the road.

"Absolutely not. Those folks are still contagious. I sure don't want any of us infected with chicken pox." Retta firmed her grip around Addie's waist. "Besides, I can't deal with her out of our sight, Harrison. Not after," she swallowed, painfully, "after what happened."

He laid a hand over her knee and squeezed. "I know, honey. And I understand." He peered ahead, where the narrow trail met the edge of town and widened. "Today's the day Morgan's supposed to leave for prison. You really want to see him hauled away?"

She heaved a sigh, rubbing at her temple where residual tension lingered. "No, I really don't, but I think I need to. Betsey said she'd watch Addie over at the mercantile. I don't want her anywhere near that bastard." At Harrison's raised brow, she stuck her nose in the air. "Well, that's what he is."

On the other side of the buckboard, Frank clucked his tongue to keep Beauty abreast. "I agree. Call 'em as you see 'em, sister."

She released an unladylike snort. "Oh, I intend to."

Addie sat up and held out her arms. "Unca Fank, wide."

Frank made a silly face. "You just want me for my candy."

In answer, she bounced on Retta's lap. "Mama, can I?"

"Oh, all right. Harrison, ease a bit." He obligingly pulled in Copper's reins, and Retta handed Addie over as soon as the wagon stopped moving. Settling into Frank's lap, she crowed happily and immediately went on a search through his pockets.

He flinched. "Damn, those bony little fingers tickle." Catching her wrists carefully, he fished for her treat, grinning when she snatched it from him and sucked the candy into her mouth.

"Tank you." She pressed a sticky kiss to his bearded cheek, then leaned against his shoulder, content.

Harrison snapped Copper's reins and the buckboard started rolling again. Retta found herself staring off into space, chewing one of her fingernails ragged.

His warm hand eased her thumb away from her gnawing teeth. "Everything's going to be fine, Retta. We won't go near the station." Shifting the reins, he twined her abused fingers with his. "We've got the proof needed to connect Morgan to embezzlement and attempted murder. Enough to keep him locked up until we can get at the truth regarding Peter's death. Morgan can't hurt anyone now. If he's found guilty for murder, he'll hang for what he's done. And even if nothing can be proved, he'll never get out of prison."

Slowly, she nodded, clinging to him.

A few minutes later, Harrison stopped the buckboard across from the jail and looped the reins. Jumping down, he strode around to help her.

Frank coaxed Addie to wind herself around his neck, and dismounted as she clung to him like a vine. He carried her to Retta.

Looking around, Harrison spotted Silas on the boardwalk near the mercantile. "Loman, you seen the sheriff?"

Silas finished locking the door, pocketing his key. "Probably still in the jailhouse." He strode over and tipped his hat to Retta. "Ma'am." Stretching out a tickling finger, he caught Addie in the ribs, earning a wriggle and a squeal. "Betsey ran over to Doc's office. She'll be right back."

"That's fine, we can wait." Retta eased Addie to the ground and retained a firm hold on her hand. Still sucking on her candy, she huddled against Retta's skirts, not inclined to wander off as she usually tried to do when in town.

"Retta, why don't you and Addie go find Cat while you're waiting for Missus Loman?" Harrison suggested. "You can have a nice visit." At her hesitancy, he drew his knuckles across her cheek. "You don't need to be out here, seeing anything *or* anyone else."

"No, Harrison. I think it's just what I need."

He rubbed the back of his neck, and for a second she felt badly for causing him extra worry.

"All right," he finally replied. "If you're sure."

"I am."

"There's your wife now, Silas." Frank pointed up the street where Betsey bustled along, her skirts swirling around her shoes.

She reached them, out of breath, her straw bonnet askew, and immediately held out her arms for Addie. "Is that Miss Adeline Carter? Why, she's almost all grown up, I'd have scarcely recognized her but for those big pretty eyes."

Addie went willingly, snuggling into Betsey's comfortable embrace. "I got a kitty."

"So I heard, and how exciting for you." Betsey winked. "I'll bet your papa just loves having a puppy *and* a kitty to chase around the house."

Retta coughed delicately. "I wouldn't go so far as to say that, Betsey."

The outer door to the jail opened, and two unfamiliar men stepped out, both fully armed with double holsters and lethal-looking Colts.

Slim Morgan hung in their grip, his head drooping down over his bedraggled waistcoat. Behind Morgan, Joshua Lang and another armed stranger kept their cocked rifles pointed at his back.

Retta eased back toward Addie and spread out her full skirts to make certain her child didn't see anything, as Betsey murmured, "I'll just take your girl to the store." She led Addie away.

Though she'd heard herself thanking Betsey, Retta couldn't help staring at the monster who had perpetrated so much evil in such a short time. He looked anything but tough and deadly at the moment, yet she knew his downtrodden appearance could instantly change to something ugly and dangerous.

But for now, chains circled his wrists and wound halfway up his arms. Another chain locked over his ankles above the hem of his tattered pants. Padlocks secured the ends of both chains.

Disheveled, dirty, one eye swollen, bruises on his face . . . The consequences of more than a week in the jailhouse showed clearly.

Just then Elijah Lambert walked up, his arm in a sling. Retta noted he advanced to Frank's left so his shooting hand wouldn't be blocked. *Smart of him.*

His presence helped to balance her emotions, and she nodded to the young banker. "How is Sarah, Mister Lambert?"

"She woke up this morning and said her stitches itch, then she asked for a soft-boiled egg." A faint red stained his cheeks. "And a kiss. I was proud to supply both."

"I am so happy for you."

"Thank you, ma'am." His smile faded to a fierce frown when he stared at the man who'd shot his beloved. "I'm surely relieved to see Morgan get his comeuppance."

A noise down the street drew everyone's attention as the prison stage approached, its wheels sending up dust. In its wake Joshua came over. "Two guards and a deputy will accompany Morgan to the state prison," he stated. "The driver is armed. Former Union captain, now working at the prison. They sent five men in all."

His deep blue eyes rested on Retta. "He won't escape. He's in chains, and he'll remain that way until this coach pulls through the prison gates and they lock behind him."

"He should hang, Joshua." Harrison tightened his hands on his guns, still in their holsters.

"I know he should."

"Attempted bank robbery. And he shot Sarah. You know damned well that wasn't an accident as he claimed. I would wager my last nickel he killed Peter, arranged the explosion that ruined Clem's life, and killed two good men."

Remembering Harrison's description of how he'd found their child, limp and unresponsive in that cave, sent a flood of fury crashing through Retta. "We all know he was behind Addie's abduction, Sheriff." Her calm voice belied her barely contained emotion.

At that moment, how she wished for a gun.

~ ~ ~

Another deputy, badge flashing in the sunlight, exited the rear of the coach and positioned himself facing the door. Harrison bit the inside of his cheek so hard it bled. His hand hovered over his right-hand gun as the pair of guards urged their prisoner off the boardwalk and into the street.

Harrison found himself longing to put a bullet between Morgan's eyes for the pain and fear the man had caused his wife and daughter.

Joshua clamped a palm on his shoulder. "Do you really want to do that in front of your wife? Put it away, Carter."

After a tense moment, Harrison relented and relaxed. "Thanks, Joshua."

"Don't mention it," he replied quietly. "Your family needs you more than you need revenge."

"That's the only thing keeping Morgan on his feet right now."

Behind him, Retta murmured, "Harrison, is he . . . can he . . .?"

Harrison was quick to reassure her. "No, He can't get loose. He's done for." Reaching for her arm, he gently pulled her to his side, intending to walk her back to the mercantile. As far as he was concerned, they'd seen enough.

Then above the murmuring crowd, a low growl rumbled, as Morgan began tugging at the chains binding his wrists. His eyes flashed over Harrison and burned, hot and hateful, on Retta.

Lips pulled back in a sneer, he strained against the hard grip of two burly, heavily-armed guards. When another animal-like hiss came out of his mouth, Harrison swept Retta behind him as Joshua and Frank crowded closer.

"Bitch." Slim twisted and writhed in the guards' meaty hands, unable to move more than a foot in any direction thanks to the restraints. He thrashed harder. One of the guards emitted an impatient grunt and cuffed him upside the head so hard his ear bled.

Slumping in their grip, Morgan's feet dragged as they carted him toward the waiting prison coach.

"God." Retta pressed her face against Harrison's shoulder. "I want to get Addie and go home."

He stroked her hair, dropping a kiss to her cheek. "We're going now, honey. There's nothing more to see."

As they started toward the mercantile, Morgan's voice rang out, ugly and mean.

"I'll be seeing you, Carter. You and your *lovely* wife. Did you hear me? *I'll be seeing you.*"

Chapter 25

Retta adjusted the sleeves of her gown, fussing with the lace. In the vanity mirror, the red silk brocade glowed, deep and rich. Betsey Loman had convinced Harrison to buy the bolt of supple fabric, then she'd helped Retta design and sew the lovely garment.

Warm hands settled on her shoulders, and firm lips trailed her skin. "You are so beautiful." Harrison's deep rasp left her shivering. When his fingers caressed her nape, her trembling increased.

She met his appreciative gaze in the mirror. "You don't think it's too fancy for a country dance?"

"I think you're perfect." He nuzzled her ear as his hands slipped up the boned bodice and cupped her breasts. "Besides, I scrubbed my neck just for you. If that's not fancy, I don't know what is."

Helpless laughter bubbling in her throat, Retta turned in his arms. Her fingers stroked his clean-shaven jaw as she rose on tiptoes to kiss him, a chaste caress that became impassioned when his lips parted and his tongue sought hers. Harrison groaned and took the kiss deeper.

Endless seconds later, he broke free with a bite to her bottom lip, then eased back to look her over. "There, now. Got that pretty mouth all rosy to match your dress. I think we're ready to go."

He looked so handsome in his starched dress shirt and knife-pleated trousers, Retta's heart melted. How she'd ended up such a lucky woman, she'd never fully understand.

If it took a lifetime, she'd make sure her husband felt loved and cherished by her.

Starting now.

"You're a wonderful man, Harrison Carter." She slid her hands over his collar, straightening the string tie that had loosened, smoothing the lapels of his waistcoat. Urging his face closer, she pressed her cheek to his. "So wonderful. I just thought you'd like to know."

"Thank you, honey." He kissed the tip of her nose, then offered his arm. "Ready to collect our daughter? I'm sure her pinafore is still in one piece, and mostly clean."

Retta took his arm. "I wouldn't bet on it." At the high-pitched squeal that echoed through the house, followed by Noodle's frenzied barking and the yowling Doppy, she sighed dramatically. "No, I wouldn't bet at all."

~ ~ ~

The Lucky Lady looked a lot different tonight. Harrison gave the dance hall a thorough onceover as he escorted Retta through the double doors. Addie had already spotted Frank and leapt on him. Her excited chatter and his teasing responses echoed in the expansive room.

Tables and chairs had been pushed back to allow for the dancing that would begin soon. In one corner, Dub rosined up his bow and tuned the fiddle tucked beneath his bearded chin. Couples clustered here and there amongst unattached miners and some of the older townsfolk. Somebody had sprinkled sawdust over the planked floor, and Harrison winced, imagining Addie plopping her little rump down—then rolling in it—the way several children had already done.

"You do know her new outfit is going to be ruined by the time we leave, don't you? All that pink and white flounce is guaranteed to collect dirt, real fast," he murmured in Retta's ear.

She glanced down at the floor and groaned. "Sawdust. My favorite thing in the world to scrub out of clothing. I might have to burn that dress tomorrow."

"Well, it'll light up nicely. Maybe we can use it for kindling." He swung her into a spin, enjoying how gracefully her skirts belled out, then brought her close, his arm banded around her waist. "You going to dance with me, Missus Carter?"

"Why, I just might." Her eyes glowed as she fluttered her lashes at him. In the soft lantern glow her beauty struck him like a lightning bolt, and he swallowed a lump of emotion. *My wife.* It still amazed him at times, how fate altered everything . . .

"Papa, dance." Addie's sweet demand broke in, and Harrison looked down at his daughter, who had grabbed hold of his leg and planted her tiny slippered feet on the top of one boot. She bounced, her big eyes mischievous. "Dance."

Harrison patted her tousled curls. "You bet, sweetpea. Dub," he called over, "my girl wants to dance. How about a little 'Turkey in the Straw?'"

"Comin' up." Dub set his foot to tapping, plucking out the first strains, and Harrison caught Addie's hands, keeping her balanced on his toes as he stepped lively around the room. Amidst her excited squeals, his gaze found Retta's.

The misty tenderness he saw in her blue eyes clutched at his heart.

More and more folks took to the dance floor as Dub slowed the music, the stately 'Down by the River' giving courting and married couples the chance to hold each other in a waltz. With Addie sitting on the floor as Retta had predicted, playing with a little girl close to her age, Harrison took advantage of the situation and swept his wife into the dance.

She seemed to float on his arm, her red skirts swaying each time he spun her around. He brought her closer and laughed aloud at her attempts to place a few inches of decorum between their bodies.

"Stop wiggling, wife," he admonished in her ear, then bit the tempting lobe. "You're getting me all fired up."

She shivered deliciously. "Behave yourself, Harrison. And you're holding me far too close. People will talk." When she squirmed harder, he groaned under his breath. "They're probably staring at us too," she fretted.

A fast perusal of the room netted him a few grins and a wink or two, but not a single look of disapproval. He bent to her and kissed her blushing cheek. "They all envy me." To distract her, he nodded toward the edge of the dance floor. "Look there. Ben and Cat are dancing, and Frank's about fit to be tied."

She glanced in that direction, and blanched at the dark fury evident on Frank's face. "Oh, Lord. You don't think they'll come to blows over Cat, do you?"

"I think our Cat knows exactly what she's doing. And I think my brother probably deserves it." Harrison snuggled her closer as they passed a proud Ben swinging Cat in his arms. Seeing the ample space she maintained between their bodies, he doubted Frank had anything to worry about.

As one waltz blended into another, the sound of lively conversation and boisterous miners rose above the smoke from candles and kerosene lamps. The awful events of a few days ago dissipated into nothing as Harrison scooped Addie into his arms and made a circle hug with Retta, dancing with both his ladies, uncaring who saw him steal a kiss or two from his wife.

~ ~ ~

Harrison tucked the blanket around Addie, as Retta kissed her forehead. It'd been a long evening for everyone, with plenty of food and fun, and socializing with the townsfolk.

His wife and daughter were fast becoming favorites among everyone, with their sunny smiles and generous hearts.

Frank had voiced some concerns about the budding friendship between Retta and Cat, worried the more sophisticated barmaid would be a bad influence on his wife. Harrison thought his brother had Cat Purdue all wrong, but telling him so proved pointless. There was more to the woman's story than met the eye. If Frank crawled off his high horse and opened his eyes, he might just figure that out.

Retta turned to him and held out her hand. "Ready for bed?"

Soft and feminine, her eyes shone with contented happiness. He felt like the luckiest bastard alive.

His gaze swept over her, enjoying the pretty picture she made.

The rich fabric of her gown formed gently to her lush curves, and he hadn't been able to keep his eyes off her all night. It seemed like forever since he'd held her, kissed that perfect mouth, and buried himself deep inside her body.

His fingers felt along his trouser pocket for the item he'd been carrying around all evening. Jack Jaworski, the smithy, had pressed it into his hand earlier at the dance, with a knowing wink that Harrison couldn't take offense to.

Maybe the timing was off and he should have had this done months ago. Then again, this moment might be just right.

Stepping to her side, Harrison took her left hand. "Close your eyes."

She regarded him suspiciously. "What are you up to, Mister Carter?"

He gave her fingers a squeeze. "Indulge me."

"All right." As her lashes swept down, he reached into his pocket and drew out the shiny circlet. Bringing her hand to his lips, he kissed her ring finger, then slid the band home, where it belonged.

Her eyes opened wide and she glanced down at her hand. "Oh, Harrison. Is this my—"

"Wedding ring. I think it's about time, don't you?" He traced the pretty little bauble, a single, perfect ruby set in etched silver.

"It's beautiful. It's—oh." She raised teary eyes to his and cupped his cheek, the ring sparkling as she stroked his jaw. "It's one of my mother's rubies, isn't it?"

Emotion clogged his throat, but he managed a nod. "I know you consider your mama's jewels part of Jenny's dowry. But one of them needs to stay with you."

Retta flung herself into his arms. "You wonderful man."

He pressed her head to his shoulder as she clung, kissing her hair, unable to speak for the emotion clogging his throat.

For long moments they held each other close, until with a final squeeze Harrison stepped back. "Let's go to bed."

This past week had been rough for everyone, and there was no missing the lingering shadows under her eyes. She was still recovering from the ordeal.

Slow and easy, jackass.

Arm in arm, they walked to the bedroom.

Harrison pulled off his boots and unbuttoned his shirt while Retta sat before her mirrored vanity and pulled out the jeweled pins holding her hair, then brushed the long tresses until they fell like sunshine silk down the back of her gown.

She faced him with a smile, and his heart clutched. There was no denying he loved his wife. And his daughter. With everything in him, and he'd spend the rest of his life making them happy and keeping them safe.

Thank you, Jenny, for sending them to me.

Retta presented her back. "Unfasten me, please."

His fingers actually trembled as they fought with the row of hooks. Never had so few felt like so many. At last the heavy silk loosened, the dress falling to the floor. She turned, a thin chemise and pantalets her only covering. Her hands went to the tie holding the fragile linen together, and Harrison pushed them aside.

"Let me." Losing himself in her glorious blue eyes, he pulled at the ribbon, then slid his thumbs under the dainty straps and eased them off her creamy shoulders. A few more buttons and one stubborn hook later, the garment hit the floor along with her pantalets . . . and she stood, bared before him.

He almost swallowed his tongue when she murmured wickedly, "My turn."

The cotton drawers he wore against his skin scraped like sandpaper over his engorged cock. Jaw locked and tense, he forced his hands to remain at his sides as she worked at freeing him from his restrictive garments.

Finally, naked as well, Harrison urged her toward the bed and followed her under the sheets.

Turning onto her side, she snuggled up to him, her body soft and warm. She palmed his face with one hand, tilting his head toward her. A tender smile curved her lips. "I love you."

He stilled, his world realigning with those three small words.

Life was like a winding trail, and no one knew where they might end up. He'd had hopes and dreams with a girl named Jenny, a future that never came to pass. Instead, she'd sent him Retta. A substitute wife that turned out to be the biggest prize of all.

A lifetime with Retta flashed across his mind. His beautiful bride. His sweeter-than-candy Addie.

A wagon full of more children, God willing.

His chest bursting at his good fortune, he rolled over to tug her beneath him. Framing her face between his hands, he stared into her misty blue eyes.

"And I love you, Retta." He dropped a tender kiss onto her smiling mouth. "You and Addie are my world." He nuzzled her ear. "You're everything I didn't know I was missing." His hand trailed to her breast, swirling his thumb around the tight peak, loving the sound of her throaty moan. "I'll spend the rest of my life cherishing you."

His mouth moved to her other breast as she threaded her fingers into his hair and arched into his touch. "Loving you." He suckled hard, and she quivered and cried out his name.

Lowering his hand further, Harrison reached between her legs and found her wet. He flicked her bud, causing her hips to jerk as another moan burst from her lips. Her legs fell open in invitation and he slipped two fingers inside.

"I want to spend the rest of my days making love to you, honey."

"Yes, Harrison, yes," she cried, lifting her hips so his fingers could slide deeper.

Bringing his mouth back to hers, he nibbled her lower lip, before probing inside to tangle her tongue with his.

His adorable wife made love the same way she lived life. Holding nothing back from him, her kisses grew passionate and wild, frenetic, as if each moment on this earth could be their last.

He loved it.

He loved her.

Swallowing her moans, Harrison curled his hand around the back of one knee, raising it up and out, opening her completely.

"I'll never hurt you, nor make you unhappy." As he made the vow, he positioned his cock at her soft center, and stared into her passion dazed eyes. "Today, I take you, Retta Carter, as my love. My life. From this day forward, forever."

Harrison sheathed himself to the root in her moist heat. Her needy moan felt like a stroke to his cock, already throbbing with the urge to empty everything he had into her.

She clung to him, tilting her hips to meet his slow, steady thrusts.

"Today," she said breathlessly, "I take you, Harrison Carter." Another moan as he quickened his pace. "My love. My life. Oh God, yes . . ."

Harrison palmed her hips to lift her higher so he could delve deeper still. Her silken flesh clutched at him, and he groaned at the exquisite torture. Reining in his lust, he held back long enough for Retta to catch up with him.

"From this day forward," she promised, arching up as her body stiffened with her impending release. The snug muscles of her core rippled along his cock.

With a groan, he lowered his head and laved her breasts with his tongue as his own release bore down on him. Their bodies damp with sweat, they moved together, passions rising, breaths panting, hearts beating as one.

As the first vibrations of her release gripped him tightly, Harrison threw back his head as he exploded, filling her with his seed.

Legs coiled around his hips, Retta managed to gasp out, "Forever," before she convulsed beneath him.

Epilogue

One Year Later

Sitting across from Retta, Harrison held the note from her Aunt Millie. Swallowing against burning emotion for the lovely girl he remembered, and once thought to marry, he met Retta's watery gaze. "I'm so sorry, honey."

"Aunt Millie said she went peacefully." Tears she could no longer hold back rolled down Retta's cheeks. "She died months ago, Harrison. It took all this time for my aunt's letter to reach us." A sob hitched in her chest. "All she ever wanted was for us to be happy."

Harrison took a seat next to his wife on the sofa and pulled her into his arms as she wept at the loss of her sister. Holding her close, he murmured words of love and comfort, until she finally calmed.

"At least Jenny received our letters. Aunt Millie said she was happy we found love in our marriage. And Jenny wouldn't want us to grieve." She gave a hiccup, wiping the dampness from her face.

Desperate to touch her and offer comfort, Harrison rubbed his hand up and down her arm. "We'll celebrate her life, Retta. She'll never be forgotten."

"Aunt Millie's all alone now."

Addie came running into the room. "Mama, Jenny's up."

Retta's face broke into a real smile this time, and Harrison's heart warmed. Their daughter, born three months earlier, looked a lot like her namesake, with her warm-brown hair and blue eyes. "I think your sister would be pleased that we're using the dowry she sent with you for the girls' education."

Retta swiped the last tears from her face with both hands. "I'm sure she would be."

Addie threw herself onto Harrison's lap. "Papa, Jenny can sleep with me now?"

He stood, lifting his daughter with him. "Let's head into Little Creede and see if Silas can order us a bed."

Addie clapped her hands in excitement. "I want a bwother, too."

Harrison kissed her forehead. "Soon, Addie girl."

Leaning in to their daughter's other side, Retta nuzzled her silky cheek. "How does seven months sound, my angel?"

Harrison's eyes widened and his heart pounded hard as he glanced at his wife. "Are you sure?"

She smiled up at him, her eyes overflowing with love. "Yes. Mostly sure."

A grin split his face, and he lifted Addie high in the air. She squealed with delight. Bringing her back down to his chest, he hugged her. "What do you think? How about we send for Aunt Millie to help your mama?"

Addie nodded vigorously, giggling as he bussed her neck with a noisy kiss before setting her back onto her feet. Smiling, he watched her run over and plop down next to Noodle in front of the fireplace, coaxing the skittish Doppy into her lap.

Looking back at Retta, he caught her dabbing at her eyes. At his arched brow, she said, "I just— Have I told you today how much I adore you?"

She had in fact, just that morning after he'd loved her silly before breakfast. But he never tired of hearing it, or telling her what a lucky man he was to have her and their daughters.

Their baby took that moment to squawk at being ignored.

Harrison reached for his wife's hand. "Someone's hungry."

Retta's tinkling laughter filled their home. "Someone's always hungry in this house." She pulled him toward their bedroom to collect Jenny from her cradle.

Settling onto the bed, Retta lowered her bodice so their baby girl could have breakfast. Caught by the sight, for a moment Harrison lost track of what she was saying, then her words hit him, and his gaze shot back up to her. Her eyes danced with amusement.

"Come again?" he asked, not sure he'd heard her right.

"I said, it's official. Cat is the new owner of the Lucky Lady Saloon, and she's turning it into an eatery."

"Hmm." He mulled it over as he sat beside her and their nursing child. Cat had been keeping the place running over the past year, since Morgan's arrest, by offering meals along with the liquor. Shutting down all prostitution within the establishment, the women had the choice of staying on as cooks or waitresses, or moving on. Most stayed.

There'd been some grumbling from the men in town, who had to ride over to Silver Cache for their needs, but surprisingly not a word of complaint from Frank. His brother had concentrated on the mines, which were running smoothly and making them both rich.

Rich enough to send back east for their mother and sister, arriving as soon as Vivian received her teaching certificate and Mother finalized the sale of their house back in Bolster. Harrison figured in less than six months, he'd be holding his beloved womenfolk in his arms at last . . . and introducing them to the new loves of his life. He couldn't wait.

Cupping the side of Jenny's downy head as she suckled, he mused, "The cabin is almost finished. Would have been sooner, if not for this pretty little scrap demanding to make an entrance a month early." He stroked Jenny's rosy cheek, earning him a grunt as she waved a tiny fist.

"Do you think your mother and sister will take kindly to living in the wilds of Colorado?" Retta moved the babe to her other breast, wincing as she latched on. "I swear, this child was born with teeth." She relaxed against the pillows, her free hand smoothing over Harrison's thigh. "I have bedding to bring over. Dishes, too. I just hope they like everything. They've always enjoyed the advantages of town."

"They'll do fine. My mother is from sturdy stock. Frank takes after her." He winked at the confused look on her face. "Lucinda Carter is a lovely woman, but strong and tall. She'll dote on you two seconds after she meets you."

"I feel as if I already know her. She's written me such wonderful letters." Retta expertly burped Jenny, then snuggled her close as the babe yawned and dozed. "And Vivian's notes are a delight to read. I predict your sister and I will become great friends."

"Vivian is a shy one. Always been a bookworm and a dreamer. But if anyone can draw her out, you can." He pressed a kiss on her temple as she rested her head against his shoulder.

Seconds stretched into minutes as they watched baby Jenny sleeping in the crook of Retta's body. Addie darted into the room, barefoot and bouncy, quieting instantly when Harrison held a finger to his lips and nodded toward her slumbering sister. Smiling widely, Addie clambered onto the bed and snuggled into his lap, as Noodle chased Doppy, then his own tail, finally stretching out on the rug for a nap. The cat hissed and dashed under the highboy.

Arms full of the ones he loved and a slumbering pup at his feet, Harrison sighed contentedly. Soon, the rest of his family would join him and Frank. The future unfolded before him, bright and bountiful.

Can't ask for anything more.

THANK YOU for reading THE SUBSTITUTE WIFE, Book One of *Brides of Little Creede*. We hope you enjoyed Harrison's and Retta's story.

The series continues with Frank Carter and Catherine 'Cat' Purdue, in Book Two, THE DANCE HALL WIFE, scheduled for release October 2018:

CAT . . .

Cat Purdue has come a long way from the days when her father used her as partial payment for a gambling debt to a ruthless man. Reacquiring the saloon Father had lost, and turning it into a successful restaurant, is only the beginning of her drive for success.

FRANK . . .

Unable to reconcile the new, sophisticated Catherine Purdue from the saloon girl he once dallied with and foolishly spurned, Frank Carter finds himself blocking his growing attraction with sharp words and sarcasm. But when the Carters' old nemesis escapes prison and comes back to Little Creede for vengeance, Frank's only thought is to protect Cat, as well as his family.

A PAIR OF HEARTS . . .

Determined to lead separate lives yet bound together by danger and their growing desire, Frank and Cat will leave their mark in the new state of Colorado.

LINKS FOR CICI CORDELIA:
CiCi Cordelia, Writing From The Heart:
https://ccromance.com/
www.amazon.com/Cici-Cordelia/e/B01AJ5EM90
www.facebook.com/HeartfeltRomance

Want to Find Cheryl and Char?

Cheryl Yeko, Where Love Always Wins:

Website: http://www.cherylyeko.com/
Amazon: http://tinyurl.com/qzsks8q
Facebook: https://www.facebook.com/ProtectingRose
Twitter: https://twitter.com/cherylyeko
Pinterest: http://www.pinterest.com/cyeko/boards/
Goodreads: http://www.goodreads.com/author/show/5406425.Cheryl_Yeko
YouTube Channel: https://www.youtube.com/playlist?list=PLjitsNVe3r5oq5kMKM3zA49z083bjXYi5

Char Chaffin, Falling In Love is Only the Beginning:

Website: http://char.chaffin.com
Facebook: http://facebook.com/char.chaffin
Amazon: http://tinyurl.com/pvscu7w
Twitter: http://twitter.com/char_chaffin
Goodreads: http://www.goodreads.com/author/show/5337737.Char_Chaffin